DESERT SKIES II

A Story of "Warriors" in Operation Iraqi Freedom

MICHAEL T. GREGORY

ISBN
978-1-958122-91-4 (Paperback)
978-1-958122-92-1 (eBook)
978-1-958122-90-7 (Hardcover)

Thanks goes out to
Lori, Amy, Kelly, and Rachel
for putting up with all my absences
and the times I wasn't there for them in the last 17 years.
Thanks to the United States National Guard,
citizen soldiers each and every one.
It is with much appreciation I recognize your sacrifice.
THANK YOU ALL!

Thanks to my family and friends;
I could not write without your support.

Special "THANKS" to the following 'bookworms.'
This book doesn't get to you, without them.
Thanks to Anne Castro at Quantum Discovery.
Your help is greatly appreciated.
QD is a great team. It's MY TEAM!
Special thanks to Ryan Reeves for having faith in me!
Thank you, Brother. "LET'S DO THIS!"
Super special thanks to "Dave" wherever you are!
I owe you a brew, too. You are our "trusted agent."
And to Evan Trumeter, Thank YOU for your time, your effort
and your belief in the story.
You all are first class!

Thanks to Pat Green and the Pat Green Band, Les Dudek,
Walt Wilkins, Gary P. Nunn, Dana Jacobson, Django Walker,
The Marshall Tucker Band, and George McCorkle.
Special Thanks to Shannon Hoge at Djangold Music,
Miss Susan at Tried and True Music,
Mike at 823 Management,
Tina Wilkins, Ruth Nunn, and Betsy.
And for Dru Blair: You are the best!

TABLE OF CONTENTS

PREFACE

HAVING RECENTLY RETIRED FROM THE UNITED States Army with over twenty-two years of service, I have been afforded some time to catch my breath, look back on a wonderful career, and ponder what the hell it was all about. My time of reflection has afforded me the opportunity to ponder questions I never even bothered to ask back in 1981 when I joined the military.

First and foremost: Why did I join the military? Why did I serve my country in this way? There are dozens of other ways to serve America. After looking back at what I accomplished and the people I met and with whom I served, I think I now know why.

I served because it needs to be done. While military service is not a job for everyone, it was a duty I could perform. I think I performed well. It's in my blood. My father served and his father served. I like to think that's why this country that is my home continues to be the best place in the world to live. Millions of people have served selflessly in this fashion and millions more will follow. It has been an honorable and often enjoyable journey.

The highlight of the trip has and always will be the people with whom I worked. They come from everywhere with one mission, one goal that unites us: to protect the freedoms Americans enjoy.

Defending this freedom has and always will require sacrifice, and since the active army component has been stretched so thin, reservists will continue fighting as long as the current war on terrorism persists.

The citizen soldiers of the National Guard are reflective of this sacrifice. The majority of Guardsmen (and women) have full-time jobs, yet still make or find time to perform military service requirements. This creates hardships on employers, family members, and the Guardsmen themselves. I, for one, greatly appreciate every Guardsman in the US.

The second thing I discovered since I've retired is an understanding of what we've been fighting for. It's very easy to say family, friends, and the citizens of this great country, but that is a given for every one of us. That is and always will be worth fighting for. Understanding the bigger picture is a greater challenge. What defines the freedom that I've been fighting for? I think I finally understand.

I've been fighting so that Americans may live by the laws we have, the Constitution of the United States (The forefathers got that thing pretty damn near perfect!), and for ALL Americans to be able to speak and act freely. It is with great pride that I dedicate *DESERT SKIES II* to the citizen soldiers across the United States that protect our freedom. They are integral and much needed for this current fight. It is with heartfelt regard that I say thank you for their dedication to duty. From Maine to California, Florida to Washington State, and of course, Texas, I appreciate the efforts of our reserve forces.

Desert Skies II is a work of fiction based on my knowledge and concept of how National Guard units function, operate, and are employed, and my following of Operation Iraqi Freedom.

"Check your six and I'll see ya on the high ground!"

MTG
April, 2022

ACKNOWLEDGMENTS

IN ONE OF MY LAST "FIGHTS" on active duty, I was searching for something called "Measures of Effectiveness" (MOE) in certain operations we were conducting. I found a fascinating MOE in Afghanistan.

US Forces asked an old woman in northern Afghanistan what she thought about the Americans coming into her country. She summed up the effort with a magical perspective. It was a good thing when the Americans came because she could "hear the beautiful music again." We did some research and found out that the Afghani population had not been permitted to listen to music. The woman had not heard music play in nearly fifteen years!

American forces broadcasting native Afghani music from a C-130 Commando Solo aircraft provided the music the old women had heard. Pennsylvania National Guardsmen fly these aircraft.

Therefore my first acknowledgment goes out to all those military folks who are bringing liberty and the sounds of democracy to people around the world who hadn't previously had the opportunity to enjoy freedom.

Inspired by an old woman in Afghanistan who reminded me how significant music is in my life, I tried something different in Desert Skies II. I used lyrics from songs I love to set the scene for each chapter. Footnotes identify each artist and explain how to obtain the music.

Among the artists, writers, and musicians I would like to acknowledge for contributing to this project are Pat Green and the Pat Green Band. Pat Green's music, in my opinion, is the current voice of Texas. It resonates with the power, imagination, and spirit that distinguish the state.

I would like to recognize Walt Wilkins for his work, time, and contribution. He is a writer and musician that I am certain you will hear more from in the near future. I absolutely love the song "Some Men Fall," so it was very easy for me to set the scene of Chapter 5 with those beautiful lyrics.

I first heard Les Dudek play in the '70s. He had played guitar with many artists before he recorded his own work on vinyl. I remembered a song called "Old Judge Jones" from Dudek's album Say No More; and it's a perfect fit for Tom Lawton's troubles. To me, his guitar style is a fusion of country rock and blues that cannot be duplicated. One of America's great guitar players, Les Dudek is a hero of mine.

A new voice in Texas comes from Django Walker. Being from Oneonta, New York myself, I am very familiar with Django's father, Jerry Jeff. Texas kind of grows on you and once you live here, you don't realize how much you miss her until you're gone for a while. Django's song "Texas On My Mind" is destined to be a classic and I could not get the melody out of my head when I put my lead character in Iraq.

While writing this book, I also had the pleasure of discovering Gary P. Nunn's work. Already a Texas music legend, he was kind enough to let me use lyrics from "London Homesick Blues/Home With the Armadillos." If you've never heard the song, you need to get to Gruene Hall, have a couple Shiner Bock beers, and get a whole new perspective on the "Texas Thing". Thanks, Gary P!

A close personal friend of mine is Christian musician Dana Jacobson. His work is contemporary Christian and two of his songs fit in this work. Dana is an underrated musician and a talented writer that we will hear more from as he is working on a second CD. He fights for us all in the Air Force Reserves in his spare time!

Some other musicians that contributed to this project with their writing are David Neuhauser (Pat Green Band), Billy Montana ("We've All Got Our Reasons"), Mark Winston Kirk ("Who's To Say"), Mark Irwin and Josh Kear("Some Men Fall"), and the great Radney Foster ("Three Days"). Although their lyrics are not used in this book, I would like to recognize and thank the Caldwell brothers and George McCorkle of the Marshall

Tucker Band ("Desert Skies"), and a new voice familiar to Texans, Gary Allan. A sincere thanks to all these artists and writers.

Some of these artists have family members or relatives that serve in the military. Pat Green's brother is in the Air Force, Walt Wilkins's father flew jets in Vietnam, and Les Dudek is a military brat. Dana Jacobson is a lawyer in the Air Force Reserves. Even George McCorkle did a hitch in the Navy.

I would also like to recognize three organizations that were instrumental in getting life into this book. Tried and True Music in Austin, Djangold Music in Austin, and 823 Management in Kerrville, Texas. Without their assistance and patience, I could not have pulled this together. Frequent their websites, listen to their artists, and buy their records!

I cannot say enough about the beautiful paintings of Dru Blair. He has supported me from the start of my writing and I am forever grateful. His work recognizes and supports the military warriors everywhere.

Websites used to gather information for this book include:

www.patgreen.com
www.lesdudek.com
www.danajacobson.com
www.drublair.com
www.djangowalker.com
www.hepcat.com/campfire/gpnunn
www.823management.com
www.garypnunn.com

Acknowledgments from contributing artists:

Djangold Music would like to thank all the men and women who serve our country to protect our freedoms. I cannot imagine living in a place where I was not allowed to do what I love. The greatest reward for me would be knowing that something I've written or sang made just one day away from home easier for anyone. Thank you very much.

A huge thanks to Michael Gregory for using my material in this project.

Sincerely,
Django Walker and the Djangold Music Staff

A sincere thanks to the Air Force Judge Advocate General's Corps and the USAF Reserves for their support.

Dana Jacobson

PROLOGUE

IT WAS AN EARLY AUGUST SUNDAY evening and Joe Petty was drunk. As Texas Monthly reporter Anna Mercado walked out onto the patio that overlooked the river, Petty asked, "Can I get you something to drink?"

Ms. Mercado, always a professional, declined the offer and took a seat in a chair at the edge of the deck. A slight breeze blowing up the cliff stirred the cedar. This was Joe Petty's home in Marble Falls, Texas. Ms. Mercado grabbed a Kleenex and dabbed at her nose. Something was triggering her allergies. She began, "Would it be okay if I recorded this?"

Petty sat down, popped the top on his Shiner Bock, and said, "No sweat, Ms. Mercado. I ain't got anything to hide."

Ms. Mercado was interviewing the 7/17th Squadron (Attack Helicopter, Texas National Guard) Standardization Instructor Pilot, Chief Warrant Officer Four Joseph Petty. She was asking questions about Lieutenant Colonel Thomas Lawton's activities while serving as the commander of Petty's unit, the 7/17th Cavalry, in the Second Gulf War. The interview took place on August 11, 2003.

She smiled, reached over to the table, and turned on her pocket-sized recorder. "I'm here discussing the command of Lieutenant Colonel Thomas Lawton with his primary pilot, Joseph Petty. Tom Lawton was the commanding officer in the 7th Cavalry Squadron, 17th Cavalry Regiment during the second war with Iraq. Mr. Petty, did you witness any war crimes?"

Petty slowly finished his sip of beer. He placed the bottle on the table, then reached over and turned off the cassette recorder. "Ms. Mercado, you're gonna have to do better than that!" The reporter flushed bright red and started to rise from her chair. "It's obvious to me, you have already researched what you're here for. You know about the events that led up to the trial."

Ms. Mercado quickly recovered and sat back down. "Of course I do!"

"By all accounts, it is a perspective that is... unbiased?"

The reporter tapped her pencil against her chin. "Are you going to tell me about the drinking and all the criminal activity that went on last year?"

Petty shook his head. "Ma'am, I'll do better than that. I'm going to tell you the truth. Because I know Colonel Crane won't say anything about it. You did try to interview him, didn't you?"

The reporter pulled the eraser from her mouth. "He was not the... most interesting of subjects."

Petty chuckled. "He didn't tell you shit, did he?" She nodded. Petty shook his head, grabbed his beer, and took a big drink. He leaned back in his chair as he looked at the sunset. "I'll tell it to you, Ms. Mercado. I'll tell it to you straight. You probably won't be able to print it." He paused, looked directly at her, and added, "But it will be the truth."

She nodded. *All right, Mr. Petty. But I intend to print the story, no matter what you tell me.*

Petty eyed the reporter cautiously. Somewhere in the back of his mind he remembered how much he hated reporters, but there was always a chance she would be different. He took another drink of his beer and said, "Just tell the truth, Ms. Mercado."

"I will, Mr. Petty. Trust me."

Petty sat back in his chair and looked again at the setting sun. "How 'bout I just tell you the story and you take what you want from that?"

She nodded, "That's what I'm here for, Mr. Petty. The story of Tom Lawton and the Warriors."

Petty took one long draw on his beer, swallowed, and leaned back. "It all began last June during the handover ceremony..."

CHAPTER ONE

If I ever get to heaven and I got one question
Hope the Good Lord ain't offended
Gave me a world of pain between the cradle and the grave
Is that what was intended?
I don't have to know why he put the stars in the sky
Or fooled with the change of seasons
I guess we've all got our reasons.

"We've All Got Our Reasons"
-Walt Wilkins and Billy Montana

17 June 2002
Montgomery County Airport
Conroe, Texas

"I WILL ALWAYS BE A WARRIOR!" With those final words, Lieutenant Colonel Harold Earl turned over command of the 7th Squadron, 17th Cavalry Brigade, Texas National Guard, to Lieutenant Colonel Thomas Lawton. It was a moment that Tom Lawton never thought would come. He had all but given up on commanding anything other than a scout troop. Now he was taking command of one of only five attack helicopter squadrons in the Army National Guard.

39-year-old Tom Lawton, 10 pounds over Army weight standard, might stretch to 6-feet tall. His brown hair was turning gray at the temples, but a boyish grin hid his age. He stepped to the podium and cleared his throat. "Major General Walker, Colonel and Mrs. Crane, distinguished friends of the 7/17th Cavalry, let me say thank you for attending our ceremony today. Troopers of the 'Warrior Squadron,' you look fantastic! It is both an honor and a privilege to take command of the best attack helicopter squadron in the National Guard." Lawton surveyed the squadron before him in the hanger and quickly estimated their number. *Maybe there are 170 soldiers here; about 70 percent of the personnel a regular squadron had assigned to its ranks. He quickly put the thought away.*

"I swear to each and every trooper out here today, I will give you my best. I ask no less from each of you. I look forward to both the challenge of command and the opportunities we have to attain success. Thank you all for coming." With that, Tom snapped to attention. The soldiers and the crowd were stunned by the brevity of the speech.

He yelled, "Sergeant Major! Take charge of the Squadron!"

Sergeant Major Trino Martinez smiled broadly, saluted, and did an about face toward the unit. "DISMISSED!"

The troopers yelled in unison, "WARRIORS FIGHT!" It didn't seem like much of a motto back then; more for show than an indicator of their demeanor. The troops made a collective sigh and fell out to shake hands with their new commander.

Tom and Cindy Lawton spent the next hour floating about the hanger meeting and greeting people who had driven as much as six hours to witness the change of command. Tom was especially thankful that Major General Jerrold "Jerry" Walker, the Texas Adjutant General or TAG, had come all the way from Austin to witness the ceremony.

When Tom met Major General Walker, they seemed more like friends than a chain of command. Tom stuck out his hand and said with a broad smile, "Thank you for coming, sir!" General Walker, the senior National Guard member in the state of Texas, was beaming with delight. He was proud to see a Texan and a fellow citizen soldier take command of the only National Guard attack helicopter squadron in their state.

"I wouldn't have missed it, Tom!" smiled the general.

Tom pulled his hand from the general and moved it toward Colonel Crane. Crane was a different story. Tom sensed some sort of invisible force field around that guy. The handshake came, but it was brief and awkward. "Sir, thanks for comin' down from Hood!"

Colonel Crane, the active duty representative from Ft. Hood, had come to the ceremony representing the 1st Cavalry commander. Colonel Crane was a tanker by trade, an Armor officer, who was, in a word, focused.

Crane just grunted. "Pleasure, Lieutenant Colonel Lawton. This is a nice little command you have here."

At least he was professional enough to fake his enthusiasm, Tom thought to himself, taking the "little" insult in stride and handling it in his typically good-natured way. "Hell, sir, little, big! It don't matter! A command is a command, right?" He eyed the active duty officer with a cautious smile.

Crane just nodded. "Sure it is." He looked at his wife, Dorothy, and said, "Any command is a good command."

It was painfully obvious he did not want to be there. As a matter of fact, he would have rather been knee deep in al-Qaida terrorists than be at that ceremony. Crane was the type of officer that wants combat, wants to smell the burnt powder, an officer that felt his career would not be complete without a combat patch on his right sleeve.

Dorothy Crane replied by looking as if she was going to throw up.

Tom shrugged off the grim exchange with Crane and turned to the General. "Sir, will you be able to stay for the barbecue?"

General Walker's smile disappeared. "Sorry, Tom. I have to get back to Austin. But don't let that hamper your party."

Tom smiled, "Not a problem, sir!" He turned to Colonel Crane and said, "Excuse me, sir. I hope you two can stay, but let me get the general down the road!"

Colonel Crane nodded to the general and then to Tom. His smile appeared difficult to maintain and his words seemed coerced. "I suppose we'll be staying here for a while longer. We wouldn't miss it." He quickly grabbed his wife, turned, and headed for the refreshments.

Tom watched as they walked away. Crane pointed his wife to the refreshments and then moved over to a group of captains. Lawton noticed the colonel was very cordial to Tom's subordinate commanders, friendlier than Tom had expected. It was as if he knew one or two of them. Tom watched for a moment longer, just long enough to see the Colonel place his arm around the shoulder of one of the captains. *Crane is no Mr. Nice Guy. Is he pumping the junior officers for information?* Tom shrugged off his suspicions and faced the general.

Major General Walker broke the silence. "I'm sorry I have to leave you here with that shithead, Tom. I've got about three feet of crap to go through in my inbox. That's just the paper. I ain't talkin' about that stupid computer on my desk."

Tom looked at the general with a smile. "Not a problem, sir." He glanced over at Crane and said, "At least he took the time to come down here to see the ceremony." He looked back at Walker and added, "I don't think he likes me too much."

Walker stuck out his hand and said, "You better watch that guy, Tom. He is hardcore and way too absorbed in himself. Guys like that are dangerous for their troops. You use your judgment and everything will be all right. Don't let him make you do things you don't want to or can't do, okay?"

Tom let the general's comments sink in, then he smiled. "Roger, sir. I guess I need to drink your beverage for you, then?"

The general smiled, "I thought you weren't drinkin' anymore."

Tom wasn't aware that Walker knew of his past problems with alcohol. The National Guard Aviation Community is small. There were no secrets. Tom maintained his smile. "Once in a while, General."

Walker grunted. "Me, too, son." The general turned and started to walk away. "You better get these guys of yours in shape for combat. I wouldn't be surprised if you all got called up for the next one."

Tom suppressed a laugh. The thought of his National Guard unit getting called up for war was the furthest thing from his mind. *Hell, we only have seventy-five percent of the unit manned.* Tom snapped to attention and said, "I'll get 'em ready, sir!" Not for the slightest moment did he think that would be necessary. He was never more wrong.

The barbecue was held in a park on the quiet side of the airfield. The wives had put together some side dishes for the troopers and Tom Lawton had sprung for the meat. The smell of grilled ribs over mesquite filled the air. Even his wife Cindy was happy with the choice of a barbecue. She wouldn't have to clean up afterward.

The officers had decided to provide some entertainment. There were a couple of short skits and lots of handshakes. Congratulations were in order and Tom was quite pleased with himself. He had confidence that the 7/17th was going to become a damn good unit.

The first handshake he received at the barbecue was from Sergeant Major Martinez. The sergeant major was a full blooded, 100-percent Texican. Martinez, who spoke with just a slight Hispanic accent, said, "Sir, I just want to be the first to tell you that we are gonna have a good time with you as the boss!"

It took Tom a moment to interpret what he had just heard, but after it sank in, a big smile came across his face and his hand went out. "I'm looking forward to working with you, Trino. I've heard a lot of good things. Harly Earl told me you were the best NCO he'd ever worked with." Harold Earl was the previous 7/17th Commander. He'd explained to Tom, in detail, the situation of the Warriors prior to the change of command. "This command is gonna be tough, but I'm counting on you," Tom said.

"No problem, sir! We're gonna do just fine!" shot back the five-foot-ten Warrior.

Tom's troopers were all enjoying stuffing themselves on brisket and ribs, and drinking more than their share of Shiner Bock beer. Most of the troopers worked "real" jobs and the National Guard gig was just another paycheck.

Taking time away from the normal job was usually a burden for the employer and some Guardsmen took a calculated gamble by serving in the Guard. Most really enjoyed serving their state or country, and to a man, the Cavalry troopers would say they loved the camaraderie the unit provided. The change of command was a great break and most made the extra effort to show up for a Friday afternoon ceremony.

Some were actually on active-duty status and had a little more time to fly and train. Others, especially some of the junior enlisted troopers, just got by. Time away from work was something they couldn't afford. Tom understood, and the number of attendees he had for his ceremony was more than he had anticipated.

Tom carried a beer over to Colonel Crane. The colonel looked at the beer and said, "No thank you, Lieutenant Colonel Lawton. I've got to drive later."

Tom offered the beer to Dorothy Crane. She received a frown from her husband, and so declined Tom's offer. He shrugged, popped the top, and said, "Here's to a safe and successful command!" Crane nodded, but acted inconvenienced.

To his credit, Tom didn't give up. "Sir, I'm looking forward to training with you and your Brigade at the National Training Center. I haven't been there in years."

Crane shot back, "It's a lot tougher now. I don't think you and your part-timers will be able to provide much support out there."

Tom felt as if he had just been punched in the gut. To cut him down was no big deal, but Crane lobbing a cheap shot about his unit being part-timers was uncalled for. He didn't know this colonel very well. But the comment spoke volumes. Crane was obviously unaware of the Guards' ability to perform their duties and did not have faith in the unit. Even worse, he was not tactful enough to keep his concern on a professional level. The 7/17th was the roundup unit that would augment Crane's unit if and when it went to war. He proved he didn't care for his new subordinate command by laying the snide comment out there for the new commander to handle.

Tom remained tactful. "We may just surprise you, sir. We have two months to train. I'll have them ready." He wanted to add, "You'll see," but decided discretion was much better when it came to dealing with an active-duty colonel, especially this prick.

"You do that, Lieutenant Colonel Lawton. They're gonna need every bit of training you can give 'em. Now, if you'll excuse us, Dorothy and I need to get back to Ft. Hood. We'll see you next month."

"Roger that, sir." He saluted and watched the couple head towards their car.

Cindy walked over. "I see Colonel Crane has to leave." She put her arm around her husband. "That's too bad. Now you can have fun." Tom smiled at her, and she added, "That guy's a jerk, isn't he?"

"I can think of another term, but you're a lady."

She smiled back and playfully smacked him. "Come on. I think that Joe and the Ramrods are gonna play you a song." Tom did as he was told.

A few of the troopers had formed a country band called The Ramrods. Joe Petty played lead guitar. They got together two or three nights a week and still managed to fly attack helicopters in their spare time. Petty had talked Tom into letting the band play at the barbecue.

Petty grabbed hold of the microphone and said, "On behalf of our new commander, Lieutenant Colonel Thomas Lawton, we'd like to play a song he sang for me about twelve years ago when we were in Iraq together. I worked for him before and I'm damn glad to work for him again. The song was originally performed by the Marshall Tucker Band. We have Sergeant Duane Taylor on saxophone, so bear with him if he misses a note or two. It's only the fourth or fifth time he's played it. This song is called, 'Desert Skies.'"

The crowd gave the band a polite clap and Tom gave a fake bow and smiled. Joe was older, but still respected him as the best leader he'd ever worked for. Lawton sang with them for the first verse, then went and danced with Cindy. She grabbed Tom and pulled him out into the crowd. He rarely danced and found the initial going very rusty. But Cindy was patient and gently led him around the grounds.

When the song was over, the Ramrods received a standing ovation. They played three more songs and had to pack it up. It was getting dark and the unit had to train early on Saturday morning.

Tom and Cindy said their thank yous and good-byes. It was a thirty-minute drive up highway I-45 to Huntsville. Their three girls were away at

Scout Camp and the animals needed to be fed. *Maybe I'll get to see a little Sports Center and find out if the Astros won before I crash for the night.* He would be right back down to Conroe in less than eight hours.

That Saturday would be different. He had a new job. Only it wasn't just a job, it was a duty. Someone had faith in Tom and thought he would be a damn good commander. That person was undoubtedly Major General Walker. Tom had worked for him in Austin, when the general was a colonel on the headquarters staff.

Tom enjoyed his duty in the Guard but he enjoyed his civilian life as well. He wasn't very excited to be called up for full-time service until he found out what the job was. He was sad that he could not still coach the women's high school basketball team in nearby Willis.

It had been a long time since he had been a commander. That command had gone well while he and his troop were in combat. Tom had led his troops, The Champions, into the lion's den of Iraq back in 1991. The war was the most intense week of flying, fighting, and surviving he had ever endured, and all his men respected what he had accomplished. It was adjusting to a new commander and the subsequent peace that was hard for him to manage. He never really adjusted to the bullshit after the return. That was the most valuable lesson of the first Gulf War. The bullshit goes away when the bullets start to fly.

This squadron was a responsibility he had never anticipated. When he left command after the first Gulf War, he never expected to lead young men and women again. It was both an honor and a curse.

CHAPTER TWO

Tell me the truth Avatar,
What to do
Don't let these people
Bring me down.

"Avatar"
-Les Dudek

18 June 2002
Montgomery County Airport
Conroe, Texas

TOM WAS IN HIS NEW OFFICE by five o'clock that morning and Sergeant Major Martinez already had the coffee made. Lawton and Martinez took the first thirty minutes of the day to go over the daily activities. The first item was the accountability formation at 0700. At 0730, Tom held a staff meeting. At 0900 was the meeting with the enlisted soldiers and at 1000 came the meeting with all the officers. The afternoon would be devoted to observing training and maybe getting lucky enough to fly around Texas.

Tom stood off to the side in the hangar and watched as the squadron gathered for the accountability formation. It was already ninety-five degrees and the humidity was ninety percent. He told Trino to keep it short. The personnel accountability was taken by the troop commanders and the squadron was told to report to their troop areas. Trino Martinez came over to Tom with a smile on his face.

"We're doin' all right, sir. We got 219 bodies in the formation. That makes seventy-eight percent for a drill weekend. That's damn good, sir!"

Tom smiled at the news. Seventy-eight percent was nothing to sneeze at. "Good deal, Sergeant Major. I'm gonna get ready for the staff meeting. I'll see you upstairs."

Tom walked into the conference room and found the executive officer, Major Bryan Suggs, a black, full-time Guardsman, who had been in Conroe with the 7/17th for ten months. He was a six-foot-two, 220-pound mountain of muscle. The only thing more impressive than his frame was his smile. In the month Tom had known him, he had never seen the major without a huge grin.

Tom walked over and stuck out his hand, offering his own smile. "How we doin' today, Major Suggs?"

"Hell, sir! Just another fine day in the Cavalry!"

Tom chuckled and looked across the room at Major Jonathan Wright, the squadron operations officer. Major Wright was probably best described as the exact opposite of Bryan Suggs. He was a wiry five-foot-nine, bundle of perpetual motion nicknamed "Ping," as in ping-pong ball. He also lacked confidence and had a short temper, neither of which sat well with Tom. *If Wright is nervous in this environment, how the hell will he be at the National Training Center?*

Tom walked over to Major Wright slowly, afraid he might scare him. "How ya doin' today, Jon?"

"Fine, sir, fine!" Wright's hand was wet. "I have all the handouts ready and the Troop commanders should be here any minute."

Tom nodded. "Good." He looked over at Suggs who was still smiling. "I'd ask you guys if you want coffee, but I think you both are charged up enough already!" Both men nodded in unison.

Into the conference room came two captains. Tom had met them before, just briefly. The first one was Maintenance Troop Commander Darren Hodges. Hodges carried two notebooks and was already wet with sweat. Lieutenant Colonel Earl had given Tom the background on all the commissioned officers in the squadron. He had studied their Officer Record Briefs and knew them all on paper. Now it was time to match the paper to the face. Hodges was an Aggie, a product of Texas A&M University. He worked as a loan officer in his real life, but according to Earl, was surprisingly competent.

The second captain was Headquarters and Headquarters Troop (HHT) Commander, Captain Jason Wills. Wills sold real estate in Dallas. Maybe it was his sales background, but Tom always felt Wills was trying to sell something. Earl had given Tom a heads-up on Wills, noting that Jason Wills was the son of Major General Robert Wills, the retired TAG that Walker had replaced. For some reason, the expression "all hat and no cattle" popped into Tom's mind.

"Good morning, gentlemen!" Lawton received a "morning" back from the pair and they promptly took their seats.

Two more captains entered followed by two lieutenants. This group seemed so young; Tom wondered if they shaved. The captains were the Bravo and Charlie Troop commanders.

The B Troop was led by Captain Chase Freeman, a schoolteacher who had just finished the Apache Course. He had taken a year off from teaching to attend the Aviation Advance Course and the transition. Chase Freeman loved being an army officer. His uniform was always perfect and he could easily serve as poster child for recruitment. He had just turned

26 and most of his flight time was in Blackhawks. Earl was confident in his abilities and had told Tom he was probably his best officer.

The C Troop's commander was Captain Hector Sanchez. Hector had just gotten off active duty and already had two hundred hours in the Apache. He was a graduate of Texas A&M at Kingsville and called Corpus Christi home.

The two lieutenants were S2, Intelligence Officer, Lieutenant Samuel Gash, and S1, Personnel Officer, Lieutenant Anthony Harper. Both lieutenants were new to their jobs and could have passed for privates, except for the gold bars on their uniforms.

The S4, Captain Jack Bartlett, popped in the door, signed some paperwork for the NCO that was trailing him, then quickly took his seat. Jack Bartlett was another fulltimer, but he was being outgunned and outmaneuvered by paperwork and lack of personnel support. He appeared burned out, but he was still very capable at his job.

The clock showed 0730 as Tom took his seat. Sergeant Major Martinez started to close the door, but a loud crash outside followed by someone saying, "Excuse me! I'm sorry!" stopped him.

Sergeant Major Martinez looked at Tom with a frown. "Sir, I believe Captain Talbot is arriving." Captain Bartholomew A. Talbot came to a sliding stop in the middle of the doorway. "Sorry, sir! I had some paperwork to sign."

"Come on in, Captain Talbot. We haven't really started yet." The captain quickly took his seat. Tom was never happy with people that were late. He filed away that Talbot was tardy and started the meeting.

Tom looked around the room at the young, fresh, and highly anxious faces. "Good morning, everyone." After receiving the customary cordial response, he continued. "I want to start off by telling you all how happy I am to be the new 'Warrior Six.' It is my intent to make this tour the best tour any of you have ever had. We will do two things. We will train hard, and we will play hard." He couldn't help but notice the smiles that appeared on their faces.

Tom handed some three-by-five cards to Martinez. "I'm going to give each one of you two cards. On the first card, I want you to write the three things this unit does well. On the second card, write down three things we don't do so well." Tom watched as the staff members looked at each other quizzically. Captain Talbot and Major Suggs immediately began writing.

Tom looked at Suggs and said, "If that's the bad ones, XO, make sure you only have three!" Bryan Suggs laughed. Five minutes later, the men had returned all their cards to the sergeant major.

Tom said, "Thank you all. I'll check through them later this week, and give you all feedback at our next meeting." Then he stood and started walking around as he got down to business.

"I want to make sure we get to flying. That is, and always will be, the priority for this unit: To get aircraft in the air, safely. We need to train. We need to train hard, day and night. The most important person in this unit is," Tom stood behind Captain Darren Hodges, "the D Troop Commander." Tom looked at the faces to make sure they understood.

"Squadron maintenance is his problem. If he doesn't have aircraft fixed for you, it becomes your problem. If you can't fly, it becomes my problem." Tom continued to walk around the room. "Troop commanders, you need to let him know what's going on with your aircraft. You absolutely need to let your maintenance officers know what's going on with your airframes."

He stopped, looked at Hodges, and said, "You come to me immediately if you don't get the support or answers you need from these guys." Hodges was beaming.

"My second priority is owning the night. I know it's the most dangerous time. And I know you guys don't get enough flight hours to get out there as much as you need to. But it has to be done. Fifty percent night flying, at a minimum." He saw two captains shake their heads while Bart Talbot smiled broadly.

"The third priority is being able to hit what you shoot at. Your pilots must have confidence in themselves and their equipment when they pull the trigger. One hellfire, one kill."

Tom stood behind his chair. "That sums it up. The rest is all minor stuff for an Attack Helicopter Squadron." He looked at Executive Officer Major Suggs, and for the first time, found his smile absent.

"Why, Major Suggs, where is that beaming smile? Have I said something to scare you?" It was Tom's turn to smile. He could tell Suggs was nervous.

The major looked around the room as if he was gathering strength from the audience. He didn't have to say he was speaking for everyone. Tom knew he was. "Sir, we have an operational readiness that's less than fifty percent. We only get three to four crews from each Troop here on any particular weekend. And the enlisted soldiers haven't done any—"

"Let me guess! Any ARMY training?!" Tom laughed. "You think it's any better in the active duty right now? Trust me on something. The only thing they have is more bodies. They don't fly more than you, they don't maintain more than you, and they aren't doing anymore military task training than you, either." He let the comments sink in. He could see the staff's doubt.

"You have ten active duty divisions. They are broken down into three Brigades, with three missions. One is ready, one is getting ready, and one is recovering. Right now, I would bet my oak leaf cluster that we are in that middle third. The challenge is to get to the ready-for-war state of operations. That's the third that can go fight a war on the modern battlefield and come home alive. All of us. That's the challenge, gentlemen."

He walked to the door. "My door is always open to each of you." He stopped and turned around in the doorway.

The sergeant major brought the staff to attention with a loud, "TEN-HUT!"

"If any of you can't do what I ask of you, let me know so I can get somebody else in here who can." No one moved. "All right then! Get your butts to work!"

At 0900, Tom met with all the enlisted troopers in the hangar. The first thing he did was tell them to fall out and gather around him in a horseshoe so they could hear him. He started slowly. "First of all, let me say 'thank you' to each and every one of you. I know a couple things about the troopers in the Texas National Guard. Number one, you could all be someplace else this weekend. That means on a beach, going for a ride on a trail, or maybe floatin' down a river in a tube." He looked at his troopers' faces and saw the smiles and a couple nods of agreement. "But you're here. You're serving your state and you're serving your country.

"Second item is business. My priorities are twofold. This unit will fly. Its purpose is to put attack helicopters in the air to defend the state and the nation against enemies that would do her harm. I know you don't have time to have all the aircraft ready to fly." He paused again and got closer to the crowd. "Just give me your best effort. That's all I want." The sergeant major stood behind him with an intense look, supporting his new boss. Martinez liked the way Lawton did business.

"If it gets too tough, or somethin' is buggin' you, just use your chain of command. Your commanders will listen to you. If they don't, you come see me. I'll listen."

And that's what Lawton did for the next forty-five minutes; he stayed with his troopers and answered questions. The easy ones, the tough ones, and the ones nobody else would answer. For that, the troopers were truly appreciative. For once in their short military careers, somebody gave a damn about them. Even if Lawton couldn't change anything, he listened.

The officers were a little tougher. At 1000, he met in the conference room with forty-two officers. Most of them were warrant officers. He knew them, he understood what they did for a helicopter unit, and he appreciated them. They could be a cantankerous lot, often gruff or short-tempered. Sometimes they were more inquisitive about the operation than they needed to be, but they were always consummate professionals about their job and their country. It has often been said in the army that if you want the truth, you ask a warrant officer.

"Gentlemen and lady," started Tom. The lady was the chemical officer, Second Lieutenant Mary Lynn Crandle. Crandle was a product of the University of Texas with a degree in chemical engineering. The army had paid her way through college with a Reserve Officer Training Corps (ROTC) commission. The army had failed to call her up to active duty. Their loss would prove to be a tremendous gain for the Warriors.

"I suppose you've already received the brief from your Troop commanders on what my priorities are, what I think, and how I feel. Just so we're clear on this, they are exactly right. I believe this unit needs to fly. It needs to fly at night. I'm absolutely positive that we must be able to execute our missions in the dark." He looked around for responses and saw a couple of heads bob. "If you want to survive in a combat environment, you must be able to fly night system, in the dark, and employ your weapons system.

"The second thing you have to understand is the National Guard is equal to the active component." He caught a few disbelieving glances. "I'll explain that. You have to fly just as many hours a month as the active component guys and you must do it in an inconsistent time frame. I understand some of you can't get away from work for two or three weeks at a time. But when you show up here, you have to be ready to go. If you are behind in hours, or just in ability, you need to get here earlier and get caught up. No one here can afford to wait on you to catch up.

"Here's the deal. You have one month to get up to crew level proficiency. Next month, we start collective training." He heard a few low rumbles that he disregarded. He looked at Major Jon Wright, the operations officer, and said, "Plan on multi-ship operations next month, got it?" Wright was frowning, but nodded in agreement.

"Time is a luxury. We don't have enough of it. In the Texas Guard, we need to work harder than anybody, I mean anybody, to be the best attack unit …" Tom could tell he was starting to push too hard and caught himself. He smiled and concluded with, "How 'bout being the best unit we can be. No comparisons, no judgment. We'll know good enough when we see it.

"Now I've got about an hour before you guys are released for lunch. I'll take any questions you have."

It didn't take long for the warrants to turn loose with both barrels. The first question came from Chief Warrant Officer Two Gary Shamus. "Sir, I know you want us to fly, but how are we gonna do that when we don't have any aircraft in our Troop available? We have one in maintenance, four down for parts, and one reserved for the instructor pilot to fly the new guys."

"Captain Hodges," Tom pointed to the maintenance troop commander, "has recommended a squadron-level maintenance allocation flow that will work best for the next two months." Hodges did an excellent job hiding his surprise. He was not aware Lieutenant Colonel Earl had briefed Tom on his idea for more flights.

Tom continued, "Two Troops don't have enough aircraft up to fly the flights they have scheduled. Right now, Charlie Troop Cowboys have the best status with four aircraft up. We, the squadron, will use those airframes primarily until the other two Troops get their aircraft up."

He looked at Captain Hector Sanchez and saw the quizzical look on his face. "Trust me on this, Captain Sanchez. Next month you will probably use an Outlaw aircraft from A Troop or a Bandit airframe from Captain Freeman. We are not in a position to allow one unit to fly and two Troops of pilots to sit on the ground waiting for airframes. I know it sucks to run the squadron as a collective and share airframes, but there is no other way to accomplish the mission with the number of aircraft we have flyable right now. If any Troop commanders have a problem with this decision, come see me after this meeting. I'll listen to you bitch the appropriate amount of time before I tell you to shut the hell up!" Tom was smiling when he said it. The warrants laughed, but the captains and Major Wright remained expressionless. The tone was set.

Lawton continued to answer questions until lunch-time. Most tough questions came from the warrants. Some softball lobs came from the captains and lieutenants. When it was over, Tom thought the sessions with his soldiers went well. His strongest point was his ability to work with and listen to his troops. There was a reason he was picked to command. This unit needed him.

Lawton's afternoon was a maze of running through the hangar and the training sites to get a picture of how well trained the unit was. Deep down, Lawton could tell the unit needed a ton of work to be ready to support Colonel Crane's Armor Brigade at the National Training Center in September. He didn't see it as an impossible task, but the truth was the squadron was way behind the level they needed to perform well in the California desert.

Lawton flew for the first time late that afternoon. He flew in an aircraft not night-system capable. All the fully mission capable (FMC) aircraft were saved to fly at night, because they had night systems that worked.

Lawton knew he was rusty. He spent the first thirty minutes getting his control touch back, often behind the aircraft on his maneuvers. They flew north toward Huntsville and took a turn to the west over the forest. Tom was surprised at how few houses there were in this part of Texas. At 500 feet above the ground, he knew, the trees below would not be kind to the seven-ton helicopter or its occupants if they had maintenance problems.

After getting comfortable with the controls, he flew some nap of the earth (NOE), below the tree tops and slightly faster than a run, in a remote location. Just as he was getting the feel for the aircraft, it was time to head back to Conroe. He climbed to altitude, performed an unusual attitude recovery, then a precision radar approach back into the airfield. *Sure, I'm rusty, but not completely broken.*

That night the unit flew five aircraft using night-system devices two times each for a total of more than twenty-six hours of Night Vision System

(NVS) time, the same amount of NVS time they had flown during the entire previous month. Lawton was pushing them, but they needed it.

19 June 2002
Montgomery County Airport
Conroe, Texas

MORE FLIGHTS AND MORE TRAINING SPACED between hectic personnel actions, individual soldier training, as well as aircraft and vehicle maintenance, dominated Sunday. The plate was piled higher than any active-duty unit would attempt in a twelve-hour period.

Tom spent the day moving from location to location, checking on his troops, their training, and their needs. Where he could, he made spot corrections. Where he could not, he took notes in his ever-present notepad.

At 1800, he called Major Suggs, Major Wright, and Captain Hodges into his office. He wanted to discuss the positive things he saw as well as the not-so-positive things. Tom had made a list, and it started and ended with maintenance.

He sounded fatigued when he began, but he was smiling. "The best thing I saw was that everyone was working. That is very important. Lots of good troops doing the right thing." He walked around the room. As tired as he was, he couldn't sit still.

"The bad thing was they were not working on aircraft. The majority of our enlisted soldiers are mechanics. They need to be working on aircraft so the airframes can be ready to fly. If we don't get them more opportunities to work on aircraft, they won't know how to do their military occupational specialty (MOS). If they can't learn it here, they will get out and learn it somewhere else. Heaven forbid they join the Air Force!" Tom tried to lighten the mood.

"It seems to me they are well along on soldiering, medical, and weapons assembly and disassembly tasks. I simply have no idea if they can perform routine maintenance on an Apache," explained Tom.

Hodges, fresh from his kudo of the previous day, pounced on an opportunity. "Sir, the civilian maintenance personnel who fix the aircraft during the week don't like having crew chiefs working on them during the weekends."

Tom was immediately angry, but did his best to control it. "What are you talking about?" He stopped next to Suggs and saw him nod.

"They think the crew chiefs will do more damage or make more work for them if the crew chiefs start maintaining them," said Hodges.

"You believe that?" asked Tom incredulously.

Hodges answered, "No, sir."

"What do you really think?" asked Tom.

Hodges breathed in heavily. Lawton could tell the answer would at least be a stab at honesty. "I believe the civilian maintenance personnel will be out of a job if we fix the aircraft."

Tom tilted his head and looked hard at the Captain. "An interesting observation, Captain Hodges. I will be sure to bring that up to the facility manager, Mr. Briggs. He will no doubt disagree with your assessment."

William Briggs was the contract maintenance supervisor at the Montgomery County Airport. He was directly responsible for the readiness status of the unit. If the aircraft were "up," meaning ready to fly FMC, it would be a good thing for the unit and the pilots. Not so good for the maintenance personnel, because if they can keep a high readiness status with thirty people, next year they might be able to do it with just twenty-eight or even twenty-five. It was a 21st-century form of Catch-22, the irony being if you work too well, you work yourself out of a job.

Major Suggs coughed before adding, "They don't have any requirement for keeping a high readiness rate."

"You mean it's not in their contract? No bonus for seventy-five percent up, or seventy percent FMC?" asked Tom.

"Not that I'm aware of, sir," said the executive officer.

"I'll check into that next week." He thought for a moment. *Hell, I'm a squadron commander. I can do whatever I want.* "Here's what I want you guys to do. Plan on having the crew chiefs work on helicopters two weekends a month. I'll work it out with Briggs."

Tom finished the meeting and told them how happy he was with the first week. He looked forward to flying more in the next week and getting up to Ft. Hood to talk with Colonel Crane. From that meeting, he would let them all know what to expect from the training they were to conduct at the National Training Center (NTC).

19 June 2002
Huntsville, Texas

TOM ROLLED OVER AND LAY NEXT to Cindy.

"How'd it go, Mr. Squadron Commander?"

Tom smiled. "About as I expected. They had some good points and a couple of not-so-good points. They don't get to work on aircraft and they don't fly enough because the aircraft are down for maintenance all the time. We have to fix that or they won't get any better."

She playfully smacked his arm. "Well, get on it, Colonel!"

"That's 'Lieutenant Colonel'! Not full colonel. It makes a difference."

Cindy Lawton turned off the light. "Not to me it doesn't." She rolled over and gave her husband a big kiss. She sat up and looked at him, rubbing his chest. "As long as you don't change this time. You know?"

Tom knew exactly what she meant. "I know better this time, honey. It's a Guard unit. There's no way we're going to go to war. I don't care if Saddam was in Mexico. The Texas National Guard isn't going to the desert." He pulled her close and kissed her. Then he rolled over and turned out his bedside lamp.

Cindy smiled. This was the way it was supposed to be. The Guard was more like a job than the regular army. Tom could play his little military commander soldier role, and he would still be home.

CHAPTER THREE

"Put me on a cool river,
Take my worries from me.
Fly me high on a big blue sky
Well, there's no one here but me!"

"Guy Like Me"
-Pat Green, David Neuhauser and the Pat Green Band

21 June 2002
1st Cavalry Division Headquarters
Ft. Hood, Texas

COLONEL CRANE WAS THE HOST OF the Final Planning Conference (FPC) for the Second Brigade of the 1st Cavalry Division area at Ft. Hood. He invited all the commanders and operations officers that would be involved in the rotation to discuss the final timetable, operational training goals, objectives, and his personal expectations. He was all business, all the time. Crane's Brigade would be the last in line to change out to the latest equipment in the Army inventory. Theoretically, while the rest of the unit changed to fully digitized equipment, Crane's Brigade would be the only one capable of going to war. In the meantime, the Division still had to go through its rotation in the desert. Crane's Armor was the only Brigade in the 1st Cavalry available.

Crane explained to all the Battalion commanders that a Texas National Guard unit would be supporting the 1st Team (1st Cavalry Division) at NTC because the division's standard attack battalion, the 1st/227th, was focused on getting new equipment upgrades.

Crane's lack of enthusiasm for the support from 7/17th was evident as he spoke to the assembled commanders. "Unfortunately, it has been decided we must take an antiquated Apache unit. In this case, the 7/17th Texas Guard from down in Conroe," he pointed at Tom, "commanded by Tom Lawton." Some in the crowd nodded. Tom just smiled and nodded back. "The unit has a lot of problems. Between low-flight time, poor maintenance, and about a sixty-percent personnel manning, I don't see them as being the key to our success when we get to the NTC." He changed the subject and continued on. Tom went from uncomfortable to fullfledged pissed off.

Between meetings, Lawton reviewed the three-by-five cards his men had filled out. After reviewing their opinions he quickly established what he would share with the sergeant major and what he would share with the staff and troop commanders.

Tom Lawton did his best to avoid Crane. Unfortunately, he couldn't avoid him forever.

He was in the hallway getting a Diet Coke when the colonel came over. "So how is your first week as a squadron commander going? Fired any slackers yet?"

Lawton couldn't nail down if the colonel was insinuating his unit was full of slackers or if he was failing as a commander because he hadn't fired anyone. *Simple bullshit from a simple man*, he decided. "How's it going, sir?"

Colonel Crane was already beyond Lawton's not-so-rhetorical question. "Are you going to be able to have ten aircraft join us? I've already explained to the commanding general (CG) that I'm not counting on your guys to be full up."

Tom grabbed his soda from the machine and looked the colonel directly in the eye. "We'll be there with every aircraft we have ready to fly. If I were you, sir, I'd count on more than ten." Tom didn't wait for more snide comments. He popped his soda top and walked away.

Their command relationship required excellent communication because Tom was so far away from the flagpole, but their different styles, personalities, and attitudes would not help improve that communication anytime soon. The colonel didn't expect anything from his roundout Attack Cavalry unit, and that was okay with Tom. If he could enjoy his command without ever having to talk to Crane again, that would be fine too. Unfortunately, that's not the way the system worked. He would hear from his active duty boss more than he ever wanted.

23 June 2002
Montgomery County Airport
Conroe, Texas

TOM BRIEFED SERGEANT MAJOR MARTINEZ AND Major Suggs on the results of the cards. "I've got mostly good news. The staff thinks the most important positive aspect of the unit is the morale. Almost to a man, and woman, morale was mentioned as the top one or two best things the unit has going for it. The second was safety. That is a tremendously positive thing. It's good to hear the staff say they think we are doing things safely.

"As for the bad things." Tom pulled up the cards and read directly from them. "Don't fly enough. Can't fly multi-ship operations. Not good enough maintenance!" Tom looked at Suggs. "That came from Hodges! Nothing like saying you aren't doing your job!" Suggs shook his head.

"He followed up with 'not enough parts to fix broken equipment. Vehicles are not properly maintained.' " He pulled up another card. "Not flying enough to maintain proficiency." Lawton paused. "You can see the trend here."

Tom pulled out a final card. "This one got me. 'Not enough support from the chain of command.' You gotta give the lad credit for writing that one."

Suggs lost his smile. "Who the hell wrote that?"

Tom read the card. "Lieutenant Jack Bartlett, the S-4, Supply Officer."

Suggs became angry. "He never said anything to me about not getting support."

Tom put the cards down. "Did you ever ask him if he needed help?" It wasn't an attempt to lay blame; he just wanted to know.

Suggs was honest. "No, sir. I had no idea he needed help."

"I guess we can get him some now. Next week, you pull him off to the side and see what he needs. He needs you to work that side of the house, not me. You have the S4 and the S1 for handling personnel matters. Sergeant major Martinez has oversight of all enlisted matters, but I'm the one on the dotted line for them." The sergeant major nodded. "I'm on the line for intelligence and operations."

Suggs asked, "What about Major Wright? Shouldn't he be responsible for operations?"

Lawton shook his head. "He's only been an S3 for a couple months. I don't think he's comfortable in the job yet. I'm very comfortable as an operations officer. It's the loggy side that I'm behind the power curve on. That's where you get the big bucks, Bryan. You and the sergeant major." They both nodded.

"Like I said, the best thing we seem to have is good morale. I think morale can get a unit through some things that experience and luck can't cover. Granted, we'll need both of the last two, but I'll take the morale over any other factor a unit can have."

Sergeant Major Martinez was beaming. "We got a lot of that!"

"It's up to us to keep it that way," said Tom. He walked over and looked out the window. "We have the makings of a damn good unit."

24 June 2002
Montgomery County Airport
Conroe, Texas

"MR. BRIGGS!" LAWTON HOLLERED DOWN THE hallway at William "Billy" Briggs. Briggs was a 55-year-old supervisor who looked 80. He had been at Conroe for twenty years and had seen ten commanders pass through the command. To say he was set in his ways would be an understatement. Lawton couldn't help but notice Briggs did not approach him. The supervisor barely lifted his head. Lawton exhaled as he closed the distance between them. He wasn't used to not being responded to. Even as a captain, people had given him more respect than Billy was now offering. But Tom had done his homework and was ready. To get his aircraft fixed and his unit to the level it needed to be, this meeting had to happen.

"Can you come to my office for a couple minutes?" He caught on that the other two maintenance workers standing nearby were waiting for Briggs.

Briggs grunted. "I ain't got time right now." He handed some paperwork back to one of the men.

Lawton preferred to talk to the older man in private, but it seemed Briggs wanted the support that witnesses would offer. *So be it.*

"All right then. Here is fine." Tom opened up his notebook. "I understand the squadron only has a sixty-two percent operational readiness rate, and the FMC, not counting weapons systems, is only at forty-six percent. With weapons systems accounted for, we're down to about twenty-five percent." Briggs looked at his support and back at Tom. Tom continued, "I can't train my unit with that kind of maintenance. So here is my question. What kind of help do you need from me to get the unit up to seventy-five percent FMC?"

Briggs slowly responded. "I don't need any help from you, unless you know how to turn a wrench!" He chuckled and looked at his two assistants to make sure he got a chuckle from them as well.

Lawton was an extremely patient man, but at this point, he couldn't control his temper. He took a step closer to Briggs and pretended the others weren't there. "I can turn a wrench, shitstick! And so can each and every one of my crew chiefs. I understand you are preventing them from doing that!" Briggs' smugness evaporated.

Tom glanced at the two witnesses. "Go fix somethin' or find a new job!" The two witnesses looked over at Briggs, then quickly scurried away.

He turned back to the older man and stepped closer. "I am a phone call away from having you replaced! You got me?" Tom pulled out his cell phone and said, "The TAG is only this far away. If I ain't got the power to get you to work, he does. He wants this program to work. I'll call him in a heartbeat."

Briggs came back with brass that Tom had not expected. "You can make all the phone calls you want, Lawton. I got a contract." He stepped back one step and added, "And there ain't a damn thing you can do about it. You know, we can only do so much with the folks we have."

Tom stepped closer yet again, trapping Briggs against the vending machine. "Then maybe you need to get some people that can do the work. Maybe some of my crew chiefs need to fill those high-dollar contracts you control." Tom squinted and cocked his head for effect. "Maybe they need a newer, younger supervisor with a fresh outlook. Maybe you're just too damn old to do the job." That one hit home.

"I can do the job just FINE, YOU SON OF A—"

"THEN FUCKIN' DO IT!"

Tom's comeback took the older man by surprise. Lawton could see Briggs looking for excuses. "My contract says I don't have to produce any numbers for readiness." Lawton knew this was the truth.

Tom stepped back and let him off the hook. "How screwed up is that, Billy?"

The older man's gruffness dissolved with Lawton's softer tone. "It is pretty screwed up."

"I need those aircraft up. What do I have to do to fix this?" Billy exhaled loudly. "You really want to know, don't you?"

"My pilots have to fly. I gotta have aircraft that work. With night systems and weapons systems that work."

Billy nodded. "First I need the parts. We have to get a higher priority within the system. We got two hangar queens here that haven't flown in six months. I need more people to turn wrenches on the PHASE[1] aircraft.

---

[1]   Complete maintenance overhaul accomplished after every 300 flight hours.

It's been in the hangar forty-five days. I don't have any people that are qualified to do weapons adjustments." Tom was scribbling furiously. "And if you can get more funds to pay my guys overtime, we would work longer."

Tom finished writing. "I think I can handle these. One is doable right now. My Delta Troop has qualified weapons maintainers. Why not let them work on the aircraft, boresighting the wing stores, systems checks, and all the other things that go with it?" Briggs hesitated, but finally nodded.

"Also, I think I can get some help with PHASED maintenance. I have friends at Hood that are looking for work and this is what they do." Tom continued on the subject. "I want to put two more birds in PHASE now before NTC. That will get two airframes into the flow with 300 hours of flight time each. Those 600 hours will fix our flow chart." Tom showed him two tail numbers in his notes and to his surprise, Billy Briggs nodded in agreement.

"That one still has thirty hours to fly until PHASE?"

"I think we can fly it off this week. It's only a day aircraft, but we have ten guys that need any kind of stick time. I can use the second bird to fly all ten on pre-PHASE maintenance checks. Doable?"

Briggs nodded. Lawton could tell he was winning Briggs's respect with good ideas.

"Also, we can exchange maintenance training. Your guys come in and teach my young enlisted guys how to keep the aircraft up, and they'll train your guys how to fix the weapons systems?" Tom could see that Briggs was considering nixing the idea. "If your guys learn weapons systems, they can work that into next year's contract."

Briggs liked the sound of that. "You got a deal." He stuck out his hand.

Tom took the hand and stared into Briggs' eyes. "Good. Just one more thing." Briggs was smiling. "Don't ever call me Lawton," Tom squeezed his hand a little, "like you got shit in your mouth again, and don't call me colonel. I'm a lieutenant colonel." Briggs's smile faded and his hand went limp. Tom let go. "If you are so inclined and you have a beer in your hand, you can call me Tom. If you can't be my friend, don't call me at all. If that's the way you want it, I can live with that. Just do your job and I'll do mine." He turned and walked away.

Lawton sat at his desk and reviewed his notes. He made a call to Ft. Hood. He had some maintenance friends at the 21st Aviation Training Brigade, and he was hoping for assistance with PHASE maintenance for the Apaches. To his surprise, they had a space available to hangar an aircraft and do the 300-hour PHASED inspection.

Then he called Major General Walker. The TAG was extremely happy to hear from Lawton and wanted to know how everything was going. Of course when the general asked was there anything he could do for the 7/17th Cavalry, Lawton was ready. "Well, sir, now that you mention it, we seem to be having trouble getting parts. I guess the Texas Guard doesn't rate high enough in the priority system to get the parts we need to get aircraft fixed. We have a couple hangar queens." He paused because he thought the general was writing, but then continued. "I know the active duty guys need parts, but when we carry an airframe down for over sixty days, it doesn't help anyone."

Walker said, "I understand completely, Tom. Let me run with this one. I'll talk to the folks at Ft. Hood and we'll explain that with NTC coming up, we need to have an increased priority. That should be sufficient."

Lawton smiled. That was an excellent reason for an increased priority. No wonder Walker was a general. "Any help you can provide, we appreciate, sir."

"It's nice to know that wearing these stars can help. At least, I hope they can."

Lawton smiled. "I'm sure they will, General. Thank you, very much. And you come on down and see us if you get time. Maybe I can get you up in a fifteen-million-dollar helicopter." The general laughed and said his good-byes.

Tom smiled. *That call went better than I expected.* Now it was time to make the call he didn't want to. He needed to call Crane and ask him for more money to pay the civilian contractors overtime. He didn't think he'd stand a chance. But the NTC rotation surely couldn't hurt.

He dialed the phone and waited. Luckily, the colonel was there. "Hi, sir. Lieutenant Colonel Lawton here."

"What do you need, Lawton?" came the terse response.

Damn, I hate this guy. No sense beating around the bush. "Sir, I need more money." He heard the scoff on the other end.

"You need more money? What for?"

"Sir, I need to pay my contract personnel overtime so they can work longer hours to get my aircraft fixed." He listened to the pause and expected a flat "no." As subtly as possible, he added, "I have to get my aircraft up so I can support the NTC rotation." He closed one eye and listened for the explosion.

"You think by paying contractors more, they'll get your aircraft ready in time?"

"Yes, sir."

Crane paused again, "How much?"

Tom ran some quick numbers in his head. "Without hiring another man, we can convert one salary for the overtime." He got the number and said, "One hundred fifty thousand."

"DAMN! You aviators cost too damn much!" The colonel was obviously doing some math on his end. He had a budget for NTC, but only he knew how much it was. A few seconds later, he said, "Let me talk to the general. As a supported commander for this exercise, I have the latitude to get you some money." Tom smiled. "So you owe me, Lawton." Tom's smile faded instantly.

"Thank you, sir." He swallowed hard. "I guess I will, after I get the money."

"Oh, you'll get the money, Lawton. You see, us active duty guys know what the hell we're doin'!" The fact that Tom knew enough to call Crane and explain he needed help seemed to Tom like he knew what he was doing, too.

"Again, thanks, sir. We'll see you next week." He hung up without waiting for a response. What a jerk.

Tom called his new best buddy Billy Briggs and told him the outcome. Briggs was stunned that Tom had come through on most of the request almost immediately. Briggs got aircraft 456 a maintenance flight and the next day it was headed to Ft. Hood to enter PHASED maintenance. Aircraft 834 began to fly 30 day hours and was in PHASE the next weekend. Within a week, parts began to arrive for the two hangar queens. By the end of July, money had been transferred to cover overtime work of the contractors.

Best of all, the crew chiefs got to work on aircraft alongside Billy's contractors on the weekend. The aircraft weapons systems were getting much-needed maintenance and the pilots were flying. Morale continued to climb. Briggs referred to Tom as the lieutenant colonel or Mr. Lawton and every once in a while he even smiled at Tom. They didn't much like each other, but at least they had come to respect each other.

On the training front, the unit began to fly aggressively. They were getting down into the trees in the daylight hours. They flew some multi-ship operations and were beginning to work on crew night-system training by mid-July.

On the last training day in July, Tom reported the results of their hard work. In the last month, their OR (Operational Readiness) rate had improved to seventy-one per-cent, the FMC (Fully Mission Capable) rate was up to sixty-three percent, and they had flown 312 hours, over 165 at night or under night-system conditions. This was unheard of numbers by a Guard unit.

Tom was pleased with the effort, and as a reward he sponsored another barbecue. The sergeant major cooked up some "Martinez Valley Chili," a recipe from his mother down in Brownsville. The twenty-gallon bucket lasted only ten minutes. Suggs had Captains Bartlett and Wills cook the ribs, and the mess folks took care of the rest. The Ramrods played about five songs. All's right with the world. For Tom, it was great to be able to make decisions that directly affected his troopers. He was having fun. This was the way command was supposed to be.

25 July 2002
Huntsville, Texas

JUST AS THINGS IN THE UNIT were coming together, things at home started to slip. Although Tom didn't realize it, Cindy was picking up on her husband's longer hours and his lack of concentration. She couldn't let his failure to remember their anniversary slide. The 19th of July came and went, and after 16 years, this was the first time he had forgotten. To her credit, Cindy didn't make a big deal of it, but she was hurt.

Tom showed up on the evening of the 25th, late, with flowers. He crept into the kitchen. Sarah, fifteen, was talking on the phone, and Cindy was at her laptop two feet down the counter. "Wow, Dad! What are the flowers for?"

Tom shook his head, too late. Jenny, eight, ran into the kitchen. Tom said, "What are you doing up? It's past nine o'clock."

"Dad, it's summer, I get to stay up until ten!" Alicia, their three-year-old, was obviously in bed, or she, too, would have entered the kitchen.

Tom frowned. "I knew that."

Cindy saw the flowers and held back her urge to cry. Not from joy, but from a week's worth of pent-up anger. Her cheeks flushed.

Tom saw Cindy's reaction and blocked out his daughter's voice. She pulled on his leg and yelled, "DAD!"

"WHAT?" Tom snapped. Cindy had seen enough; she turned and walked from the room.

Jenny was taken aback by Tom's harsh response. "Sorry, Daddy. I just wanted you to come read with me."

Tom shook his head. He was screwing up by the numbers. Sarah hung up the phone, looked at her father, then the flowers. She frowned, shook her head, and followed her mother.

Tom knelt down to Jenny's level and said, "Let me go change clothes and then we'll read in the living room, okay?" That satisfied Jenny. She smiled and skipped towards the living room.

Tom laid the flowers on the table. He was in a world of shit and knew it. He got a vase and some water and set the flowers in them. He took a deep breath and headed down the hallway, vase in hand.

Sarah watched Tom enter the bedroom. She looked at her mom, who was dabbing at her nose with a tissue. Sarah got up off the bed and walked past Tom without a word.

Tom put his flight bag down and sat next to Cindy.

"I guess those are supposed to make me feel better?"

Tom sensed the anger in her voice. "Look, honey, I am so sorry! I absolutely forgot—"

She cut him off. "Our ANNIVERSARY, Tom?" She started crying. "How could you forget that?"

He tried to hold her but she got up from the bed. "NO! Not now!" She walked to the door. "You said the Texas Guard would be different. You said you would be home more. But you aren't here anymore now than you were twelve years ago, before your last command! Before you went to Iraq!"

"Honey!" Tom got up.

She stopped him dead in his tracks. "I'm not gonna talk about this now." She pursed her lips. "I'm gonna go check my email. We will talk about this later, but not now." She quickly walked back to the kitchen.

Tom stood in the bedroom with his mouth open. *First round, TKO for Cindy.* He slowly changed his clothes and tried to figure out what to say. No good answer came. He headed to the living room and got a smile from Jenny. *At least she's not mad at me.* Tom sat on the couch and pulled Jenny up on his lap.

"You want to start, Daddy?"

Tom smiled "You go ahead. I'll help you out if you get stuck." He grabbed the remote and turned off the TV. Jenny smiled even more. That meant he was really listening. She opened the book and began to read.

Tom tried to focus, but his mind kept drifting to Cindy's comments. "She'd seen it before." He had gone off to his own little world before the first Gulf War when he had been a Troop commander. He had hoped she had forgotten that. It was the only time in their marriage that they had ever really had a fight. He had wondered if he was wrong then and if he was wrong now. He hadn't realized he was heading back into that solitary world.

"The armadillo fell fast asleep." Jenny finished the book.

Tom snapped out of his trance. He had missed the whole book. "Good job, honey." He stood her up and said, "I see you have a couple more minutes until bedtime. How about getting your pajamas on, then feed the cat." He bent over and kissed her. "Love you." She beamed and headed upstairs.

Sarah came into the room, grabbed the remote, and plopped down. The TV came to life. "You're in pretty deep, Dad."

Tom knew better than to play games with Sarah. "How deep?"

Sarah looked at her father. "I don't think it's sleep-on-the-couch deep, but you pretty much stepped in it."

Tom wasn't sure if Sarah knew what "stepped in it" meant, but he would discuss that at a later time. "How 'bout with you? Did I step in it with you, too?"

Sarah stopped changing channels and looked directly into his eyes. "For cripes sake, Dad! Your anniversary! I always thought that was sacred!"

Tom nodded, "It is."

She shook her head and looked back at the TV. "This one is gonna take a while."

Tom walked over and bent down. He took the remote away and looked at her. "So am I in deep with you, too?"

Sarah shook her head, "Nah. But you probably need to pay more attention to Mom."

"And you?" Tom tilted his head. "You're sure?'

"I'm okay. It's not my birthday that you missed."

Tom kissed her on the cheek. "Thank you, sweetie. I'm sorry." He turned and walked towards the kitchen.

Sarah hollered after him, "You do know when my birthday is, don't you?"

Just like her mother, never misses the chance to turn the blade when it's down to the bone. "September 23rd." He was proud of himself.

Sarah yelled, "That's Jenny's birthday, Dad!"

Tom stopped and turned around. "May 22nd." Sarah smiled and shook her head. She turned her attention to the TV.

Under his breath, Tom said, "I am such an idiot."

Cindy was back at the kitchen counter typing on the computer. Tom walked in with a plate of microwaved leftovers. He sat at the table and slowly ate.

"You know, if you got home on time, you wouldn't need to eat micro waved food."

Tom was happy just to hear her voice. "Yeah, I know. It's kind of tough to get away."

Cindy stayed quiet for an entire minute. As Tom put another bite of cold potatoes in his mouth, she said, "You're not going to take me for granted again, are you? I hate it when you take me for granted."

"I know, honey."

"If you know it, why do you do it?" She paused just long enough to give the silence extra weight. "You've done a great job being a squadron commander, but I wouldn't know! You don't come home till late, you work weekends." She slapped her leg and turned toward him. "It's like I don't have a husband anymore! I have a strange man that comes into my bedroom, lays down, and starts snoring!"

Tom stopped eating. His appetite was gone. "I've got to get the unit ready for NTC, honey. For thirty days, we are going to be put in a position where our every move will be scrutinized. What we put into training now will pay big dividends out in California." He tried to sound excited.

"What about dividends at home?" She turned back to the computer and began powering it down. "What about dividends from investing in your family, honey?"

Honey is encouraging. At least she isn't totally pissed at me. "I know I need to ..." Invest isn't the right word. "I know I need to make more time for you all. And I promise I will."

"When?"

Tom hesitated. "After I get back from NTC. I swear it."Cindy looked at him with a cocked head. "And what about this weekend?"

Tom was confused. "What about this weekend?"

"Damn it, Tom!" She got up from the computer and headed towards the doorway again. "This weekend is my family reunion!" She shook her head. No tears came this time. "You forgot, didn't you?"

"Um, not really." He tried to clear his throat. "I have drill this weekend."

"YOU—" She didn't finish. "We're goin', Tom! Even if you can't make it! We, the rest of your family, are going to go!" She headed to the bedroom.

Tom tried to rationalize and say he didn't really want to go to the reunion. The truth was, he did want to go. He wanted to be with his family. For all the fun he was having being a commander, he was getting failing marks as a husband and a father. Was this the price one had to pay to command? Tom had not expected this.

While he did not have to sleep on the couch that night, he did sleep on his side of the bed, untouched by the woman he loved. She wouldn't even slip her feet over to keep his toes warm. He had truly stepped in it and was in deep at the same time. He wouldn't be able to repair this specific hurt. It was up to Cindy to forgive him, and she apparently was in no hurry.

Tom now knew he had been neglecting his family. During the Gulf War, when he had given Cindy the same treatment, she'd come around and understood that command required sacrifice. What Tom failed to see was that, this time, it was up to him to figure it all out.

11 August 2002
Montgomery County Airport
Conroe, Texas

THE SQUADRON RALLIED ON FRIDAY AFTERNOON. After roll call, they broke down to prep for the deployment to Ft. Hood for the gunnery exercise. Because a significant number of troopers could not get away from their work, the unit would go to gunnery with ten aircraft. However, most made a conscious decision to attend the NTC rotation, taking them away from their jobs for the month of September. Tom and Sergeant Major Martinez were very satisfied.

The ground assets of the unit left early on Saturday morning, while the aircraft arrived at Ft. Hood late on Saturday afternoon. They set up a garrison environment just south of Gatesville. To Tom's surprise, Hodges had the maintenance people working late that night to get the aircraft ready for eight a.m. gunnery tables. The rotation was Alpha Troop (Outlaws), B Troop (Bandits), then C Troop (Cowboys). The goal was to train the crews in the first three days with day and night tables, then shoot multi-ship tables later in the week.

With ten aircraft, it would be tough to get everyone through, but that's all the aircraft the unit could muster.

Of course, no training of that magnitude ever comes off as planned. There were delays on the range and aircraft broke, so the individual tables slipped from three days to four days. The fifth day was scheduled for multi-ship with some active-duty ground artillery support. There was no way the unit could meet the deadline.

That evening, Lawton got a surprise visit from Colonel Richard Crane. He popped in as Major Jon Wright debriefed his boss. Lawton did not see the colonel at the door. He was in the middle of responding to Major Wright's explanations for the delays.

"Damn it, Jon, I don't care about that!" He gained his composure and paced around the room as he tried to think. "Those sound more like excuses than reasons. We've known we were going to have these ten airframes for a month. These are the horses we brought and these are the horses we'll ride. Got it?"

Major Wright nodded. "Roger, sir." The major looked away and suddenly snapped to attention. "GROUP, ATTENTION!"

Lawton was confused but snapped to. Colonel Crane slowly entered the room. He waited until he was all the way in before he quietly said, "At ease, gentlemen." Inside, Lawton was steaming. Whatever Crane was doing at North Ft. Hood on a Thursday night, it wasn't good.

Lawton put on the smile and said, "Welcome to Warriorville, sir!"

Colonel Crane put his helmet on the table and grabbed a seat. "Warriorville, eh?"

"Yes, sir, Warriorville." Tom kept his smile. "Can we get you something to drink?"

"Ah, no, Lieutenant Colonel Lawton." Crane looked around the room. Tom got the impression he was about to get dressed down in front of his own men. But it was worse than Tom expected. Crane went after the unit.

"I've been to a lot of gunnerys in my twenty-three years of service to my country, but I have never seen anything as fucked up as you guys!" He stood up. "Warrior-ville?!" He shook his head in disgust. "More like, Cluster-fuckville!" He smiled at his own stab at humor.

"Lieutenant Colonel Lawton, are you ready to do live fire with the artillery tomorrow?"

Tom didn't hesitate. "No, sir."

"How much more time do you need?"

"Sir, we will need both tonight and Friday night to get through tables for fourteen crews."

Colonel Crane seemed surprised that Tom didn't try to blow smoke up his ass. He walked around the room slowly.

"Gentlemen, this is not a playground for the unprepared. I'm not going to bring my active-duty artillery guys out here this weekend when you all couldn't get ready in the time you had allocated. You failed."

Tom was biting his lip. He did not for a moment feel the unit had failed. They had not performed as well as they had intended. They were not on schedule. But there were extenuating circumstances that Crane didn't know about. Lawton wanted to say something, but he presumed Crane's display was more for show than an attempt to malign his troopers.

He should have known Colonel Richard Crane better. The verbal assault continued, moving from the unit to the commander. "Do you gentlemen think your commander didn't have you prepared?" He wasn't looking for an answer, just sticking a knife in Tom's back. Lawton walked toward the colonel with his face flushed. Crane saw him and smiled. "I know you had 'em a little better prepared than this, but it sure isn't showing, is it?"

Tom was mad enough to spit. But he knew that Crane, as big an asshole as he was, was absolutely correct. The military system is not designed for a subordinate to reach around a superior's neck and squeeze. Tom did what the system expected of him. He accepted the truth. "No, sir."

Crane walked over and smacked him on the back. "You guys get your little clubhouse in order and have fun playin' army. The artillery live-fire is cancelled." He looked at Tom. "Take all the time you need to get your crews trained. You don't need to shoot the live-fire CALFEX at NTC. We'll do it without aviation." He started to leave.

Tom looked around at the rest of the Warriors. Their spirits had been trashed by harsh words from an outsider. *If anyone's going to hammer my troops, it's going to be me, not some schmuck that doesn't know what's going on.* Tom followed the colonel outside.

"Sir, a moment of your time, please."

Crane stopped and turned. "Sure, Lieutenant Colonel Lawton. I have a lot more time now that my calendar is free for tomorrow."

Tom looked around to make sure no one else was listening. He stepped closer to his active-duty rater. "Sir, if you have a problem with me, I can handle it. If the unit is not up to your expectations, that is totally my responsibility. So you can fire me if you want." He looked for a response. There was only a blank stare.

Then he said something he would regret. "Whatever you do to me is fine," he took a step closer and said quietly, "but if you ever come into my area and chew out my unit again, I will personally kick your ass." He bit down hard and looked for a response. Colonel Crane was stunned by the comment. "Don't you ever talk to my unit like that again!" Then Tom added through clenched teeth, "sir."

Taken aback, Crane struggled to respond. He was angry, but knew better than to push Tom too far at that particular moment, it had the potential to get much uglier than it already was. Tom Lawton was insubordinate, but Crane had no witnesses. He cracked a small smile. There would be another time. If Lawton couldn't handle this little gunnery, he wouldn't be in command very long.

Through an unaccustomed smile, Crane sneered,

"Why, Lieutenant Colonel Lawton, I will be sure to ask for your permission,"—he stepped towards Tom and through his own clenched teeth hissed—"before I rip their hearts out and send them home for their unemployment checks."

Lawton squinted and bit his lip again. Crane was trying to provoke him. Tom decided not to let Crane get to him this time. "I'll get them ready. You'll have your 15 crews next month. Just lay off my unit, sir." *Crane doesn't deserve sir. Shithead is more like it.*

"Not until they are ready to fight, Lawton. I don't see them getting that way with you in charge." He backed away and added, "Not an accusation, just a fact, Tommy." He turned and shouted over his shoulder, "Go back to coaching basketball, because you suck as a commander." He hollered at his driver to crank the Humvee and climbed in for his drive back to the post.

Tom was pissed and depressed, a bad combination to have when talking to troops. He shook his head as if that would clear his anger, then noticed Petty standing in the doorway.

"How much of that did you catch?"

"Enough to know you need a break," Petty said with a smile. "Follow me, sir! You ain't in any mood to see troops." Tom suppressed curses as the two walked to the parking lot. Petty opened the door to his new 2002 Thunderbird, climbed in, and started her up. "Come on, sir. We're going for a little ride."

For an instant, it looked like Tom would say no, then, without a word, he climbed in and sat down. As they pulled out of the parking lot, Petty turned the CD player up loud. Tom recognized the CD immediately. It was Pat Green singing "Who's To Say." Petty tapped along with the beat as Pat Green sang:

> *"Who's to say and who are you to judge me anyway*
> *This is my road, I take the corner as fast as I can go!*

> *Who's to say at how I got so lucky anyway*
> *I am my own at least until the Man come and take me home!"*

Lawton started tapping with the music. The wind started to feel nice, as if it were blowing away all the crap that Crane had laid on Tom's mind. He caught a glimpse of the moon starting to come up. He laid back and relaxed as they sped away from North Ft. Hood toward Gatesville.

The song finished as they entered Gatesville, and Petty turned down the stereo. "Like the song says, 'Who are you to judge me anyway?' That guy doesn't know us. He doesn't know the unit." Lawton was still frowning.

Petty tried a different approach. "You know, if he added a couple letters to his last name, it would be 'Cranium.' "

Lawton nodded. "If he shortened his first name, you could call him Dick!"

Tom smiled broadly. Petty said, "That's right! Dick Head!" Tom laughed out loud. The anger was gone. They pulled the T-bird into the Dairy Queen.

"How 'bout a big ol' Blizzard, sir?"

Lawton exhaled loudly. He knew he was overweight by Army standards, but a Blizzard sounded great. "What the hell? My boss thinks I suck. He thinks my unit sucks! I might as well splurge a little!"

"I don't call it splurging because I don't see us getting this at NTC."

"I don't see us getting squat at NTC. I don't even think California has Dairy Queens!" They laughed, then were quiet for a moment.

"You're doing a great job so far, sir, without sounding too much like a kiss-ass. This is one of the crappiest positions a commander can be in. You only have two days a week to work with your unit, the aircraft are just now getting so they work, and you've got a boss like Dick Head pushin' for results that we can't get for him."

"Yet!" added Tom.

"Yet! You are correct, sir!' The ice cream arrived. "Guess we better head back."

Lawton nodded in agreement. "Yeah. Suppose so."

"Sir, what would you have done if Colonel Crane—"

Tom interrupted, "If he'd have pushed it any further? Joe, I'll take a lot of crap for my own actions, but nobody"—he looked at Petty to reiterate—"NOBODY is going to fuck with the Texas Warriors. Not the NTC, not some fuckin' hard-ass wannabe, and hope to God not some poor schmuck enemy that we have to fight!"

This was the Lieutenant Colonel Tom Lawton that Petty knew and respected. He was good at fighting. It's a shame it had to be with another US Army officer.

It took two more days, but the unit came together and finished the gunnery much stronger than they started. The aircraft seemed to perform better later in the week, and the improvement in the scores was evident. As the availability of attack airframes became more consistent, the pilots were able to have confidence in the machines and focus on shooting the weapons systems. The August heat took its toll on the crews in the daytime, but Tom used this as a motivational tool to remind the crews how hot the desert of NTC would be.

Lawton recovered from the blow-up with Crane and was back to normal by the end of the gunnery exercise. That semblance of normal applied to his state of mind as a commander, not his emotional state as a husband. He missed two-weeks' worth of summer activities at home with his wife and daughters. It would be time he would never be able to make up to his family. Cindy dealt with his absence by maintaining her silence. As Tom grew closer to his unit as a commander, he slipped further away from his family.

CHAPTER FOUR

Some men fall, some fly,
Some men stumble, some shine,
In the grandest scheme sometimes it seems,
There ain't no scheme at all,
Some men fall, some fly.

"Some Men Fall"
-Walt Wilkins, Mark Irwin, and Josh Kear

26 August 2002
Montgomery County Airport
Conroe, Texas

THE UNIT RECOVERED BACK TO CONROE in better shape than when they left. The aircraft had flown surprisingly well in the second week, and the crews that could make it to gunnery were qualified. Tom had six crews that could probably be considered expert as their performance was well above established standards. The unit had improved dramatically in a very short time.

Lawton was pleased and looking forward to making up for lost time with Cindy and the girls. But one of the first things he needed to learn as a commander was that his time is never his own. A commander's time is the unit's time.

After such a training exercise, it was normal for the soldiers to blow off a little steam. Tom and Sergeant Major Martinez expected it, yet neither of them anticipated what happened.

27 August 2002
Saddles and Tramps Saloon
Cut 'N' Shoot, Texas

"HEY! HEY, FLY BOY!" YELLED THE drunk.

Three Warriors were casually perched at the bar, all three wearing crew flight suits. The youngest looked over the shoulder of the man sitting next to him. "You think he's talkin' to me? Or one of you guys?"

"That's right, you sons o' bitches! I'm talking to you!"

"I know he ain't talkin' to me, 'cause I know my Momma," said the pilot in the middle.

As the drunk approached, he continued his rage. "I'm talkin' to all of you!"

"Oh shit, man! Here he comes!"

"Maybe you should buy him a beer, LT," said Chief Warrant Officer Two Jason Early to his young companion.

"Buy this jerk a beer? What are you, nuts?" fired back the lieutenant.

The mountainous drunk approached the three pilots flanked by three friends. He stood at least six-feet-two, and carried two-hundred-sixty pounds including the beer gut. That weight didn't include the chains or his two-foot ponytail. His three friends, not as drunk but just as large, weren't necessarily encouraging their drunk compadre. Yet, they weren't discouraging him, either.

The four drunks lined up behind the pilots. The leader tapped Early on the shoulder. "Hey, boy, I'm talkin' to you!"

The bartender finally appeared on the scene. "Fellas, we ain't havin' any of this shit in here tonight. Understand?"

"FUCK YOU, FAT MAN!" yelled the drunk.

Jason Early, ever the diplomat, said, "Look, perhaps we could buy the gentleman a beer." Then he turned around and saw his tormentor was by no means a gentleman. The rowdy drunk looked like a Marilyn Manson fan on steroids. Early started to stand up, but a hand slowly came from his left. The pressure it applied indicated he should hold his position and remain calm.

The hand belonged to the oldest of the three pilots. The quiet one. Still facing the bar, he continued to slowly drink his beer. He held the longneck Lone Star up to eye level and appeared to watch the moisture drip down the side. Actually, he was looking into the mirror behind the bar, assessing the situation, evaluating his enemy, preparing his battlefield. The intelligence indicators revealed diplomacy was not going to work. He identified target weaknesses and the attack sequence he planned to employ.

For a successful operation, he needed his wingmen to take out the far target, but he knew his fellow aviators were not ready mentally for what had to be done. The four metalheads were undoubtedly drunk enough to be looking for blood, thinking they had found soft targets. They thought wrong. Chief Warrant Officer Four Brian Trant was a veteran of Greneda and the Gulf War. In his spare time, he competed in Ironman competitions. If he could eliminate the leader first, that would increase their chance of tactical success. With a little luck, they might just survive the night.

The lack of space prevented the long distance targeting the gray-haired pilot was used to, and his alcohol level was reducing his ability to track his target, but he still had an idea of how to get his first round down range. He needed a diversion.

"What do you think, Brian?" said Jason Early.

"YOU GOTTA ASK YOUR DADDY WHAT TO DO, BOY?" yelled the tattooed drunk. Then he reached into his back pocket and pulled out a knife. With a small amount of pressure from his thumb, the six-inch blade snapped out. The drunk slowly moved it back and forth in front of Early.

Brian Trant resisted the urge to strike. When the blade came out, Trant's buzz immediately disappeared. His eyes narrowed as he rescanned the reflection in the mirror. He focused on the drunk's hand and the shiny blade. Because of the movement and the shine, Brian reasoned it was for show. He took a deep breath. It was time to find out. "You gonna use that thing?" he said dryly, as his eyes caught the drunk's gaze in the mirror. "Or am I gonna shove it up your ass?"

The drunk was shaken by Trant's audacity, but he recovered quickly enough. "OLD MAN!" The drunk shifted his focus from Early to Trant. "I think I'm gonna stick you first!"

That was all Trant needed. Like lightning, he turned and threw the lieutenant's bottle of beer about five feet in the air over the drunk's head. As the drunk instinctively tried to cover himself, Trant slammed the drunk in the side of the face with his longneck bottle. With his left boot, he kicked the second man in the groin, dropping him to his knees. With his right hand, he clocked the third drunk in the nose. Trant's action took less than three seconds. Considering his age, and the amount of alcohol in his system, he was remarkably fast—as if he had done this type of thing before. Drunk number four didn't wait for guidance. He punched the young lieutenant square in the eye, knocking him to the floor. Early seized the opportunity to tackle the larger man. As they wrestled, 2nd Lieutenant Jonathan Whorley, all pissed off one-hundred-sixty pounds of him, shook off his daze and joined Early in pummeling the prone enemy.

Trant wasn't done. The loudmouth drunk was holding the side of his face as blood streamed from the cut beside his eye. Brian Trant grabbed the bleeding man by the hair and pulled him backwards onto a table. One hand moved around the drunk's throat and the other around the switchblade the drunk had dropped. He pointed the knife towards the drunk's face. The drunk was terrified. He was bleeding profusely from a four-inch gash, and tears were streaming down his cheeks. Trant leaned over and whispered, "Now look at you. Ain't so cocky without this little toad stabber!"

What was left of the man cried out, "Don't! Don't do it, mister!"

"So now I'm MISTER?!" laughed Trant.

BOOM! The shotgun sounded like a howitzer. "FREEZE!" The bartender came from behind the bar holding a double-barrel twelve-gauge. Brian Trant stayed focused on the bloody face before him. "Especially you!" said the bartender, glaring at Trant. The gun came toward Brian, who didn't flinch.

Jason Early and Jonathan Whorley slowly got up from the floor, leaving behind the crumpled, bloody body of antagonist number four. They slowly put their hands in the air and stepped away from the pile that one minute before was a fellow human being.

Early looked at Trant, who wasn't moving. "Brian?" At least he got a blink. "Brian, ease up, buddy!"

Trant exhaled audibly. He released his grip, and slowly straightened up. He never took his eyes off his victim. "I believe we'll go where we want and drink what we want," hissed Trant at his wounded adversary, "whenever the hell we want to!" He paused and bent over the bleeding drunk once more, "You don't have a problem with that, do you?" Then he stood and threw the knife into the wall, nearly causing the bartender to let loose with round two from his shotgun.

"That's ENOUGH goddamn it!" screamed the bartender. "That is ENOUGH!" The bartender approached Trant and looked down at what was left of the four drunken men. He saw Brian Trant had not calmed down one bit. He looked at the nametag on the flight suit. "I don't think he's gonna bother you fellas anymore, Trant." The bartender told the waitress to call an ambulance. "You all need to get the hell outta here. The cops will be here and you've done enough damage tonight already."

"You don't understand. We're not through with our beers yet," declared Brian Trant. He turned, walked towards the bar, and sat down.

The bartender exploded, "THE HELL YOU AIN'T!"

The light came on for Early and he knew Trant was pushing it into the red zone. He quickly stepped over to the bartender and nodded as he put his hand on the barrel of the shotgun. The bartender was still pissed, but slowly lowered the gun.

Early sat down on the stool next to Brian. "Hey now, buddy! This guy is givin' us the chance to slip on outta here." Early bent closer to Trant. "After what just went down here, we need to be glad he's lettin' us move out!" Jason Early looked for recognition in his friend's eyes. He only saw anger.

"I ain't done drinkin'," said Trant. He stared into the mirror behind the bar. He could see the young lieutenant talking to the bartender. "I didn't need to hear any bullshit from some metal-head drug addict that doesn't respect me!"

Jason Early looked into the mirror to meet his friend's eyes. "I know that, bro." He could see Trant coming down from his adrenaline rush. "Other battles to fight, man. Let's declare victory and live to fight another day." Finally, the words sank in. He could see the light come back into Brian Trant's eyes. The friendly smile was slow to come, but at last it appeared. "Come on, buddy. Let's go."

Trant nodded. "Okay."

Lieutenant John Whorley walked up to his partners. "The bartender said he'll let us go if we just get the heck outta here! Can we go?"

"Oh! Now you think we should go, LT?" smiled Early. "I don't know, Brian, you think we can blow this popsicle stand now?"

Brian Trant looked at Jason Early and nodded again. He looked at the young lieutenant. "Roger that! Sounds like a fine idea to me!" The two warrant officers smiled at each other and stood up. Brian came to the position of attention. Jason Early followed the lead. Both warrants saluted at the boyish-looking lieutenant.

"THE HELL WITH YOU GUYS!" said the young man loud enough for the bartender to look up. He turned and started out the door.

Jason Early smacked Brian on the back. "He'll appreciate us more when he sees how black and blue that eye gets!" The two men laughed and started to follow him out the door.

Brian stopped and looked at the man lying on the table. The bartender and the waitress were attending to the other three injured men. The bartender stood up and yelled, "Just get outta here! And don't come back!"

Brian looked at the bartender. "You tellin' us what to do now, too?" The bartender became quiet. Trant glared at the bartender, who turned back towards the injured men on the floor. Trant turned to the injured, drunk man leaning on the table and said, "You pull out a knife, you better use it. Because the next guy will probably kill you with it."

Trant looked at the bartender and his customary smile returned. "I'm just an all right guy that wanted a beer, friend." He turned and started to follow Early out of the bar. Trant glanced over his shoulder and hollered at the bartender, "I'll be back for that beer, Johnny Ray!"

"You stay the hell away from my bar! Don't you come back here!" yelled the bartender.

Trant got to the door, turned, and smiled, "SEE YA!"

3 a.m.
28 August 2002
Outside Saddles and Tramps
Cut 'N' Shoot, Texas

"YOU CAN'T BE SERIOUS?!" SAID JASON Early.

"Let's go! Come on," said Brian Trant. He tilted his head and batted his eyes as he pleaded with the other two troopers to join him. "I'm buyin'!"

The other two men looked at each other. All three could barely keep their heads up. They had been drinking since they left the bar. Some might say the biggest curse of alcohol is the amount of courage it creates. Others might say it's the stupidity. When it becomes a combination of the two, the law is never far behind.

Jason Early cranked up the chainsaw and laid it into the wall beside the back door of the bar. The loud buzzing cracked the silence of the night as the blade penetrated the wall about a foot from the doorknob. As Early sliced through the door, Brian Trant roared with laughter. He could barely stand as he watched the chainsaw rip away.

Lieutenant Whorley, one year out of Texas A & M University, covered his ears and squinted as the sawdust flew around Jason Early's silhouette. He yelled at Trant, "Don't you think we should be going?"

Trant was still laughing. "At this point lieutenant, it just don't matter!" He smacked the younger man on the back, smiled, and continued to watch the master woodsman cut a hole the size of Houston in the back of the bar.

Whorley would have left, but he was in no shape to drive. Plus, he had no clue where the hell he was.

His masterful task completed, Early turned off the chainsaw, stood back, and admired his work with a smile. He looked at Trant and said, "You or me?"

Trant smiled, "Hell, why not all of us?" Whorley was confused.

Early put the saw down. He and Trant each grabbed the lieutenant by an arm and started running full speed towards the door. Whorley knew better than to object, less he become the battering ram for his drunk companions.

The trio hit the door at the fastest speed the three drunks could muster. The door immediately collapsed. They stopped, looked at their handiwork, and then at each other. "WHOA!!!" yelled Whorley. "I'm not sure why we did that!" He stepped into the bar and said, "We are totally screwed, aren't we?"

The two warrant officers nodded in agreement. "There's only one thing to do now," said Early.

"Want that beer?" asked Trant.

The warrant officers followed Early into the bar. Whorley and Trant sat at the bar as Early poured three glasses of Lone Star draft from the tap.

They were still sitting at the bar when the Montgomery County sheriff's deputies, with pistols drawn, came through the gaping hole in the wall.

4 a.m.
28 August 2002
Huntsville, Texas

THE PHONE RANG AT JUST AFTER four in the morning. It was Sergeant Major Martinez. He had just received a phone call from a poker buddy of his at the Montgomery County Sheriff's Department. Seems three members of the 7/17th Squadron were picked up for unlawful trespass, illegal entry, criminal mischief, and at least seven other violations, including an 1867 noise ordinance.

Tom was shaking his head in the darkness as Cindy rolled over to hear the end of the conversation. "They did what?" Tom listened and started to rub his forehead. That told Cindy it was bad.

"Jesus Christ! What were they thinking?! Hell, they weren't thinking! I'll meet you there in an hour!"

"Christ, honey!" He hung up, went to the closet and quickly grabbed some clothes. "I have three guys in the Montgomery County Jail."

Cindy was now fully awake. "Jail? What did they do?"

Tom was shaking his head. "They used a chainsaw to break into a bar!"

"Oh, my God! That's—" She didn't know how to finish her thought. Finally it came to her, "They could go to prison!"

Tom stopped in his tracks. He hadn't considered that. His instant analysis as a commander had been, *What would the loss of three personnel do to the manning report and how could I replace the crews?* He quickly dismissed the thought and became Tom Lawton again. "Not if I can help it!"

He kissed her cheek and headed out the door. Cindy lay back in bed, but an hour later she was still awake.

5 a.m.
28 August 2002
Montgomery County Sheriff's Office
Conroe, Texas

LAWTON MET SERGEANT MAJOR MARTINEZ IN the lobby. The sergeant major explained everything he knew about what had happened. And he'd written down the list of charges. He also had collected three bail bondsmen's numbers and two attorneys' phone numbers just in case the situation was unsalvageable. Tom was shaking his head when the sheriff came into the office. He and Martinez were acquaintances and Martinez talked to the sheriff off to the side.

Tom paced as the older men discussed the situation. The leader part of him wanted to run over and try to help his men any way he could. The realist in him knew it was better to stay out of Martinez's way. The two men headed down a hallway to talk more privately. Tom stayed in the lobby and paced.

An hour later, the pair returned. The sergeant major was not as upset as when they originally went down the hall. He shook the sheriff's hand and headed over to Tom. "It ain't good, sir. But it ain't as bad as it could 've been!" As the deputy took Lawton and Martinez back to the jail cells, Martinez told Tom it would not be necessary for lawyers or even bail bondsmen if certain conditions were met. Martinez explained to Tom exactly what had to be done. Tom nodded in agreement.

The three men were sitting in the cell separated from the rest of the prisoners. Tom looked through the gate in silence. His trusted Warriors. His anger built as he watched the three obviously still-intoxicated men.

Early was the first to notice Lawton and Martinez standing at the cell door. "Damn, sir! Am I glad to see you!" He got up off the cot and started towards the gate.

Trant rolled over on his cot and started to get up. He swung his feet over to the floor, sat up, and grabbed his head.

Lieutenant Whorley was sitting in the corner with his chin laying down against his chest. When he heard Early speaking, he slowly looked up to see who was there. Upon seeing Tom and Sergeant Major Martinez, the lieutenant slowly came to his feet. But he did not walk towards the bars.

Early stopped at the closed gate and put a hand on it. It did not come open. His smile immediately faded.

Tom said, "You ... gentlemen have a good time last night?"

Early was the only one to answer. "Uh, we just had a little fun, sir."

Tom was pissed, but kept his voice low. "A little fun, huh?" He stepped closer to the cell. "You cut a hole in the wall of a bar, trespassed, stole alcohol." Whorley stepped closer. "And you put two men in the hospital!"

"THEY STARTED IT!" yelled Whorley.

"So you guys finished by damn near killin' one?"

That brought Trant off the cot. He was the first one to realize how much trouble they were in. He walked toward the gate and looked at Tom. "We didn't think we hurt them that bad."

"One guy's gettin' twenty-two stitches in his cheek and the other guy has," he looked at Martinez for help.

"Three broken ribs and a broken nose."

"DAMN!" squealed Whorley.

"That about sums it up." Tom wasn't finished. "You guys are looking at no less than four felony charges and God only knows how many misdemeanors."

Trant was still drunk, but he was sharp enough to notice Tom was talking in present tense. "Are looking" was not the same as "were looking." "Do we need to get lawyers?"

"Oh shit, man!" yelled Whorley. He turned and walked back to the far wall of the cell. "SHIT!" Early stepped back and sat on the cot.

Tom exhaled and looked at Trant. "You should. But thanks to the sergeant major, we worked out an agreement with the sheriff." Whorley got quiet and came back. "You might not like it, but it could keep you out of jail."

Early popped off the cot and came over to the bars. "Anything, sir. I can't stay in here!"

Tom looked at Trant and said, "What about you, hard-ass?"

"It depends on the conditions," said Trant.

Early looked at Trant and said, "Are you shittin' me, Brian?" He smacked Trant on the arm and said, "If it means we don't have to go to jail, we should jump on it!"

Whorley agreed, "I'm up for it, sir!"

Trant looked at the young lieutenant and shook his head. He turned towards Martinez and then Tom. "What's the so-called agreement?"

"Three conditions." They were listening. "First, you go back to the bar, apologize, and either fix it or pay for the damages."

Early said, "That sounds reasonable."

"Second, you pay for the hospital bills for those stupid bastards you fought with."

That one didn't sit well with Trant. He stepped towards the gate and put his hands on the bars. "Sir, those guys started the fight. We just finished it."

"You finished it by putting two of them in the hospital! I don't give a shit about who started it! What I care about is my soldiers, in their flight suits no less, fighting in a bar with the local populace! It sets a bad example. It creates a negative perception for everyone in the state that walks, talks, eats, breathes, works, and lives here to see someone in the military screw up like you guys did!" He let the comment hang in the air. "And you're lucky to get what's being offered!"

Early said, "Maybe that ain't so bad either, Brian!"

Trant stepped away from the door. "What else?"

Tom stepped towards the cell door and waved his hand for Martinez to come forward. The sergeant major reached into his pocket and pulled out some cards. "You need to go to AA meetings."

Whorley came over to the door and looked at the business card Martinez was handing through the bars. "Go to AA meetings?"

Early took a card and read it. Trant hesitated. "You need to do this, Mr. Trant."

Trant said, "I don't need the card, sir." Tom started to get pissed again. Trant cut him off before he said anything. "I know where the meetings are."

"Are you an alcoholic, Mr. Trant?" asked Tom. Trant slowly nodded "yes." "I'm sorry, I didn't know."

Trant blew out a breath up to the ceiling and said, "Haven't admitted that in a while!" Tom thought he saw a tear form in Trant's eye just before he turned around and walked toward the cot.

Early said, "So we need to go to AA meetings?"

Tom answered, "And the other things. You need to stay in Alcoholics Anonynmous at least until I leave command."

"You all need to agree to these conditions, or we walk out of here, and you're on your own." He looked at Martinez, stepped away from the cell, and let the men talk.

"I know this sucks, Brian," said Early. "But, considering the alternative, I gotta admit, I'm for it!"

Whorley agreed. "I'm not too happy about the AA thing, but that might actually be a good thing. Hell, I don't even remember half of what went on. My face hurts like crap. I never want to do this again."

Trant was the hard sell. Deep down he knew what the agreement meant. It meant staying sober. For an alcoholic, it was the hardest thing in the world to do. But Jason Early was correct about one thing. The meetings did beat going to jail.

Tom threw in another bit of incentive. "If you sons of bitches don't agree, I will tell the flight surgeon and you're all grounded!"

Early looked at Trant. "Come on, man!"

Trant was steadfast. If he was grounded, he might as well go to jail.

Tom threw peer pressure into the equation. He looked right at Trant and said, "It's all three, or none of you."

Whorley spoke this time. "Come on, Mr. Trant! Let's take the agreement!"

Trant exhaled again and said, "You wouldn't last one day in prison, LT!" Then he looked at Tom. "Okay, I agree to the conditions. I ain't exactly too keen on prison myself."

Lawton raised his voice, "Deputy Johnson!" The deputy came and let the three men out.

As they were walking out, Early said in a particularly loud voice, "Damn good thing we're outta here. We ain't never gonna see any of you poor bastards again!"

Tom turned and jumped into Early's face. He laid into him with both barrels of pissed off. "Listen to me, you dumb shit! You are about this close," Tom put his finger and thumb an inch apart directly in front of Jason Early's eyes, "to bein' left here. I've got relatives that work in Huntsville, Mr. Early. And when Trant said the lieutenant wouldn't make it a day there, he wasn't kiddin'! But a loud-mouth shit-for-brains like you wouldn't last an hour!" He stepped closer and hissed, "So get a case of SHUT THE FUCK UP!" Tom stepped back again. "Or so help me, you can stay."

Early's lip was quivering. He nodded and said in a low voice, "Yes, sir."

The five men walked out of the jail in silence. The sun was up, and it was going to be a hot, humid scorcher in east Texas. Tom stopped. "Sergeant Major Martinez is going to take you all to the hospital, then back to the bar to ensure the first two steps of the agreement are taken care of. The third step is up to you all. If you don't participate in the program, I'm sure it will just be a matter of time until we meet under these circumstances again." He turned and looked at his Warriors. "If we do, not even a lawyer will be able to help you." He turned and walked away.

Tom arrived home and explained to Cindy what had happened. She could tell he was upset, as upset as she'd ever seen him. Then he said something that made her cringe. "I don't know what those boneheads were thinking. What are people gonna say about the unit?"

She frowned and had to ask, "The unit? Or are you worried about what they will say about you?"

Tom got quiet, then frowned back at her. "About the unit, honey! I don't really care what people say about me."

"About Tom Lawton, or about the commander of that Guard unit, Lieutenant Colonel Tom Lawton?"

Tom got angrier. "What the hell does that mean?"

"You heard me. You're worried about what people think of you as a commander. The Tom Lawton I married could care less what people think about him."

Cindy went silent. He was too angry to argue so he headed to the door. "I've gotta go in and do what I can to get the unit ready to go to the NTC. We leave in a week. I don't have time for this."

It was Cindy's turn to be pissed. "Oh, no you don't!" She started after him. Tom was nearly running out the door. "Not today, Tom!" She hollered out the door as he jumped into the truck. "Please, Tom!"

He put the truck into gear and stepped on the gas. Cindy stood alone in the doorway. A tear traced down her cheek. Lieutenant Colonel Tom Lawton, Commander, had taken away her husband, just like twelve years ago.

CHAPTER FIVE

Get off of the bench, get into the game.
nobody rides the pine in Jesus' name.
Everybody lookin' for a Savior's waitin' out on the field.
If you're gonna suit up, come ready to play.

"Get Into The Game"
-Dana Jacobson

7 September 2002
The National Training Center
Ft. Irwin, California

THE NATIONAL TRAINING CENTER (NTC) AT Ft. Irwin, California, is a massive slice of desert set aside for large-scale US military units to conduct force-on-force training. These units are usually divisional assets of Brigade size, either Armor or Mechanized Infantry. The training unit will generally be composed of the ground element, artillery support, designated support or logistics elements, and an aviation element. Usually this force numbers around 4000 personnel.

Tom's unit would go up against the home team, the Ft. Irwin OPFOR, or opposition forces. The OPFOR was created to give the unit training a look at a simulated enemy. The Ft. Irwin OPFOR, a unit that executes its mission against the best ground units the US military has to offer, may be the best-trained military force on earth.

To execute the force-on-force training, all equipment used in the "box," or training area, is rigged to transmit signals that depict exactly where that piece of equipment is located. The signals are displayed on huge screens in the "Star Wars building," where Observer Controllers (OCs) monitor the fight and subsequently provide feedback to the training audience.

A training session generally follows a four-week pattern wherein the trained unit equips and deploys to the box in the first week, exercises defense in the second week, performs a live-fire gunnery and executes offense in the third week, then finishes training, and redeploys to home station the fourth week.

September was a fairly opportune time to deploy to the NTC as the desert heat was not at its peak and the nights weren't freezing. The worst obstacle for the 7/17th would be the fine orange-brown dust that would cover everything and attempt to ruin the equipment. The OPFOR had a distinct advantage because they knew every inch of terrain and had seen it in all conditions day and night. Plus, they were funded to train aggressively with a larger budget than the incoming unit could ever typically muster. The OPFOR at NTC has been called the 4th largest and best army in the world. They know they are that good and present the training units with a great training scenario with every rotation.

The Observer Controllers are usually the best officers by branch or career path the Army has to offer. That is to say, the Infantry OCs are hand-picked, top of the line, just like the Armor officers and the Aviators. Even the best active units in the Army have a tough time satisfying the NTC's instructors.

Crane's 3rd Armored Brigade of the 1st Cavalry Division would not normally be the first unit to train during the rotation. They were picked after the 1st Brigade moved up to receive their new digitized equipment early. The unit only had four months to prepare when most units have a year. Crane looked forward to the challenge, knowing he had nothing to lose and only a golden opportunity to get his unit ready for war. But he had not counted on needing second-string support units to fill out his rotational requirements. He was sure his combat-arms grunts would excel in the training, but Crane had no intention of relying on support units—especially his National Guard Attack helicopter unit.

The 7/17th managed to get fifteen helicopters self-deployed all the way to southeastern California, but one broke hard upon arrival. For the first two weeks, the unit had only 14 aircraft to fight in the defense. That was only the tip of the setback iceberg. Due to their reserve status, the unit missed some early meetings and was late to a few exercise-focused training requirements. This did not endear them to Colonel Dick Crane who saw this as proof of his critical opinion regarding the use of reservists in the "real Army."

On the third day of the rotation, the entire 7/17th was inexplicably given a urinalysis test. Tom understood how a unit might have to get a urine test in the first day or two; but after three days, no one would come up 'hot.' Only a rare, hardcore abuser or someone sneaking in alcohol, which was totally prohibited to any unit in the box, would get caught. He checked with other Battalion commanders and no other unit was subjected to a urine test.

Tom was the first one in line for the urinalysis. His unit was generally good-natured about the requirement, but some minor grumbling occurred as word passed that they were the only unit subjected to the "random" sample.

Once the planning meetings started, Tom Lawton usually bore the brunt of the Colonel Crane's wrath. By the time the exercise was set to kick off, the Texas Warriors were relegated to a reserve roll for the first two days.

The second day of defensive operations, Captain Hector Sanchez's C Troop Cowboys got into the fight on the eastern flank. They were promptly destroyed in less than ten minutes, and the 3rd Brigade was quickly routed. The OPFOR rushed full speed into the right flank of the Blue Force Brigade, and within fifteen minutes had overrun the Brigade headquarters. Tom arrived too late with B Troop, only to witness the dust cloud hanging over Crane's headquarters as the OPFOR rolled through.

At the nightly battle review, the OCs were quick to chastise Brigade Commander Crane for not employing his aviation assets earlier to plug the breach on the right flank. Crane was steaming as he acknowledged his shortcoming. Tom sat silently in the back and ate a Snickers bar that allowed him to cover his smile. At the end of the review, Crane stormed by Tom without so much as a good night.

The next day, the Brigade Blue Forces got their ass kicked again, but it came right up the middle. This time, a one-star general named Carlson performed the debrief. He was tactful, but the fact that a general came in to tell Crane he was screwing up meant something.

The next fight was during late afternoon, and Tom and Major Jon Wright, the S3, were better prepared. They had discussed contingency plans for OPFOR breaches and did not wait for guidance from Crane, who never called for aviation support. Tom monitored the battle on the command frequency (FM) and predicted where the breach would be. He sent B Troop with Captain Chase Freeman around the western flank and set up a screen.

Freeman, inexplicably, called on the Ground command FM to notify Crane that he was in position for his screen. A somewhat surprised Crane responded with, "Uh, Roger, C35, this is Gunfighter Six! Hold your position and do not engage unless you get clearance from me!"

Tom listened to the exchange like a quarterback coach on the sideline, noting that Freeman had not reported to Lawton or Wright but had called Crane directly. Even more surprisingly, Crane apparently understood who was covering his flank without having called Tom to get an update on other aviation assets. Something stunk.

After twenty minutes, the OPFOR engaged heavily on the western flank. Tom swore it was the main effort. He heard Crane say so on the radio and he heard him call his reserves to the west to prepare for the breakthrough.

Tom reacted by sending A Troop, the Outlaws, to back up Freeman. The smartest thing he did was keep Sanchez and C Troop with him. As the fight became heavy in the west, Freeman ran out of gas and ammo. He called to reposition to the FARP (Forward Area Refuel and Rearm Point), which Tom quickly approved. The Outlaws, already in position, moved in to replace Freeman. But, for some reason, there were no targets left.

That's when it dawned on Tom. The western effort was a feint. The call came on the radio from a frantic armor company commander on the eastern flank. He was engaging a massive force to his direct front. Crane had committed his ground forces to the west and was frantically calling to reposition the reserves.

Tom didn't wait for the request order. He called Sanchez, with all six Cowboy aircraft, and Major Wright, who had just exited the FARP headed east. He fell in at the trail position and they made it into the fight with eight Apaches just as the flank was about to collapse. All eight aircraft engaged for 12 minutes and managed to blunt the OPFOR enough for Crane's ground forces to arrive and save the fight.

At the debriefing, Brigadier General Carlson gave Crane an "attaboy" for tremendous employment of his aviation assets to prevent a rout. He received a standing ovation from the assembled body. Crane was quick to acknowledge that a certain Captain Chase Freeman, from B Troop, 7/17th was in the right place at the right time to stop the penetration. Captain Freeman was beaming from the accolade. What he failed to mention was that the captain was on the western flank, where the feint was, and that Sanchez and the C Troop Cowboys had stopped the penetration in the east. Sanchez turned and looked at Tom as if he had been stabbed. Tom smiled and gave him a "thumbs up." He knew who had done the work.

Lawton watched the spectacle unfold and eyeballed Crane with an icy stare. The colonel didn't bother to tell Carlson that the aviation commander had done the entire maneuver without a word of guidance from his Brigade commander. From the back of the assembly area, Tom spit his gum out, turned, and headed for chow.

Something wasn't right. He couldn't quite figure it out, but he would soon enough.

19 September 2002
The National Training Center
Ft. Irwin, California

AFTER A DAY OF REST, CRANE slipped into the Squadron TOC (Tactical Operations Center) unannounced, like a snake quietly slithering into a henhouse. The operations NCO, Sergeant First Class Dominguez, called the tent to attention. Everyone snapped to. As was his annoying habit, Crane waited until he was all the way into the tent at the center of the light before he gave "at ease." The commanders and staff officers tried to relax, but most found it impossible with Crane there.

"I just wanted to tell you guys I saw a lot of improvement in you all during that last engagement. That was some good work by you captains in defense. I decided that you all are going to join us for the live-fire exercise tomorrow and I look forward to continued improvement next week when we're on the offensive." Colonel Crane stabbed at the dirt with his left foot. It was obvious he was not used to showing appreciation to anyone, much less this unit. Lawton thought, *It must be killing him to acknowledge a National Guard unit saved his ass.*

"That's about all I can say." He exhaled loudly and said, "I'll see you guys tomorrow."

Lawton looked at Martinez and shook his head with a smile. He followed the colonel out of the tent. Tom was the first one to speak. "Well, thanks for coming out here and telling my guys they did good, sir!"

Crane merely grunted, then said, "They did good for one mission out of five, Lawton. That's nothing to write home about."

Tom was still smiling. "I ain't writin' home, sir. But it's a step in the right direction for a Texas Guard unit!"

"I'd say you got lucky, Lawton! As far as I could tell, your captains were out there running around the battlefield without supervision. They just happened to be in the right place at the right time for one fifteen-minute stretch."

Tom's smile faded. "I chose not to talk on your radio as you had it pretty well tied up talking to your out-of-position tankers."

"They were where they were ordered to be, which is more than I can say for you!"

Tom didn't want to get into a pissing contest. He decided to change the subject. "So it's been over a week. Did I have anyone come up hot on the piss test?"

Crane shook his head. "We didn't catch any of your drunks this time." The statement clearly insinuated something more. Then Crane let one more comment fly. "It's just a matter of time until one of your alcoholic outlaws steps in deep Kimchi, Lawton. And if you can't do anything about them, I will." He turned and headed towards his Humvee without even saluting.

Lawton was stunned. *What the hell brought that comment out? "Alcoholic outlaws" and "If you can't do anything about them, I will!"? A light came on in Tom's mind. Someone told him about the incident with Trant, Early, and Whorley! I have a spy in my camp.*

He was quiet as he went back into the TOC. For the rest of the night, he was cautious of what he said and how he said it. Martinez was the only one that noticed. At the end of the night, Lawton pulled him off to the side and told him about his conversation with Crane. Martinez was unaware of any snitch, but vowed to find out who it was and screw him up big-time if it was true.

Both knew that the one thing that will crush a unit is lying. Another is disloyalty. Neither could be tolerated.

21 September 2002
The National Training Center
Ft. Irwin, California

THE GUNNERY WENT MUCH BETTER THAN expected. Lawton and Wright decided to only use four crews for each of the five live-fire exercises. That reduced the number of airframes in the sky and prevented the chance for accidents, mishaps, or delays. The strategy paid off and they earned some well-deserved compliments from the ground commanders. Crane, not one to give praise to anyone, only found fault for rounds that didn't hit and the inability of the firing units to synchronize their engagements and fight like a team.

At the end of the gunnery, the colonel found time to pontificate. Crane gave a forty-five-minute lecture on the value of digitization and how 21st-century technology would allow the 1st Cavalry to portray the equivalent of a 20th-century Corps on the next battlefield. He insisted that SA (situational awareness) would be so dramatically improved that general officers would be able to direct the fight of platoons from the Airborne Battlefield Command and Control Center.

He concluded his lecture with, "In the future, the United States Army will be able to go beyond the standard Shoot, Move, and Communicate concept that you and I grew up with!"

Tom made a mental note to himself. *Crane is definitely an idiot if he thinks such time-tested techniques are out of date.*

Crane looked skyward through the ceiling of the tent for dramatic effect and stated, "We can achieve unbelievable simultaneity, agility, and situational awareness, which will allow us battlefield domination never before conceived!" The sycophants applauded enthusiastically at the melodramatic speech by their rater.

Lawton, in his customary place at the back of the tent, afforded a small "golf clap."

Lieutenant Colonel Jack Thompson, the Artillery Battery commander, turned to Tom and said, "Do you suppose he thinks he'll be the general officer dictating direction to some poor private in a fighting position?"

Tom chuckled and shot back, "You know how much money we can save by eliminating the entire non-commissioned officer corps?" Thompson smiled broadly and rolled his eyes.

The two men gathered their equipment and started out together. They were almost clear when Crane walked up behind them. "What do you think, Lawton?"

Tom was dumbfounded that Crane even wanted to talk to him. He decided to play dumb. "About what, sir? The NTC?"

"NO!" Tom thought Crane had cursed under his breath.

"About my ideas on digitization."

Tom had the inclination to really tell him what he thought, but knew better. "I think it has a lot of potential, sir. But today's military isn't ready for it."

"I beg to differ, Lawton. You aren't. You National Guard guys with your old equipment will never be able to keep up with active duty forces."

Tom wasn't too sure how much of Crane's statement was bravado and how much was wishful thinking. "Within two years, the National Guard won't be able to deploy with frontline fighting forces. They will be relegated to homeland defense and border security."

Tom nodded in agreement. "In the next two years, those are both probably going to be highly necessary missions." Jack Thompson nodded in agreement.

Crane shook his head. "No, Tom. You just don't get it, do you? Modern technology will reduce the need for anyone to do that mission. UAVs (Unmanned Aerial Vehicles), cameras, satellite imagery, and technological developments will make the mission of the National Guard and other security entities inefficient. There won't be any need for them. Active duty forces will be able to destroy any and all enemies. No one on the planet will be able to oppose US forces. Not traditional standing forces, and not state-sponsored terrorists."

He looked at Tom and saw the combat patch on his shoulder. "We'll be able to kill our enemies even more efficiently than you did in Iraq."

Lawton looked at Thompson without expression. In any other situation, Tom would have laughed out loud. Tom had noticed long ago that Crane, even with 23 years of service in the Army, did not have a combat patch. This meant that, even though it was hard to believe, he had never actually been in combat. Crane's diatribe was weakened because of a lack of credibility. What was even scarier was that Crane honestly believed what he was saying. Tom had no desire to discuss military philosophy with any high-ranking officer, especially Crane. "You just might be right, sir. I guess we'll know in a couple of years." With that, Thompson nearly begged to leave and Tom followed suit.

Lawton went back to the Warriors as soon as he could get away. He was uncomfortable with the group of active duty commanders and their staffs. Worst of all, he was getting more and more uncomfortable around Crane. He used to think it was just him and his Texas Guard unit, but Crane was a jerk to everyone. "An equal opportunity shithead" is how Martinez described him. Crane was a perfectionist totally unaware that man was an imperfect being. He was especially unaware of his own imperfections.

22 September 2002
The National Training Center
Ft. Irwin, California

THE WEEK OF OFFENSIVE OPERATIONS WENT somewhat better, but the unit still had some problems to sort out. Major Wright seemed to improve on a daily basis, and Major Suggs was nearly flawless with his logistics support. He appeared to be one step ahead of Captain Wills, the headquarters troop commander, in every requirement. It wasn't that Wills was incompetent, just ineffective.

The engagements were not without problems. The first day, the 7/17th was required to perform a continuous attack. The Squadron was supposed to rotate one troop after another until the Brigade had achieved the advantage over the OPFOR in their defensive positions.

After the first engagement, Tom rotated back to the FARP for fuel and left the squadron in the capable hands of Major Wright. Between the rotation of the 2nd Troop and the 3rd Troop, the squadron broke contact with the OPFOR; Crane didn't miss this.

The Brigade was about to have a breakthrough and Crane called for his attack troop to exploit a seam. When he called for the Warriors, Wright did not have the A Troop ready to go. It took nearly ten minutes for the B Troop to get to the front lines. By then, the OPFOR had plugged the gap with their reserves. The initiative was lost. Crane was livid at the lack of aviation support. After the OCs terminated the engagement, Crane requested that Lawton and Wright report to his position. Tom understood the significance.

As Lawton got out of his Apache, Wright came running up, visibly shaken. "I'm sorry, sir! It's all my fault! I didn't have the B Troop in place!"

Tom stopped him with one hand and said, "Before you go jumpin' off a cliff, let's just go see what the Brigade commander wants, okay?" Tom smiled. "Nobody got hurt. We didn't crash a helicopter. And whatever happened before, we can't change it now." He smacked the nervous major on the back. "We'll talk about it later, okay?"

Jon Wright took a deep breath. "Okay, sir."

Crane's face glowered over the map on the hood of his Humvee, his face flushed. Lawton and Wright saluted. Crane saluted and pounced before they had a chance to speak. "Where the hell were you, Lawton? The one time I needed you and your outlaws!"

Then he turned on Wright. "And what the hell was your problem? You had one thing to do! Have that Troop ready to fill the gap!"

Tom stood at attention during the colonel's rant. Out of the corner of his eye, he could see Wright shaking. *Time to step up to the plate.* Tom interrupted the colonel. "Look, sir! It was my fault!"

The sacrifice threw Crane for a loop. He wasn't expecting it. "Hold on, Lawton!"

"No, sir! It was my fault! I should have waited until the troop was engaged, then turned it over to the S3! Then I could have gotten fuel and been back in time for the 3rd Troop to rotate in!"

Crane obviously didn't give a shit about the explanation, but the rebuttal threw his timing off. He lost his initiative, trying awkwardly to continue his rant.

Wright was no longer listening to Colonel Crane, thinking about how his commander had just stuck out his neck for him. He wasn't nearly as nervous as before. This shored up his courage. He stood stoically at attention and let the verbal barrage roll off him.

Tom saw his S3 had "bucked up" and almost smirked. The colonel ripped them for a solid ten minutes. Then he demanded, "Get the hell out of my AO!"

It didn't take a second request. The two Texas Warriors saluted and headed toward their aircraft. They walked about a hundred yards when Jon Wright said quietly, "Are you gonna fire me, sir?"

Tom looked at Wright out of the corner of his eye. "I don't know where you ever got the idea you could get out of your job that easy." They walked a little slower. "Do you still want the damn job?"

Wright was quick to reply. "Hell yeah, sir!" He was smiling when he said it.

"Nobody gets out of here until I tell them they're done, okay?" The major nodded. "Besides, I've spent too much time training you to have you go do good things somewhere else."

"Thank you, sir."

Tom kept walking. "Next time, make sure you have the 2nd Troop ready to move forward, okay?"

Wright had a subdued smile. "Yes, sir." They walked a few more steps. "Sorry, sir. I fucked up."

Tom stopped and smiled at Wright. "We all do, Jon. Even that shithead back there. He ain't perfect. If this is the worst thing that ever happens to us, we've had a damn good life, right?" Jon Wright nodded. Then Tom added, "Nobody died and we live to fight another day! HOAAH?"

"Hoaah, sir!"

"Now get your ass back to the TOC and get ready for tonight. I'll be at the debrief getting another ass-chewin'!"

Wright grinned as he saluted. They parted and went their respective ways. Tom Lawton was a commander that had achieved a personal victory from a tactical loss: an S3 had gained respect for his boss and himself. Tom felt quite good about the whole incident. He couldn't help but think, *The only thing better would've been if Crane had suffered a stroke.* After Colonel Crane's meltdown, the rest of the week was an uphill battle. They made mistakes, but Tom saw the unit improving rapidly. On the last mission, Captain Bart "Bat" Talbot took his troop on a deep attack and caught the OPFOR napping in a holding area. He managed to score twenty-four "kills" and returned his entire troop without a loss. The crew of Chief Warrant Officer Four Brian Trant and 2nd Lieutenant Johnny Whorley scored seven kills by themselves. They received impact Army Achievement medals from Brigadier General Carlson as the outstanding crew of the rotation.

Tom was proud of them, his commanders, and the whole unit. It only took one comment from Crane to bring him back to earth. At the awards ceremony, Crane let go with a snide, "I don't think I'd let the general give any alcoholics in my unit an award. Oh, that's right! I don't have any alcoholics in my unit!"

Tom responded flatly, "Roger that, sir." He quickly turned and left the area, avoiding any further contact with Crane. Neither of them ever mentioned their scream-fest, as if it had never happened.

At the NTC outbrief, Brigadier General Carlson indicated he was pleased with the performance and activities of the 1st Team's 3rd Brigade. Carlson stood in front of the two large video screens that displayed Red and Blue Forces, his desert-camouflage uniform (DCUs) heavily starched.

Over 50 officers had assembled in the OC seats, sand, dust, and grit covered from the California desert. During his comments he mentioned some very positive things and some not-so-positive things.

Carlson was impressed that the Brigade was flexible and managed to employ all assets available against the OPFOR. In simple terms, Crane had integrated his infantry, armor, artillery, support, logistics, and, of course, his aviation units, to the fullest. Crane was delighted with the general's comments and wholeheartedly agreed with that portion of the outbrief.

As for the negative aspects, Lawton felt General Carlson let Crane off easy. "For the most part, the Brigade commander had full situational awareness. I thought your communications with subordinate commanders could have been better." The general paused at the podium and looked over his glasses at the crowd. "I thought you were a little slow to bring up reinforcements and get them into the fight." On that note, Crane turned and looked at Tom. His frown spoke volumes. Tom just dismissed the parental glance and turned his attention back towards the general.

Carlson fired one more shot at Crane. "I know in the future, the 1st Team will be the premiere unit in the US Army with the digitized force available. But, in the current environment, with the equipment you currently have, you should not be too quick to overlook the positive attributes of the forces on hand." His comment apparently confused some in the audience, so the general clarified his intent. "In layman's terms, you need to be able to fight with what you've got. If you don't have 21st-century technology, you need to adjust your war plans to the equipment available. For example, provide your staffs more planning time." Then he looked directly at Crane. "And get those Apaches some more time and bring them a little closer."

Lawton smiled. *The general didn't get his stars because he was an ass-kisser.* Tom agreed with everything he said except "bring them a little closer." Tom remembered an incident when he got his unit too close in combat in Iraq. He was lucky he had only lost an aircraft. That nearly cost him a crew.

Finally, it was Carlson's turn to get on his soapbox about the future and how wonderful the totally digitized force of the 21st century would be.

"The newest equipment we have will prevent fratricide on the next battlefield. Technology will allow a commander the ability to employ effects-based targeting, targeting directed with pinpoint accuracy at precisely the right time, when the enemy is confused, while we maintain full situational awareness!" The assembled crowd stood and applauded the closing statement. Tom watched and clapped politely as the general took his handshakes and moved through the crowd.

Tom was tiring of a system largely unproven in training, much less in combat. The general in his starched DCU had been briefed that the systems would work in the desert environment. Crane believed what Carlson said. But Lawton had been in combat. *No battle plan, not even a computer-generated one with "full situation awareness," will survive first contact.* Lawton knew that technology could not eliminate fratricide. It simply wasn't possible. *As long as war exists, people will make mistakes and friendly forces will be killed.* Tom understood it was humans that made the adjustments, humans that made the decisions, and it would be humans that died on the battlefield.

Tom waited outside the Star Wars building for all his commanders to come out. As he looked out over the assembled crowd, he saw something that made his skin crawl. Colonel Crane was standing with Captain Chase Freeman, one hand on the captain's shoulder and the other shaking his free hand.

Tom didn't break his stare until Suggs tapped to remind him they needed to get back to the barracks. They had an early pitch pull in the morning and it was a long flight back to Conroe. Tom nodded and said, "You're right, Major Suggs. How 'bout you go get that captain from the good colonel before he gets some kind of fuck-up fairy dust on him?" Suggs followed his boss's gaze and frowned. He saluted and went over to get Freeman.

Lawton had seen enough to know he had found his spy. Now he had to figure out how to deal with him.

CHAPTER SIX

Life will make sure that you got your troubles,
Life will make sure that you work too hard.
There ain't nobody that don't get tired,
Watchin' troubles pile up big in your own backyard.

"Carry On"
-Pat Green and Walt Wilkins

8 October 2002
Huntsville, Texas

THE UNIT HAD DONE QUITE WELL at the NTC. Lawton even found it in his heart to tell Mr. Briggs how wonderful the aircraft had performed. The crews had performed much better than he had anticipated, and Suggs had performed outstandingly as the executive officer. Major Jon Wright had some rough spots, but he was probably the one officer that benefited most from the entire training exercise, improving by leaps and bounds. Lawton was extremely satisfied with the whole experience.

While things at the unit were as good as they could get, home-front woes for Tom continued. One event in particular set Cindy off. A wife of one of the warrant officers called one Wednesday night. Tom tried to console her, but she was crying and talking about how hard it was to be an officer's wife. He fell for her tears and instantly thought the best way to deal with the poor woman's misery was to let her talk to Cindy. She was an experienced Cavalry wife and would do a terrific job.

Tom called Cindy over with his free hand and explained what was going on. Cindy, to Tom's surprise, wanted absolutely nothing to do with this strange woman on the phone. Tom nearly begged her to talk to the woman. Reluctantly, she agreed.

Tom sat on the kitchen counter and listened intently as Cindy and the woman talked. It took Cindy about three minutes to get her to stop talking and listen. "Look, I've been an Army wife for about 15 years now. I understand completely what you are going through." She paused and listened. She nodded in agreement with a woman that was hundreds of miles away. Cindy interrupted her and said, "Well, that is just something to be expected! They're men and they have this kind of psychological addiction to the military!" Tom raised an eyebrow and wondered where the conversation was headed. Cindy noted his curiosity and covered the phone. "If you want me to do this, butt out!" She turned away from Tom with a frown on her face and resumed the conversation.

Tom grabbed a soda from the fridge and returned in time to hear Cindy mention the Dining-Out, a traditional format dinner that included spouses. "Oh, you must come! It's our chance to get back at all the Neanderthals and enjoy ourselves for a while!" She paused, then added, "I look forward to meeting you, too, Sharon. Just remember, they're all like that. Uh-huh! Me, too. Bye-bye!"

She hung up the phone and leaned against the table. The first thing Tom noticed was her glare.

"What?"

"Look, Tom. This whole command thing is on you. I don't want any part of it. Never have and never did.

"This woman is married to one of your soldiers, so her troubles are your responsibility. I am not in your command, don't know the soldier, and don't want to know his wife. I am a mother of three beautiful children. Perhaps you remember them. I have no desire, nor the time, to babysit twenty-something-year-old wives of Cavalry soldiers that treat their families," she hesitated, "as shitty as you treat yours!"

Tom was stunned. Cindy had obviously saved that one for the right time. "I don't want you to babysit these women, Cindy."

"Then why did you give me the phone?"

"I just thought you could give her some guidance, you know? Help her out. It was clear to me she was upset!"

Cindy got up from the table. "She's upset because her husband is selfish and not paying any attention to her and their six-month-old son."

Tom tilted his head. "And you?"

"I'm not upset. I'm just annoyed because my husband doesn't know his family exists!"

"You're wrong! I know .. I .. just don't have time."

She stopped him with a hand and said, "You were gonna make time after you got back from California. Now the girls are back in school. You missed Sarah's birthday party last month. And now you've got me talking to complete strangers going through the same bullshit as me!"

Tom tried to smooth it over. He walked over and tried to put his arms around her. "But you're so good at stuff like that!"

She pushed him away. "NO! I was good at stuff like that. I gave it up when you left command after the last war. You said I wouldn't have to do this military-spouse game anymore when you got off active duty. Now I'm back in it as deep as you are." She stepped backwards and started to walk away. "That's what drove you away from me last time. This command is your game, Tom, not mine!"

Tom almost spoke, but couldn't find words. Cindy found them for him. "It's all right. I'll play the happy wife at the Dining-Out! Because, God knows, I deserve to get dressed up once in a while and go out. Even if it's with my totally-focused-on-his-command husband. But nothing, I repeat, I will do NOTHING for you, until you do something for your family!"

"What the hell would you have me do, honey? Quit?"

Cindy looked in his eyes and said flatly, "Yes, Tom. Quit! I want my husband back." She turned and quietly walked down the hall.

18 October 2002
Montgomery County Airport
Conroe, Texas

THE TRAINING CONTINUED TO GO WELL and the unit was flying regularly. Tom was at his desk going through some maintenance reports when the phone rang. To his surprise, it was Major General Walker. "To what do I owe the pleasure of the Adjutant General of the Texas National Guard calling a low-life helicopter pilot like myself?"

Walker chuckled and started the conversation simply enough. "I just wanted to check in on you. I finished reading your report on the results of your NTC rotation. I have to tell you, I liked your version a lot better than Colonel Crane's."

Tom was smiling. "I would imagine that if you believe his version, you would relieve me of duty, General?"

Walker laughed again. "It wasn't quite that bad, Tom! He did say some things about," the general must have been reading it verbatim. "undisciplined, lack of focus, with some tendencies towards irrelevance?"

"Holy crap, sir! He never told me he was going to put those kinds of terms in writing. I didn't expect it to be good, but I had hoped he wouldn't make it so damn negative, General. I'm sorry!"

"Oh, don't worry about that. Tom, the bottom line is, I need to know if you guys can fight."

A sense of dread crept over Tom. The directness of the question meant that it was not the typical, "Can you beat the OPFOR guys at NTC?" It was, "Can the unit you command fight and survive on the modern battlefield?" It was an honor for any unit to even be considered for combat. Tom had been there before. Because of the NTC rotation, Lawton was confident the 7/17th was probably a better trained Cavalry unit than his Champions had been heading into the first Gulf War. He swallowed hard and gave his honest opinion. "We can fight, General."

There was a moment of silence. Walker must have written something down. "That's what I thought you'd say, Tom."

Lawton couldn't leave it like that. "Why did you ask, sir?" "I can't talk about it now, Tom. But I will let you know when we get together at the Dining-Out."

"Good deal, sir! I'm glad you and Mrs. Walker can make it out!"

"She's actually looking forward to it. I'm guessing I better try on my dress-mess blues to see if I can still fit in them!"

Tom laughed. "Not a problem for you, General. You still running three or four miles a day?"

"Only when I can get out of this damn office! I love to get down to the park and run by Barton Springs. That's a beautiful run."

"Well, sir, when I come up next month, we can slip out and say we're going to Threadgill's!"

"That's what I like about you, Lawton! You are a damn good planner! I'll see you next Saturday."

Tom roger'd his National Guard boss and hung up. His question of whether the 7/17th could go to war still lingered. He made another mental assessment. *At least 15 crews that went to NTC are ready to go to war. That is enough to be a combat asset.*

The other questions started to pop up in Tom's mind. *Why did Walker want to know if we could fight? What isn't the general telling me?*

26 October 2002
Walburg Mercantile
Walburg, Texas

THE DINING-OUT WAS HELD AT THE Walburg Merchantile north of Austin. Tom and Cindy sent the girls to Cindy's mom's for the weekend. It was a great opportunity for Tom to make up for leaving her alone and pulling her back into the military. They had made a reservation for the Hyatt in downtown Austin.

The Walburg Merchantile is about as close as you can get to an authentic German Restaurant and still be in Texas. In the back they had set up two long tables for forty each and a head table for the special guests and the commanders. A non-stop flow of wait staff hustled in and out of the nearby kitchen, trailing the fantastic smells of authentic German cooking.

The Dining-Out started with a small social gathering in the courtyard behind the Merchantile. The restaurant was lined with dozens of imported beer brands, but most of the young guys and gals drank Texas beer. Shiner Bock was the favorite.

The special guests were General Jerrold Walker and his wife Susan. 1st Lieutenant Sam Gash and his wife Melinda did the introductions as the special guests greeted all the attendees in the receiving line.

Lawton kept mental notes of the troopers and their spouses or dates as they were introduced to the guests. Most attendees were well mannered and behaved with respect. Of course, some were more intoxicated than others. Cindy got to meet her new friend, Sharon, and her too-dedicated husband, Chief Warrant Officer Steven Werner.

Richard Crane, and his docile wife Dorothy, were stoic as expected. Tom urged Cindy to keep her eye on that couple because he didn't trust Crane. Cindy played the role of the military wife and did as he requested. She knew that one of the captains was too close to Crane and made a mental note to watch for that as well. She didn't like Crane one bit and suspected Tom's focus on his unit was in part because Crane was looking to fire her husband. She didn't like being an army wife, but she was damn good at the game.

As the dinner guests were brought their meals, the staff provided each participant a charged glass of Texas White wine or German Red. First thing was the ceremonial posting of the colors. The restaurant was silent as the flags were brought into the room, presented to the presiding official, and posted behind the head table. The troopers paid tribute to the spouses and female guests, the unit, the National Guard, the State of Texas, the President and the United States of America. One trooper was selected to give the prayer over the meal, and then the feast was on.

Things were going quite well. Tom expected nothing less for a Dining-Out. Some rules were broken and minor fines paid, but nothing was too out of the ordinary. The unit was fairly well-behaved. But nothing good lasts forever.

A couple of rolls went flying and Tom quickly dispatched Sam Gash to quell the uprising. It was a sign of things to come.

Major General Walker, as the senior ranking official, had the dubious honor of giving a speech. The crowd was relatively calm as the general began.

"I will keep this short," he started. A couple of people yelled "YEAH!" but were quickly shushed. Lawton caught the disgusted look Crane shot his way, but he blew it off. "I appreciate the invitation. Susan and I don't get out much with fine young folks like ya'll." He spent a few minutes thanking as many people as he could.

Then Walker cleared his throat. "I want to make sure I leave you all with one thought tonight." Lawton recognized the change in Walker's tone. "When you go home and lay down on your bed, I want the last thing to go through your mind to be, 'What Will I Fight For?'" The assembled crowd became silent.

"This is a critical time in history. And whether or not you realize it, it is critical for you as an individual. Things are getting very"—he hesitated—"precarious in our world today."

"A long time ago, I fought in Vietnam, an experience best described as hell. I was an Infantry platoon leader and I saw things that no man should ever see. So I know war. I know precisely what it means to commit forces to that act. Make no mistake: war is the most heinous act man can perform against his fellow man."

He paused again and looked around the room. "So why would you fight in a war?" No one spoke a word. "I'll tell you."

The crowd shifted nervously in their seats. "I'll tell you why I fight. I fight for Texas. The epitome of what America stands for. Where cultures mix and people get along. I fight for America. Because, despite all those faults that the media and some in foreign lands exaggerate and dwell on, we are the bastion of democracy! We are what is right with this planet.

"I fight for my family and my friends. I fight for those who can't fight for themselves." He took a deep breath and his voice wavered. "And I fight for you! Each and every one of you that is here tonight. You have made a commitment. You've made a commitment to Texas and you've made a commitment to me. Some of you may even die for one another. So you need to ask yourself, 'What will I fight for?'" Walker closed his notebook and looked over his glasses at the crowd.

No one knew whether to clap or not. The general smiled a gentle smile and added, "I don't mean to be so dramatic, folks. It's just that you need to be clear—positively crystal clear, on what you are doing with your life. I expect no one, and I mean *no one* in this room, to sacrifice themselves for freedom. Or America. But I do expect everyone here to understand what they are doing with their life. You need to know that what you are doing with your life is what you want to do with it. If that means being in the Texas National Guard," he raised his Shiner Bock and toasted the audience, "here's to us!"

The crowd raised their glasses and toasted the General. "To us!" They stood for a minute-long ovation. Tom looked at Cindy and noticed the tears in her eyes. All he could do was smile and nod. He rubbed his nose and quickly moved his hand up to his eye to wipe away the wetness. Walker was on target with his comments. Tom knew at that moment the 7/17th was going to war. And he knew that Cindy knew, too.

After the ovation subsided, Tom thanked the general and directed the assembled crowd, "If we could have everyone take fifteen minutes to freshen up, then meet outside in the biergarten, where we will reconvene for entertainment and more beverages!"

Tom put Walker's comments behind him temporarily and began mingling with the crowd. Cindy walked up behind him and quietly said, "I think you need to see something." She turned and walked to the back of the beirgarten. Tom was confused until she discreetly pointed to a dark area to the side of the crowd. Tom saw two figures in the shadows. One was Captain Chase Freeman. The other was Colonel Richard Crane.

He turned to Cindy and said, "Thank you, honey. I owe you!"

She smiled, "What's new?" Her duties done, her vision of the future clear, Cindy Lawton went straight to the bar and ordered a double Margarita.

Crane shook hands with Freeman and headed into the crowd. Freeman was smiling when he turned around and saw Lawton standing there. Tom's facial expression said everything.

Lawton waved his hand to indicate Freeman should follow him away from the crowd.

Freeman said, "Good evening, sir."

"Skip the bullshit, Chase. Why?"

"Why, sir? I don't know what—"

"You know what I'm talking about, so don't play with me!" Lawton's anger popped up and he took a moment to control himself. "What did he promise you?"

"Promise me, sir?"

"Scumbags like Crane don't do anything for anybody. He had to promise you something! What was it?" Tom walked slowly behind the captain. "An active duty slot ... Maybe an early promotion?"

Freeman leaned his head back and exhaled. "The colonel did mention an early promotion, sir."

Tom cut loose. "For what, Chase? For what? An early promotion? You sold me out! No! Not me! You sold the unit out on a promise from Crane?"

Tom walked directly in front of Chase. "First of all, that guy can't be trusted. Second, you can't move to active duty without getting approval from your National Guard chain of command. Third, if I told anyone what a piece of disloyal shit you are, they wouldn't want you."

"I wasn't disloyal, sir."

"What about Early and Trant?" The captain bit his lip. "You didn't know I found out about that, did you?"

"No, sir!"

"You told Crane, and he was gracious enough to rub it in my face! Told me I had a bunch of outlaws in my unit and that I wasn't fit for command."

"I didn't know anything about that, sir!"

"You don't know shit, do you Captain Freeman?" Tom didn't wait for an answer. "You saw glory and a quick ride to the top by listening to someone that didn't tell you what he was doing with the information, didn't you?"

The captain knew he was toast. "I had no idea—"

Lawton interrupted him. "You made an assumption based on his rank that the shithead would take care of you. He can't help you, Freeman. He is not in your chain of command." Tom stepped back. "You screwed me and you sold out your unit." Freeman remained silent. "What else did you tell him? Anything tonight?"

"No, sir! We just talked about the NTC and he said I did really well."

"Yeah, well he was filling you full of more bullshit, because you took credit for something that one of your peers did!"

Tom didn't give Freeman any options. "If I could, I would send you packin' right now. I can't have anyone who places himself above the unit, and I don't want anyone that isn't loyal to me."

Freeman did his best to initiate damage control. "Sir, look, I screwed up! I didn't know what he was doing with the information. He never told me! As for getting promoted, everyone wants to get promoted, sir!"

Tom snapped, "Not at the expense of a peer, Chase!"

The comment stung like a branding iron. "Sir, I'm sorry.

I want to stay in the unit."

Tom was torn. Freeman wasn't a bad officer. He had just seen a quick way to glory, based on the seduction of a superior officer. Adding to the situation, Lawton had no one to replace Freeman if he did fire him. Against his better judgment, he went soft.

"All right, Chase. You can stay. But understand two things. One, you work for me and me alone. Don't kiss Crane's ass. You stay away from him, understand?"

The captain roger'd his boss.

"And second, if you are ever disloyal to me, or this unit, or screw over any of your peers again, you will never wear the uniform again, you will never fly again, and you will never again have a job anywhere in the Texas Guard! You got me?" Again, Freeman nodded.

"Now get the hell outta my sight!" The captain turned and quickly walked away.

Tom was so angry he quickly went to the bar and ordered a shot of Schnapps and a Bitburger Pils. Both were gone within a minute.

Sam Gash at the microphone introduced the first act of the night. The A Troop's Outlaws and Bart "Bat" Talbot had put together a skit that made fun of the NTC, the rotation, and events in California. When a warrant officer implied during the skit that a certain captain was kissing Crane's ass, the colonel turned completely red.

Tom was unaware that the unit knew Freeman was brown-nosing Crane. He watched Crane squirm at the bar as the crowd progressively became louder and more confident that the humor was acceptable. Feeling the alcohol kick in, Tom moved next to Crane at the bar and watched him with a smile.

The skit ended with thunderous applause. Joe Petty came up to the bar and looked at Crane. He made a mock, half-assed salute. Crane, unimpressed, did not return the salute. Instead, he noticed a button that the chief warrant officer four wore on his dress blues. "Mr. Petty, what is that pin on your uniform?"

"Oh, this is my FUBIJAR pin, sir!"

Tom chuckled. Crane was confused. "I see that, Mister. What does it mean?"

"Oh, sir, I'm sorry. I thought you knew everything about us. FUBIJAR means, 'Fuck you, buddy, I'm just a reservist'!" The small crowd laughed uproariously at the joke. Crane was visibly angry.

"Sorry, sir! The Bandits are up and I gotta go introduce somebody." Petty turned to Tom and saluted, "By your leave, sir!" Tom stood at attention, snapped off a crisp salute, and watched Petty head to the stage. He couldn't hide his smile.

Crane turned. "Outlaws, Lawton. Unprofessional, second-class troops."

Tom smiled and said, "Yeah! Ain't they great?!"

Petty yelled into the microphone. "HOW Y'ALL WARRIORS DOIN' TONIGHT?"

There was a loud cheer. "I guess you all know the Bandits are next. They ain't got no skit for ya!" The crowd let out a mock "boo." "But they do have a guy from California that can sing a little bit. He got together with the Ramrods and he's gonna do a little song for you. I think he's an all right guy! Ladies and Gentlemen, Lieutenant Gary Prior!"

The crowd was less than enthusiastic. After all, he was a Californian and some of the Warrants had started calling Prior "The Kid."

Prior was aware he was not a local favorite. "Hi, y'all…" Um… I guess the best thing I can do is get right to the music. This song is called, 'All

Right Guy.' I heard it in a bar back home sung by a guy named Gary Allan. I hope you like it."

The lieutenant broke into the song and the Ramrods were with him from the first note. By the time the second verse came around, the crowd was smiling and starting to enjoy the music.

> *"Well this one time for medicinal purposes,*
> *they forced me to smoke some dope."*

The crowd was a mixture of rowdy howling and stunned silence. The lieutenant continued singing,

> *"Well I still think I can be the President,*
> *But I don't think I'll ever get to be the Pope!"*

Colonel Crane's attitude went from hot to full-fledged pissed off. He pointed to Tom and called him to the back of the crowd. Tom kept his smile, grabbed his beer, and finished what was left in the bottle.

"Did you hear that!"

Tom nodded. The alcohol was keeping him much calmer than he expected to be. "Yes, sir, I sure did. He sang a song that said he smoked dope for medicinal purposes."

"And you condone that?"

Tom shook his head. "I surely do, sir!" Crane turned beet red. "I condone singing songs that get my unit together, sir!"

"Not that! The part about smoking dope?"

Tom lost his smile. "It's just a song, Colonel Crane. You already gave the unit a piss test last month. My pilots all passed."

"That's beside the point, Lawton! By singing that song, it implies marijuana use! It implies that the lieutenant smoked pot. And it implies you, as his commander, by not stopping him from singing those lyrics, tolerate that behavior!"

Tom exhaled loudly. He really hated Crane, but he understood his point. He nodded, "Roger all, sir. The lieutenant is clean. You got his urine last month. I do NOT condone marijuana use and no one in the unit is a user. Or sells the stuff if that's what you're thinking! Those are the lyrics to the song. It's about wanting to be accepted for who you are. You see, the LT is an outsider. He's from California, for Christ's sake! We're not gonna hold that against him. He is trying to tell this group of Texans that he's okay, that he wants to be accepted!" Crane's eyes narrowed. "Look at the crowd, sir!"

Tom was right. The crowd was swingin' and singin' with Lieutenant Prior. They were enjoying the song and the lieutenant was now accepted into the group. He had passed an unstated initiation.

Crane was unamused. "Monday, I want all of your unit tested again. Every one of them, Lawton! You got me?"

Tom got him just fine. The beer took control of his emotions. It was Tom's turn to talk to Crane. He put his index finger up and motioned for the colonel to follow him.

When they were away from the crowd, Tom stepped close. "I'll skip the crap and get to the point. I know all about Captain Freeman. He's not going to be your butt-boy anymore. As of tonight, he is a Warrior. He is in this unit and he doesn't answer to you. Do you get me, sir?"

Crane was unprepared for the straightforward feed-back and did not know Tom had discussed Crane's "special relationship" with the B Troop commander. But he did not deny the activity. "That captain was providing me with information I needed to make judgments on the use and employment of a unit in my command."

Tom shrugged his shoulders and said, "Why didn't you just ask me?" The colonel went silent. "Why didn't you just call me and say what it was you were looking for? You didn't need to make that captain a spy!"

Crane actually struggled for words. Finally, he blurted out, "I didn't think I could trust you!"

Tom was confused. "You don't even know me! What do you mean?" Tom went silent. A small light came on in the darkness of his drunken mind. "You checked up on me, didn't you?"

After a moment of hesitation, Crane answered. "Yes."

Tom stepped back and began to pace. "Let me guess. You went back to my troop command in the desert. Right?"

"I noticed you had a somewhat 'storied' command."

"You weren't satisfied with what the paperwork said, right? You had to ask people about me?"

"Yes. I did."

"Let me throw a name out there. Lieutenant Colonel Sweat?" The colonel's silence was all the answer Tom needed. Ten years later and Sweat still haunted him. "Did he tell you I cracked up under the pressure of command?"

"He indicated you had some problems, yes."

Tom nodded. "I did, Colonel Crane." He knew the colonel had never seen combat. "Let me tell you something, Colonel Crane. I was scared. Not about me. Not about my safety, but for my men. I put undue pressure on myself because I thought my commander was pushing me beyond my limits. And you know what? He wasn't. I was pushin' myself beyond my limits. Now, I know what the limit is. The limit of what can be done by a commander and where he needs to trust his subordinates."

Tom took a pull on the fresh beer in his hand. "I took it to the limits as leader and a follower, but I brought everybody home. You see, that's what a good commander does. And he does that with truth and trust. Right now, I don't think I have yours. And you certainly don't have mine!"

Crane was expressionless as Lawson continued. "You don't need to worry about me when it comes to trust. I may not like you, Colonel, but I will always be honest with you."

Crane frowned. "Maybe I should have come directly to you and gotten my questions answered, but I had no reason to doubt my source."

Tom snapped again. "Your source is a self-serving prick!" He didn't finish with 'sir.'

"I don't need to explain my actions to you, Lawton." It was his chance to leave the argument, but Crane couldn't leave it alone.

He's got something else is on his mind. I can feel it.

"I don't want your explanations, sir. I want your trust."

Crane was biting his lip hard. Finally, he said, "I guess I can give you that." Crane looked around as if he expected someone to be watching them. There was only the sound of cheering from the crowd as Lieutenant Prior finished his song.

"All right, Lawton. I needed to know if you were mentally tough enough to lead this unit in combat. I needed to know this unit had a leader I could count on."

Tom shook his head. "If I'm not up to your standards, relieve me."

"I tried," replied Crane honestly. "You seem to have a guardian angel in Texas." Tom knew he meant Walker. "You are in for the long haul,

Lawton. I can't get rid of you, so you will be the commander of the 7/17th. Wherever we go."

Tom was drunk, but not that drunk. "Are we going somewhere?"

Crane was coy. "I'm not sure yet. But since you just finished the NTC rotation and our attack unit is not available, you may be taking a little trip with us. When and where, I'm not sure."

Tom cleared his throat. "You think maybe you can tell me when you do know, instead of my having to jump down the throat of your pet captain?"

Crane nodded. "Yes, Lieutenant Colonel Lawton. I will."

"Thank you, sir. I'm so glad you decided to let me know we will be gracing you with our presence, wherever and whenever that may be." He replied in the most ingratiating tone he could muster. Tom came to attention and offered a salute. "So, if you'll excuse me, I'm going back to have a beer with my men." One last jab before he left. "You might not trust me, but they do."

Just in case they hadn't figured it out from General Walker's comments, Lawton knew enough not to tell anyone the news. He didn't have enough information to go on anyway. Would they be going to Afghanistan? Just their luck it would be Kosovo! Anywhere they were headed with Crane, it wouldn't be good.

Lawton got back in time to see Sam Gash breaking up a fight between two junior warrant officers. Tom started to step in, but Gash gave him a look that indicated it was over and everything was under control.

At that point Petty grabbed the microphone and introduced Major General Walker to the crowd. General Walker received another warm round of applause, said a quick howdy, and added, "I ain't sung in ten years, so please bear with me."

The Ramrods started into a Texas favorite by Gary P. Nunn called 'London Homesick Blues.' Listening to the words, Tom knew right away that Walker was aware the unit was on the hook to support Crane. He didn't have to say anything. The song gave it away. On the second verse, Walker got the crowd going as he sang:

> *When a Texan fancies,*
> *He takes his chances.*
> *Chances will be taken,*
> *That's for sure.*

Tom considered the words as he headed for the bar to get another beer. For an instant, he thought maybe he should get water or a Coke. Hell, Cindy was drivin', so he bellied up and got a Corona with lime.

The crowd's clapping showed their approval for Major General Jerry Walker as he sang. It didn't take long for the crowd to get into his song, which Walker knew by heart. When he burst into the chorus, the whole unit joined in:

> *"I want to go home with the Armadillos,*
> *Good country music from Amarillo and Abilene,*
> *With the friendliest people and*
> *The prettiest women you've ever seen!"*

Tom didn't join in the song as he was busy looking for Cindy. He found her in the crowd singing and clapping with Mrs. Walker. Tom missed times like this. Unfortunately, he couldn't allow himself to enjoy the party as much as he wanted to. His conversation with Crane kept taking him away from the party. Cindy was enjoying herself so he decided to head back to the bar and get another shot. Tequila would work. Maybe Cindy would join him, if she saw him at the bar.

General Walker came over with a beaming smile on his face. "Hot damn, Tom, I haven't felt this good about the Guard in years." The general changed the subject. "Can we go over there and talk a minute in private?" Tom nodded and followed his boss.

When they were away from the crowd, Walker looked around to confirm they were alone. "This is a special group of folks you have here, Tom." Tom nodded, but wasn't certain where his boss was headed.

"You know the National Guard, essentially all the reserves across the US, have a bad reputation with the active duty guys. Crane is typical of what Guard folks have to deal with across America. The active duty perceives the Guard as second-class fighters, sucking off the government tit, not in shape for physical training or able to perform in combat."

"Citizen soldiers, sir! Most of 'em have more 'God-and-country time' than some sergeants on active duty." God-and-country time was time spent doing training without being reimbursed by the government. "Not to mention they have jobs they work during the week." Lawton's irritation was evident.

Walker continued. "They don't see that. They see the reservists as part-time help. Bodies to fill in as needed." Walker looked into Tom's eyes. "That's why I got you for these folks, Tom."

Tom shook his head. "Come again, sir?"

"I know about you. I know about your command and what you did in the last war with Iraq." Tom started to ask a question but he let the general continue. "You had a reputation as a great commander. A guy that led and took his men to the fight and won."

"You probably heard it didn't end so well?"

Walker nodded. "You mean the picture?"

"Uh-huh." A certain picture of Tom Lawton dressed in drag for Halloween had appeared on his Brigade commander's desk. The picture, plus two or three other minor incidents, contributed to Tom's decision to leave, not just his command early, but active duty.

"That includes the picture. I heard about a little jog through the desert, too!" The general laughed out loud. "I don't care about any of that shit, Tom." His smile faded. "I needed to know who in my command could lead and fight on the modern battlefield. I checked everything about you. I asked the warrant officers that you worked with and they were all highly supportive of your ability to command. You can get them ready for combat and they need you to lead them." Tom nodded, but he was frowning.

"The reserves as a whole need to be able to fight. Texas needs you to represent the state in combat, if it comes to that. It was my decision and they let me pick who I needed. I chose you." The general stood up and presented his hand to Tom. "Don't let me or Texas down, okay?"

"I won't, sir."

He escorted the general and his wife to their car and made sure they headed in the right direction. After a deep breath and a quick look at the Texas night, he said a quiet Hooah to himself. He was picked because he had been a Champion and his men had stood up for him. He thought it was a good time to celebrate. He gazed up at the stars one last time and headed back to the bar. *Life in the Texas Guard was good.*

Cindy never did make it over to the bar to meet Tom. She was having a pretty good time dancing with the members of the 7/17th. In her mind, the party was a lot more fun without Tom, the commander. She spent the rest of the night dancing with other Warriors, as Tom told war stories at the bar and drank.

Cindy had to drive to the Hyatt. Somehow she managed to get Tom from the car and into the 9th-floor room. Tom was nearly falling down as she opened the door. She didn't bother to undress him, but just laid him in the chair by the window. With a small exhale of disgust, she turned and got ready for bed.

For some reason, the thought of sex had crossed her mind earlier in the night. As she looked at Tom, laying in the chair, barely breathing, and smelling like the Pearl Brewery at closing time, any thought she had of sex disappeared. A tear formed in her eye and she wiped it away immediately. This wasn't her fault. This was all on Tom's shoulders. She laid on the bed and squeezed the pillow tightly. It was Tom's fault. It was command. She had seen this before. She carried Tom's burden twelve years ago. Command had changed him then and it was changing him now.

Maybe, just maybe, she needed a change, too.

CHAPTER SEVEN

"Poetry"
-Walt Wilkins

27 October 2002
Austin, Texas

CINDY HAD BEEN QUIET ALL MORNING. As they got in the car to head back to Huntsville, Tom couldn't stand it. *Her silence hurts more than this hangover.*

"All right, I'm sorry. Whatever it is you are mad at me about, I am sorry!"

Cindy was ready for his weak attempt at reconciliation. "You're sorry and you don't even know what for?"

Tom hesitated. "Yeah, I am."

Cindy stared down the road as she drove. "Are you sorry for ignoring me?" Then she added, "Or are you sorry because you were so drunk you couldn't get it up last night?" Tom was speechless. He started to fumble through some kind of response. She understood the situation with so much more clarity than he did. He swallowed hard and said, "Both."

They drove for another mile until Cindy said, "I can't take this, Tom. I want my husband back. I want the man I married. I can't share you while you are doing this command." She glanced out the corner of her eye. "Something has to change."

Tom tried to figure out exactly what her last statement meant. None of the options that ran through his hungover mind seemed very pleasant. She had just asked him for his decision. He thought she may have just meant for him to make a "behavior modification" like paying more attention to her instead of being the commander of an attack helicopter squadron. He exhaled heavily. He had his shot to do that twenty-four hours ago, and he blew it. *She's asking me to decide between the command and this marriage.*

Tom looked out the window and said flatly, "I can't give up my command, honey."

Cindy was a stone. She focused on the road and said quietly, "That's what I needed to know."

Tom couldn't look at her. "That's the priority right now."

Cindy looked at the road in silence. She quickly reached up and wiped the tear off her cheek before Tom could see it. The rest of their ride to Huntsville was silent.

The next day she took the girls and moved out to live with her sister in Shiro.

29 October 2002
Montgomery County Airport
Conroe, Texas

TOM STARED AT THE ORDER IN disbelief. Crane sent a message indicating he wanted the unit to undergo another random urinalysis. For a reserve unit, random meant every person in the unit you could get in at the earliest possible time. This was just another stab by Crane to demonstrate to Tom he was overseeing his unit. It was insulting. He knew his men were clean and Crane wouldn't find anyone taking drugs. So, Lawton did as he was ordered. He called in the sergeant major and told him to start bringing people in to get on with it.

The sergeant major shook his head in disgust, unable to hide his frustration. He saluted crisply and headed to his desk to make the phone calls. Soldiers would be brought in from their assigned duties, and in some cases, from their regular jobs, to provide the samples. It was a tremendous misuse of manpower.

Tom left work early that day. He stopped by a little bar on the way home for a beer or two, to relax. He stayed there until eight o'clock before he called a cab.

31 October 2002
Huntsville, Texas

TOM SAT IN THE LIVING ROOM in silence. Occasionally he would see some of the trick-or-treaters walk by, but he never got up to answer the door. He wondered if Cindy was walking with the girls or if she had stayed home to hand out candy. He got up once more to make sure the light was out on the porch. Tom thought that someone might knock on his door that didn't know the Halloween rules. Thoughts ran through his mind as he took a long pull on his long- neck. *Who made the rules about Halloween trick-or-treating? Who made the rules that said a man had to make decisions? Who made the Army and its stupid rules? Why doesn't a wife understand what a husband does during command?*

The bottle was nearly empty as it flew across the room, bounced off the wall, then fell back into the chair.

Tom had always thought of himself as a man of principles. He began to wonder if those principles would console him when he was 80. *Will they tuck me in at night when I'm an old man and need my diaper changed? Will someone write on my tombstone, "Here died a man with principles. He abandoned his family to pursue his command of honor and courage for Texas."*

He struggled to his feet and staggered to bed. *All the principles and convictions in the world don't feel as good as the warmth of the body of the person you love.*

Tom looked at the clock one more time. If he fell asleep at that very moment, he could get seven hours of sleep before he had to be at work. But he knew he wouldn't get seven hours of sleep. He rolled over, put the pillow over his head and prayed for a sleep that wouldn't come. *God how I miss Cindy!*

> During the first two weeks of November, the United States and United Kingdom used diplomatic leverage to convince the United Nations Security Council to pass UN Resolution 1441, requiring Iraq to provide all information they had on weapons of mass destruction and to completely disarm. Iraq choose to ignore the resolution. The United States, the United Kingdom, Australia, and others, choose to go to war.

8 November 2002
Montgomery County Airport
Conroe, Texas

IT WASN'T MUCH OF AN ORDER. It came in the form of an excited phone call from Major General Walker. "The word just came down. We have a warning order to"—He obviously was reading now—"be prepared to deploy to conduct operations against military forces in support of the 3rd Infantry Division."

Lawton was confused. "The 3rd Infantry Division, sir?"

"I'm not real certain at this point exactly what they are asking for, Tom."

"So it's just a warning order, right, sir?"

"So far, yeah! But get your boys together. Looks like Texas is going to war."

Tom held his breath and said, "Does it say anything about when?"

Walker was obviously reading the order since he became silent. Finally, he said, "It doesn't say anything specific; just be prepared to deploy."

Tom nodded as if someone could see him. "Roger that, sir! I'll have them ready to go, sir." Tom hung up the phone and got his thoughts together. It was the moment he had been waiting for. Going to war is what every unit trains for. Deep down, he knew his unit was ready. But there was still so much more they had to work on. He made a mental checklist and called the sergeant major. There's no time to waste.

15 November 2002
III Corps Headquarters,
Ft. Hood, Texas

TOM LAWTON WAS CALLED TO A meeting at Ft. Hood in Killeen. Lieutenant General William K. LeBeau, the III Corps commanding general, called for the meeting. In attendance were Major General Walker, the TAG of Texas, Major General Aaron Franklin (3rd ID commanding general), the aviation brigade commander, Colonel Benjamin Powell, Colonel Crane, and Lieutenant Colonel Tom Lawton. Tom sat in the back and tried to keep a low profile.

"It seems we may have a slight compatibility problem with your Apaches and the 3rd Infantry Division," LeBeau said, looking directly at Walker.

This was the first time Walker had heard anything about any sort of problem. "What exactly does that mean, General?"

"It means we may not be able to take your guys to the desert."

Walker started to get angry. "We just came from a deployment at the NTC. That unit is certified, it's trained, and it's ready. If you're going to a fight, you're gonna need every gun you can muster." His words didn't seem to be registering.

Tom caught Crane smirking but avoided eye contact with him. LeBeau replied, "I understand that, Jerry, but you've got some old Alpha-model aircraft and your pilots..." The General finally came to the point. "Your National Guard pilots may not be up to the task."

"On what grounds do you make that assessment, General?" Walker spun and faced Crane. "On the word of this ground Cavalry officer, who had his own share of problems at NTC?" Crane's face went red. Walker turned back to LeBeau and Franklin. "I will put this unit up against any enemy our country has to face. I'd stake my reputation on them!"

LeBeau looked at Franklin, who in turn looked at Colonel Powell. Powell had been ominously quiet. Franklin said, "I guess it may be your call, Ben."

Ben Powell was a mover and a shaker in Army aviation circles, a politically motivated commander, and a product of President Clinton's push for political correctness. It was clear to many that he was destined to be a division commander, something rarely achieved by an Army aviator. He was in command of the most advanced attack helicopters in the world. Powell had been handpicked to blend 20th-century tactics and 21st-century technology to create the most lethal aviation brigade in Army history.

"General, I'm not inclined to integrate antiquated machines like the Guard flies into my unit. I don't see them meshing well with AH-64 Delta models or the Kiowas. The unit doesn't even have a full compliment of eighteen trained crews!"

Tom saw an opening and spoke quickly. "We don't have to mesh in, sir. We can do other missions, like screening for the ground Cavalry. True, we may not have eighteen crews, but the fifteen we have are trained and ready for combat." Tom didn't bother to look at Crane.

Powell, irritated, replied, "You've got old Doppler navigation systems, your maintenance requirements may outweigh any advantage, and that's fifteen more aircraft that will be drinking JP-8!" Tom wasn't sure why he was so irritated. Then came a clue. "And you just aren't in tune with the 21st-century fight!"

Tom sat back and wondered about the 21st-century fight he wasn't in tune with. He didn't have to ask.

Walker cut in. "What the hell does that mean, Colonel?" He looked back at LeBeau. "The enemy isn't fighting a 21st-century fight, General. Those Republican Guard divisions will fight old-fashioned, Soviet-style doctrine. That's what Lawton's unit does. You don't need that new-fangled stuff! You're gonna need these guys, General Franklin. I recommend you take them and let them do their job!"

LeBeau looked around the room. The battle lines were clearly drawn but LeBeau was in charge.

"I can't see any reason not to send them, Aaron. They just came out of NTC. You didn't even take your aviation assets because they were getting upgraded."

Powell jumped in. "But, General LeBeau, the reports indicate that the unit—"

A quick wave of LeBeau's hand stopped the colonel in mid-sentence. "I read the report. The fact is, they passed." He stood up from the table. "Now, I have another meeting to attend." The men came to attention.

As LeBeau got to the door, he turned and said, "Now, you gentlemen play together nicely. I don't want any bullshit. It isn't the systems, or whether they are older or not in tune. The fact is, it's the men in the machines that make the Army work." He paused. "Make it work." Walker was quick to follow LeBeau out the door.

Crane scowled at Tom, but Powell seemed the most pissed off. He tried to protest again to Franklin, but he would hear none of it.

"You heard him, Ben! It's decided. They're going with you. The boss thinks they'll be an asset and so do I. Now it's up to you to figure out how to integrate them and get them into the fight."

Powell was flustered, "Yes, sir." He turned to Lawton and said, "You better have them ready to fight, or so help me, you'll be standing gate guard in a flight suit!"

Tom nodded. "We're ready to go, sir."

Powell grabbed his notebook and bolted for the door. Crane shook his head and followed Powell.

In the hallway, Walker was smiling broadly at Tom. "I'm glad that little rendezvous is over. I was worried for a minute. I needed you in that fight; we've got to show them what the Texas National Guard can do."

"Yes sir, I guess we'll get to show 'em." *Therein lay the problem; now Tom Lawton had to deliver.*

As Tom lay his head on his pillow that night, he couldn't help but think about Powell's comments. "Not in tune with the 21st century" had a nasty ring to it. Those words rang all the way up to the think tanks in the Pentagon. The "21st century" was code for RMA, the Revolution in Military Affairs that applied to the transformation of the military to a leaner, more modern force, one based on exploiting all advantages technology could provide. Advantages, mind you, only perceived on the drawing board of a think tank, not any place that mattered—like the modern battlefield.

Tom was pissed at himself for taking Powell's words like a jackass in a hailstorm. *Christ, I just sat there. I wish I had defended the unit more.* He rolled over and tried to forget the events of the day. He absently reached across the bed to find an empty space. *I wish Cindy were here.*

19 November 2002
"Cowboy's Ride Saloon"
Conroe, Texas

TOM LAWTON SAT AT THE END of the bar, alone. She was actually a very beautiful lady. Probably ten years younger, but nearly as inebriated. She asked him to dance and he said no. She took offense at his rebuff and questioned whether he was gay. Tom just laughed out loud. "Maybe!" She threw her rum and coke in his face and stomped away. Tom blew off her anger and staggered to the rest room.

After he cleaned up, he came back to the bar and ordered another Shiner. The bartender, shaking his head, still got him the beer. Five minutes later, Tom passed out. The bartender made a phone call to Sergeant Major Martinez.

When Martinez arrived he went straight to Lawton and carried him into the bathroom.

After splashing water on his face, he smacked him, first gently, then a little harder. "Hey! Wake up! You need to wake up, sir!"

Tom was slow to come around. Finally, he blew water out of his mouth and slurred, "What are you doin'?"

"I'm savin' your ass, boss!"

Tom shook his head and leaned over the sink. As the cobwebs cleared, he stared at his reflection in the mirror and started to focus. He recognized the sergeant major and said, "I'm in bad shape, Trino."

Martinez stared at the man in the mirror. "You need help, sir!" Tom rubbed his eyes. "I know she's gone, but you're gonna die if you keep this up!"

"I'm okay, Trino!"

Martinez exploded. "NO! You're not okay! You're a damn sorry excuse for a man and I'm disappointed that you even wear a uniform!"

Tom turned and looked at his trusted friend. "What the—"

Martinez cut him off. "You're screwing up!"

Tom stepped back from the sink and took a long, hard look in the mirror.

"Remember what you did to those pilots a couple of months ago? You're in the same boat, sir! This is a case of the pot callin' the kettle black. You need help."

Tom looked back at the mirror. He had passed out in a bar, he was soaking wet, and his sergeant major was trying everything he could to help him. It was time to make a hard decision. A tear formed as he looked at Martinez. "I'm such a fool." His knees buckled.

Martinez grabbed him and held him by the shoulders. "No. You're just a man. A man that needs to get his shit together. You won't get her back like this. And you ain't any good to the unit in this shape." Tom nodded in agreement. "You're gonna get help, you understand me? You're gonna check into Alcoholics Anonymous. Just like you had those pilots do!"

Tom saw that Martinez was not making a suggestion. The tear slipped from his face and he nodded. "Okay." He looked at his friend and said quietly. "Please get me out of here."

"Promise me. You promise me you'll get help, or so help me, I'll leave you here!"

Tom lay his head on Martinez's shoulder and said, "I will."

"Promise?"

Tom nodded and said, "Tomorrow. I promise you I'll get help."

Martinez grabbed Tom and turned him towards the door. "You start tomorrow, or I'll call General Walker. You got me?"

Tom nodded. "I got it. Just get me home. Get me home, Trino."

Against his better judgment, Martinez took Tom back to his house and put him to bed. He left a note by the phone with the number of the local AA chapter.

When Tom woke up at ten-thirty the next morning, he found the number next to the phone. With trembling hands, he picked up the phone and made the call that changed his life.

At the Saturday night meeting of the Conroe Chapter of Alcoholics Anonymous, Tom Lawton was one of the last people to enter the building.

He slowly walked up and took a seat next to Brian Trant and Jason Early. That night, Tom Lawton was the second new member to announce that he was an alcoholic.

After the meeting, Trant and Early took him to the Dairy Queen to get a Snickers Blizzard.

CHAPTER EIGHT

"Mama cried when you left me,
You know she's always loved you so.
She said "Hey fool, what the hell did you do?"
I said "Now Mom, I swear to God I just don't know."

"Whiskey"
-Pat Green

25 November 2002
Conroe, Texas

IT WAS A LONELY THANKSGIVING. TOM watched the Cowboys game and chewed on crushed ice as a way to avoid thinking about his desire for a beer. The game was entertaining enough to keep his mind occupied, but the physical desire to drink was maddening. He often found himself walking around the living room for no reason. He had so much energy after the game that he changed into gym shorts and his "HOOAH" T-shirt and headed out the door for a run.

Tom stopped in his tracks when he heard the phone ring. "Hello?"

"Hi, Tom." It was Cindy.

"Wow! How's it goin'?"

She sounded good on the phone. "It's going okay. We just finished watching the game and I thought I'd give you a call." She was quiet for a second then added, "I heard you went and got some help."

Tom thought for a moment. *Must have been the sergeant major.* "I needed it."

"I'm glad you did that. I could tell you were drinking. More, I mean."

"I was getting deep into work. You remember the last time."

"Yes, I do. That's why I'm at my mom's house now."

Tom bit his lip. *I don't want to fight. I want her back. I want to tell her how much I miss her.* "I'm sorry, Cindy. Look, I'm trying here. I'm taking steps to get myself under control." It sounded so weird to say, but that was exactly what he was doing. "I'm even trying to work out again."

"You need that, too." Lawton didn't miss the jab. "You should be back in shape in no time if you keep it up." Lawton noticed her attempt to soften the blow.

"How are the girls?"

"Doing great. They miss you. They don't miss you hollering at them. I get to be the bad mom all the time now."

"I know that must be tough." He nearly said it was her choice, but stopped himself in time. She had called him and he didn't want her to hang up.

She sighed heavily into the phone. "Well, I just wanted to let you know I was glad to hear you are going to meetings. And I'm glad you're trying to get yourself together."

"Me, too." *Go ahead say it.* "Do you think sometime you and I could get together?"

"It's too soon, Tom."

"Not for anything other than talking." He paused. "I miss talking to you, Cindy." The phone went quiet. He thought he heard her sniff.

"I miss you, too, Tom. I just can't see you. Not yet."

"Okay. I understand."

"I'll call you later. I love you." She hung up first.

She said she loves me. It was probably the hardest thing Cindy Lawton had ever had to say, but it was what Tom needed to hear most in the world.

He went outside and smelled a fresh breeze in the air. December was coming. A new season was dawning. Tom didn't feel as alone as he had five minutes ago.

For the first time in five years, he ran four miles.

5 December 2002
Conroe, Texas

THE WORD WAS OUT IN THE local community. The citizens of Conroe, Texas had received word that the unit might get called up to deploy. Tom's phone was ringing off the hook. Reporters from the local paper were lining up to get information and were trying to pry interviews from the soldiers in the 7/17th.

Tom found the whole situation a distraction. He was trying to train his men and get them ready. He called Walker to see if he could get the Adjutant General of the Texas Guard to turn off the media hounds. What he got was a lecture in public affairs.

"Tom, you need to think this through. The press is there to get stories. Stories that people will read and see on TV. It's all free publicity for the Guard and great for recruiting." Tom could almost see Walker beaming from his large chair overlooking the capital in downtown Austin.

"Sir, I would rather just get 'em ready to go."

"Tom, I know you. You have those guys ready to fight. You need to sell them. You need to market them. Work with the media folks. They'll tell your story better than you can. Trust me on this."

Tom exhaled as quietly as he could. "All right, sir."

Walker added one more thing. "This is just small stuff in a larger picture, Tom. It's all about money. It's about getting funding and making jobs for people." Tom actually smiled at that. *Walker, as usual, is right.*

Then Walker concluded with something quite enlightening. "Tom, you need to understand something about the three levels of the military: strategic, operational, and tactical. Of these three, only the strategic and the tactical are important. The rest, that in between ninety percent, is just stuff. The ten percent you and I handle, is driven by money."

The comment made Tom chuckle out loud. Walker wasn't laughing. Tom said, "Okay, sir. I seem to remember being told that there are some significant operational things that go on."

"You're aware that you're at the pointy end of the spear, Tom. The tactical end, the most important level. This engagement with the media is tactical. The significance of the Guard and how we get equipped, manned, and used, that's strategic. That's what I do. The in between-us stuff is all ups and downs and ins and outs. It is a bit more important than that, but not as important as what you and I have to do."

Tom began to see the light. Walker was more of a politician than Tom wanted him to be. But that's the job of the TAG. "I guess I'm just not in tune with the system, sir."

Walker grunted, "Son, you're in tune with fightin' the enemy. That will be more important than any technology those active duty boys have. You do the mission and bring your Texans home, Tom. The rest is just stuff in the middle." He hung up.

Tom looked at his phone. *Stuff in the middle, technology, and the media. What is the military coming to?* He longed for the good old days, when you gave your men whiskey and you trusted everything and everyone around you. Now he spent more time writing and reading emails than he did flying.

Lawton was a good soldier and did as he was told. He hung up the phone and starting dialing. First he called Joe Petty and found out how soon he could have a static display ready for the local press and TV stations. Then he called the local paper and offered them the opportunity to come see an AH-64 Apache up-close and personal. He drew the line at offering a ride. Then he turned off all the power in his office and went flying. It was the one place he could get away from everything.

Lawton and Chief Warrant Officer Four Brian Trant flew over Lake Conroe and put the aircraft through her paces. They found a nap-of-the-earth flight route over a swamp to the north of the lake and took the bird to the limit, soaring fifty feet above the water at eighty knots. Tom navigated the first leg. He loved to watch the water vapors fly when the rotor blades got close.

On the return route, he had the controls. Not as steady as Trant, but he was getting better. He was beginning to find his control touch and the old confidence was coming back. *When I'm good enough to do the same route at the same speed and altitude in the dark, then I'll be ready, he thought. Another month. One more month and I'll be ready for war.*

18 December 2002
Montgomery County Airport
Conroe, Texas

LAWTON WAS SITTING IN HIS OFFICE finishing some paperwork. It was almost five o'clock. He was making a habit of leaving promptly at five, trying not to be the workaholic he had previously been. He had just approved a training manual which highlighted Iraqi Republican Guard equipment, and had approved a press interview for four soldiers.

He was about to leave when Cindy called, sounding very happy.

He immediately put everything in his mind about work away.

"Hi! I was just wondering what you were up to. I admit I am a little surprised you're still in your office on a Friday afternoon."

"Just tying up a few loose ends. This is our last weekend of training and Sunday I'll probably give the squadron a data dump on what to expect next year."

Cindy knew Tom well enough to know "data dump" meant a speech, probably telling them to get ready. If they were in an active duty unit, they probably would have already missed the holidays with their families.

"Well, I hope it goes well." She hesitated before asking, "If you don't have any plans for Christmas, would you like to come up here?"

"I'd love to. I was wondering how I'd get all these presents up to you and the girls."

"They're looking forward to seeing you."

"Me, too."

"So how is it going? Everything still okay?"

Tom knew exactly what she meant. "Almost 30 days now without a drink. I've lost five pounds and almost, just almost, have had my hands stop shaking."

"That's real good, Tom." Her voice couldn't hide her happiness. "How's the unit doing? Are they ready to go?" Tom figured she must have found out what she wanted, because she usually didn't ask about the unit. "Nearly ready. We need to fly more at night, but we have most of the aircraft up and some of them can even shoot!" He didn't want to say anymore than that on the phone because of operations security. Even the reserves knew they were being watched and listened to by adversaries around the globe.

"I'm glad they're ready." She seemed at a loss for words.

"I was wondering, will you be going to that little Baptist Church on Christmas Eve?"

"Yes, we're going with Mom."

"Would it be okay if I ..." He wanted to say come up, but decided to take it slow. "Would it be okay if I stopped by? Services are at eight, right?"

"SURE! Sure! That would be fine!" She took a second to collect herself. "If you can get away, stop by. That would be terrific."

"All right then! See you then." He hung up and leaned back in the chair. *She misses me as much as I miss her. Better not press the situation.* He exhaled and looked at the clock. *Five after five.* He slid away from his desk and headed home. *If the traffic's light, I can still get in a short run before dark.*

21 December 2002
Montgomery County Airport
Conroe, Texas

TOM TALKED TO THE UNIT IN two groups. The first data dump was to the entire squadron at the three o'clock formation. He had the troop commanders break the formation and bring the men in close around him so they could hear.

"First of all, I want to say to each and every one of you how proud I am of you. You come here when you're asked to and you do things that no one will know about or understand. You've come here for long hours on hot days and cold nights. You've trained aggressively. More aggressively than I wanted to push you, but you all know why that was done." He got some nods from the assembled crowd. They knew.

"When we went to NTC last summer, we sucked." Tom glanced at the sergeant major. "But you guys embraced the suck. You made this unit better. You made it capable of fighting and surviving on the modern battlefield. All the BS is over. I got a call this week from the TAG. We need to pack our stuff. We've been activated."

A nervous murmur ran through the crowd and one possibility popped up immediately. "We heard they were callin' us up to go to Kosovo to backfill the peacekeepin' mission." Dozens of heads turned to Lawton.

He asked for silence. "Listen, for operational security purposes, they have not disclosed the location of our deployment." More mumbles in the crowd. "So, I would place such comments in the realm of rumor. If I were you all, I would plan for the worst. And trust me. The worst thing is to go to combat. We all need to be mentally prepared to go to war. If we are chosen to go to Kosovo to backfill a unit there, then we will do that mission to the best of our abilities. No whining! There's NO whining in the TEXAS NATIONAL GUARD!" That got a huge HOOOAAH!

"Now, we still have work to do. I want everyone to go home for these next two weeks and be with your families. Celebrate the holidays"—he chose his words carefully and as positively as he could— "the way they need to be celebrated. Be with your loved ones. Enjoy it. When you come back next year, we're gonna get our aircraft down to Beaumont and go where they tell us to go. We'll do what they tell us to do. And if we need to kick ass and take names, DAMN IT, THAT'S WHAT THEY PAY US TO DO! HOAH!"

The Troopers to a man roared back, "HOOOAAAAHH!" "DISMISSED!" Tom yelled, "All pilots to the ready room!"

Lawton stopped to talk with Martinez. "Sorry about saying we sucked, Sergeant Major. No offense, okay?" Martinez nodded and a smile appeared. "We were a little screwed up. I just never really accepted it, sir."

"We're better now and that's all that matters."

Martinez smiled. "Where'd you get that 'embrace the suck' crap from? I don't like the suck! I'll be damned if I want to embrace it!"

"Friend of mine in 3rd Infantry Division sent me an email. Says that's going around the 3rd ID. And it's stickin'."

"Aren't those guys—"

"They're embracing the suck, Sergeant Major."

At that point, Tom Lawton and Sergeant Major Martinez suspected they would be supporting 3rd ID. And 3rd ID was in Kuwait... waiting.

In the ready room, the pilots were a bundle of nerves. The thought they were going to war was sinking in. The young guys were excited and the old guys were quiet.

Tom started slowly. "We need to talk about history for a few minutes." He put his beret on the desk and started walking around the room. "Back in the first Gulf War, the AH-64 Apache had a checkered record. We flew dozens of missions in that war. Many were performed well. But not all were." He looked at Petty and Trant; they knew exactly what he was talking about.

"We made some mistakes in the darkness, we wrecked some planes, we shot the wrong things. And there were mental errors, too. A commander shot friendlies even before the war kicked off. Some of you didn't know that, did you? Night-system flying can trick your eyes. But the best way to avoid those mistakes is by working on your SA. Situational Awareness is the key to success on the modern battlefield. When so-called state-of-the-art technology can't help, simple, good SA can."

"In another instance, mental and tactical breakdowns led two Apaches following a Blackhawk to assume the downed aircraft had no survivors. They were wrong. They flew away and left people on the ground.

"Every one of you hear and understand me! We will NOT leave anyone on the ground. Nobody from this unit gets left behind. I can't make you any promise other than that. No one gets left behind."

He continued, "Then came ALLIED FORCE and Task Force Eagle. Again, Apaches were called on to represent army aviation and the United States of America. We did not do our best. We crashed two aircraft and killed two guys. We were fortunate to have that one end before Hellfire's started to fly. Indications are that training problems associated with the altitude may have contributed to that situation." He paused, yet continued walking. "I am confident in your training. You've got the best instructor pilots I've ever worked with, and you know your shit! Anywhere we go and anything we are asked to do, we can do."

Trant asked with a smirk, "Do we have to 'embrace the suck'?"

Some of the group laughed. Tom smiled and said, "Trust me. Based on experience, the best way to handle THE SUCK is to embrace it!" Most of the pilots laughed. They could almost see Tom going back to Iraq in '91 and remembering how much he hated the desert.

"For now, go home. Give your bosses a heads-up that you may need some time off. Probably 179 days." He let the comment sink in. "Then have a great

Christmas and come back ready to do whatever our state and our country asks of us. Happy holidays, gentlemen and lady." He nodded to Lieutenant Crandle. He never noticed how young she really looked until right then. At 22, she was just a few years older than Sarah. Something about the picture of Sarah in a uniform and headed to war scared the hell out of him. Tom mustered up the best smile he could and said, "See you in January, LT."

The fresh-faced lieutenant responded quickly with, "Hoaah, sir!" then headed for the door.

As she left the room, Lawton couldn't help but think, *I need to make sure I bring Crandle and all the rest of these kids home.* Some were so young, but they were going to do what was asked of them without reservation. His palms started to sweat.

After most everyone had left the hangar, Petty stayed and caught Tom in his office. "Howdy, sir. Just wondering if you had an option, would you 'embrace the suck' again or stay home and wash your cat?"

Lawton laughed out loud. "I think the latter. I don't even have a damn cat, but I'd find a whole herd and wash 'em all to keep away from the suck!" Petty laughed and Tom waved him towards a seat.

"Thanks, boss." He sat down but stayed on the edge of the seat.

Lawton could see something was bothering him. "All right, Joe. I give! What's on your mind?"

Petty tried to smile. "That obvious?"

"We've been doin' this for 20 years, Joe. Shoot."

Petty exhaled loudly. "I was just wondering what that little meeting at Hood was all about. I'm sure those guys in the active Army have something up their sleeve. Can you tell me what's goin' on?"

"Like what?"

"I can't help but think those bastards either don't want us or they want us to go to Afghanistan or even worse. Maybe Kosovo, like the rumors are sayin'!"

"I can honestly tell you, no one told me anything about Kosovo."

"What about Afghanistan?"

Lawton hadn't thought about that possibility, but it made no sense. They had trained with the Cav, and Powell was too political not to be involved in the main effort. If he was going to be an aviation general, they had to put him in the war, and the war was going to be in Iraq. "I can't say absolutely, one-hundred percent, no, but I don't see us going to Afghanistan."

Petty studied his face. "They say anything else while you were up there, sir?"

Lawton chuckled. "They said, 'You guys are the greatest National Guard unit in Texas and we would love to have you come fight with us!'"

Petty shook his head at Tom's answer. "Sir, you know about those bastards up there. If they're patting us on the back, it's only a recon to find where to stick the knife!"

Lawton laughed, yet the comment struck home. Petty was smiling, but his face betrayed more than sarcasm.

Lawton's laughter was muted by a fake cough. "Joe, it's gonna be all right. When we go anywhere, just like last time, we'll be in the middle of an Armored or a Mechanized Division. We're just going to be in a support role. Hell, we probably won't even see combat!"

Petty nodded again, but didn't believe him for a minute.

"I was told that we aren't even in tune with the active duty and all their modernization plans," Tom added.

Petty raised an eyebrow at the comment. "What the hell does that have to do with fighting war today? That's for the research and development guys to use their millions of dollars to fight the next one. This is the now fight! Our equipment can fight today!"

"You're right, Joe. That's why we need to have our shit together so we can be ready to kick ass."

"Kick ass? I hope it's as easy as you think!"

"Just like last time. If we get about a month over there, get used to the conditions, we'll kick their ass again."

Petty stood up. "I'm not as cocky as you about this one, boss. I don't care much for the shape of this fight. It's on his home turf this time. How would we fight if someone came after Texas?"

Tom nodded. *As usual, Petty's perspective is fresh. Warrant officer's are the best-kept secret in the United States Army.* "They aren't Texans, Joe. We'll be all right." Petty gave him a low-key salute and said, "Happy holidays, sir."

Petty's comment flipped a switch in Tom's mind. Money. *It makes sense after listening to Walker talk about strategic and tactical and how everything in between was just stuff. That stuff means millions, even billions of dollars in defense money. Money for the Guard, money for research, and money for active duty aviation. Money for generals.* Tom shook off his thoughts. His paranoia crept in to join the typical warrant officer cynicism. He had had enough for the day. He quickly got his beret and headed to his car.

On the way home, he actually pulled into a Quick Stop and started to buy a six-pack. He was bothered by all the details floating in his head. Between Powell's politics, Walker's guidance and Petty's comments, Tom's head was pounding. He had been called to Hood to be told his unit wasn't good enough to go to war with the active component. There really was no good reason why they shouldn't go. Something was going on and Tom couldn't figure it out.

There was a drunk sitting on a bench outside the store. *Here's this guy just days before Christmas, sitting on the bench smoking a cigarette, drinking a beer, and staring into space.* The thought occurred to him, *if I wasn't going to see Cindy, I might join the man.*

Seeing the bum helped him figure something out. *What is my priority in life? Easy enough question to answer. To live life free and happy.* He looked at the man on the bench. *He doesn't seem too happy.*

Lawton started the car and pulled out of the parking lot. He needed to get home. *If I hurry, maybe I can get three miles in before dark.*

25 December 2002
Huntsville, Texas

TOM SPENT MOST OF THE DAY staying in the background. He watched Cindy and the girls as they enjoyed their Christmas. He listened to all his relatives as if he had never heard them before. It was a day of pure joy. He only had to leave the living room once to go wipe his eyes. The thought that this was what living was all about kept popping up in his mind. This was the way people were supposed to treat each other.

Cindy must have pre-briefed everyone about Tom's resolve not to drink because no one offered him any alcohol.

In fact, there wasn't any to be found.

Sarah stopped by twice to ask her father if he was okay. Tom smiled broadly each time and let his beautiful daughter know he was having a wonderful time. He couldn't get over how mature, at 16, she was.

After the presents and the feasting, Tom found himself sitting on the couch watching football and talking sports with his brothers-in-law. Things were almost like before Cindy had left him. He still wasn't comfortable, but the family was making the whole situation easier for him than he expected.

When he finally thought his food had digested enough, he got up off the couch and headed out to the porch to sit in the swing. He saw Cindy talking to her sisters and just smiled. She was content and he decided not to press her to join him.

The afternoon air was a bit brisk, but December in east Texas isn't exactly the frozen tundra. He sat on the swing and gently rocked. *This is what it's all about. This is living.*

Tom started to understand a little about himself at that moment. *This is why I'm a soldier. This is why I'm in the Texas National Guard. To defend this way of life. To defend this family. They have no way of knowing how things around the world are going. They don't need to understand terrorists or brutal dictators or any of the cruelty out there.* He hoped that his daughters would never suffer the cruelty of the world as he knew it.

Cindy popped through the front door. "Well howdy, stranger! Mind if I join you?"

Tom smiled. "Not one bit." He motioned for her to sit next to him on the swing.

"You were deep in thought."

Tom nodded. "Yeah."

"Thinking about the deployment?"

Tom's smile faded. His expression must have given away his surprise. *There isn't anything going on that I don't know about,* Cindy's eyes seemed to say.

Tom knew to just go with it. "Kind of."

She came clean rather than keep him guessing. "I talked to the sergeant major last Sunday. He said you guys were getting prepared to go somewhere. You weren't sure where."

Tom nodded. "He told you the truth."

"You don't' know for sure if you are going to Iraq or not?" She was watching his face closely.

"We really aren't certain. But if I was to guess, I'd guess we are." She nodded uncomfortably. "Do you have an estimated date?" Tom frowned. "No, but I would guess the way the UN keeps procrastinating, the US will decide to do something soon. I expect to get some orders for the unit next month. Maybe right after the new year."

"At least they gave you the holidays for a change!"

Tom smiled. "Yeah! For a change!"

Cindy switched the subject. "I'm glad you went to AA, Tom. I know it was tough to admit you have a problem. But I can tell a difference."

"Sober over fifty days now! I've lost ten pounds. I ran five miles on Monday. Damn near killed me, but I made it." She smiled. "And I leave work at five o'clock. Which is new for me!"

She agreed. "Don't know what to do with all that free evening time, do you?"

Tom started to say something else but caught himself. "I can think of some things I'd like to be doing."

Cindy tilted her head. "Are you flirting with me?"

"Yeah. Got a problem with that?"

"No. Not one bit."

She looked away but was still smiling. It was quiet for a moment. Cindy exhaled loudly and her smile faded. "I can't come back just yet, you know? We have some other things to clear up. But I'm closer."

Tom nodded. "I know, sweetie."

She turned to face him. "But I will come back."

Tom reached up and gently touched her face. "As long as you need. I'll be waiting." He slowly bent towards her and kissed her cheek.

Just then Sarah came out the front door and caught her father's tender action. She stopped in her tracks.

Tom spoke quickly. "Hiya, kiddo!"

Sarah looked at Cindy with chin down and eyebrows up, smiling. "Did I interrupt something?"

"No. Just talking," exclaimed Tom as innocently as possible.

Sarah nodded and smiled. "Well, talking like that is better than talking to each other on the phone!"

Tom and Cindy smiled at each other. Suddenly, Alicia came outside. She yelled back inside, "Jenny! Come look! Mom and Dad are sitting in the swing!" She turned back. "That means you two are gonna kiss!" She ran up and jumped on Tom's lap.

Sarah caught Cindy's glance, "They don't have to kiss."

Tom looked at Jenny. "If you think I need to kiss your Mom, I can do that." He bent over and pecked her on the cheek.

"Oh, Dad! I meant a REAL kiss. Like this!" She grabbed Tom's face and planted a juicy one. "Merry Christmas, Daddy!"

Tom was laughing as he wiped the wetness from his face. "I don't think I'll give your Mom one like that, but I'll try." He turned and kissed Cindy softly on the lips. Her hand gently touched his arm and Tom moved closer.

Tom couldn't take his eyes off Cindy, remembering how much he loved her.

"That was a good one, Daddy!" yelled Alicia.

Cindy looked at Tom and said softly, "That was a good one, Daddy."

Sarah took her sister's hands. "Come on. I think they have some more talking to do." As they followed her to the back yard, Sarah smiled over her shoulder. "Just talkin', okay?"

3 January 2003
Montgomery County Airport
Conroe, Texas

IT DIDN'T TAKE LONG FOR THE orders to come. Lawton was only at his desk forty minutes that morning when the call came from none other than Colonel Powell himself. Tom didn't even know Powell knew his phone number.

"Hello, Lawton. We just got the official notification. You guys are actually coming with us. Check your secure fax for the official orders. I've already called General Walker. He was very happy and, I suppose I can say, confident in your abilities to succeed." The colonel hesitated, then tossed out, "I'm not so sure we can use you. But, as they say, orders are orders."

"Thank you, sir for that tremendous vote of confidence." *Asshole.* "If there is anything we can do to support the brigade, sir, we'll do it. We're ready."

Powell hesitated before responding. "We'll see, Lieutenant Colonel Lawton. We'll see."

Tom grabbed the orders from the fax machine, noting the orders directed them to join the 3rd Infantry Division in a support role. A support role for an Apache attack helicopter squadron could mean a wide range of missions, including defense, movement to contact, deliberate attack, and even deep attack across enemy troop forward lines. But one thing was certain. All the missions involved killing the enemy.

CHAPTER NINE

I got three days, to wash the road out of my soul,
I got three days to love you outta control.
And I wish I had a lifetime to hold onto you this way,
Love can do some healing, in just three days.

"Three Days"
-Pat Green and Radney Foster

14 January 2003
Conroe, Texas

TOM LAWTON AND SERGEANT MAJOR MARTINEZ frequently discussed news media reports. Tom had a television put in his office so he could watch Fox News. He found himself bored by most of the coverage and the information provided by the talking heads, most of them retired military officers. In the sergeant major's opinion, some of those talking heads should have been arrested and charged with treason.

Tom thought otherwise. In fact, after watching one particular broadcast, he suspected that all that information may have been an organized plan to keep the average citizen (and al-Jazeera) totally confused about what was truth and what was fiction. That way, only the Bush administration and the commander of Central Command in Tampa really knew what was happening.

He was content merely knowing what he had to do at his level to support the fight. He remembered Walker's words, "The middle ninety percent was just 'stuff.'"

The only difference between this war and other recent wars was the fact that reporters would be embedded in the units to provide actual, live coverage. Tom definitely had an opinion about embedded reporters; the unit would have enough distractions without having to deal with a reporter. So he was happy to find out no reporters were headed his way when he got into the country. As a rule, he didn't trust them.

16 January 2003
Montgomery County Airport
Conroe, Texas

THE UNIT HAD BEEN IN LINE for over an hour getting their deployment shots. Tom had gone first—all the men knew his ass hurt and his left arm was virtually useless. As the commander, he knew he had to set the example. Some soldiers in other units had refused shots, even active-duty troops. To Tom's surprise, every one of his Cav soldiers was in line and taking their required vaccinations. *No bitching, no whining, no complaining. That's the Cav way.*

As he walked around the hangar, he caught an exchange that piqued his curiosity.

"Did you do it?" asked 1st Lieutenant Gash, the intelligence officer.

"Naw! I've got three kids already," said Captain Jason Wills, HHT Commander.

"Um. Excuse me, but did you do what?"

The pair was somewhat hesitant to answer. Gash looked around to see if anyone was listening. "Well, sir. Seems some of the men have made visits to the 'bank.' You know?"

Tom looked at Sam and shrugged his shoulders. "No, LT. I don't know. What bank?"

Wills stepped in to help. "Sperm banks, sir." "What?" Tom was amazed.

Wills said, "They've heard stories about the first Gulf War. They believe they may be altered."

"What?" Tom winced. "Altered by what?"

"You know, sir," said Gash. "All the chemicals, the shots, radiation poisoning, from the first Gulf War. They're afraid their sperm might get messed up in combat!"

Tom shook his head. "I don't know what to say. I don't think my sperm was altered in the first war. My kids are just fine." He looked at Gash and Wills and saw the seriousness in their faces. "Guess I don't really see any harm in it, though. If it makes them feel better about going to war, hell, I'm for it." Tom shook his head and started to walk away.

He shouted over his shoulder, "Hell, maybe I'll go make a deposit!" Tom turned and saw the look on his subordinates' faces. "Just kiddin', guys. I'm fixed. I won't be making babies anymore!" The pair nodded.

Tom wondered to himself about the latest news. Honestly, he had wondered about Gulf War Syndrome and the exposure to toxins and potentially poisonous or lethal combinations of injections. But he and all his soldiers seemed to be healthy after the first Gulf War. He had taken as many precautions as possible to keep his men safe, avoiding minefields and areas contaminated by chemical residue. He even had them remove the flea collars they had worn to prevent sand fleas.

But if the knowledge their semen was safe and sound in a sperm bank would make the men more comfortable, it was not Tom's position disagree.

18 January 2003
Texas National Guard Headquarters
Austin, Texas

MAJOR GENERAL WALKER CALLED TOM TO his office. "I thought you would be deploying with the First Cav, Tom, but apparently you will be going with only selected units from the Cav."

Tom understood, but still had questions. "Just what kind of units and who will our higher headquarters be, sir?"

"You're going to join the 3rd Infantry Division."

"The 3rd ID?" *So ... we will be "embracing the suck" after all.*

Walker looked over his bifocals at the orders in his hands.

"It seems they need to have aviation and artillery augmentation. They want the 1st Team Divarty (Division Artillery), the Longbows, and—" he looked up at Tom with a smile, "—the Texas National Guard attack helicopters."

Tom nodded. "That'll work, sir. Do we have a date for departure yet?"

Walker shook his head. "Not yet. I would imagine any day now."

'Any day now' could mean tomorrow. Or weeks. Tom saluted and headed out the door.

Lawton did the mental rundown on the 3rd ID. 'The Rock of the Marine,' as the Division was known, had a tremendous history. Since World War II and the Battle of the Marne, the Division had been honorably decorated and never left Germany. It was being tagged to spearhead the attack into Iraq. As the premier United States Army mechanized division, it would bring 665 combat vehicles to war, including 203 M1A1 Abrams tanks, 54 Paladin self-propelled howitzers, 267 Bradley fighting vehicles, and 24 of their own Apache helicopters.

The Division also had 4300 support vehicles, most tagged for fuel support. An M1A1 tank drank two gallons of fuel per mile. Tom started to add Bradley fighting vehicles, over 1500 Humvees, and over 40 Apache's to the gas line. The amount of fuel needed to conduct the war would be astronomical.

Tom was glad he wasn't the 3rd Infantry Division G4. Resourcing a division with over 17,000 men and women, while managing logistical support seemed an overwhelming task.

And they were now the standard for Army Force 21, the epitome of digitization. Moving a division of that size across Iraq seemed an insurmountable task.

Tom shook his head. The new program supposedly offered, "simultaneity, agility, and effects-based targeting." Lots of fancy verbiage, but he wasn't sold.

The Guard aircraft would still have compatibility problems with the Division, but if it was the 3rd ID that got him into the fight, he was more than happy to join them. The Texas Guard may not have been the most advanced attack unit in the world, but it could still kick ass.

By the 25th of January, the unit's aircraft had been flown to Beaumont, sealed in shrink-wrap, and loaded onto ships bound for Kuwait. They wouldn't fly again until they arrived in the Middle East.

28 January 2003
Huntsville, Texas

TOM WAS SITTING ON THE COUCH when the doorbell rang. He opened the door and was shocked to find Cindy standing there. "I heard you were fixin' to deploy soon."

Tom nodded. "We have three days left. I was gonna call you, but—"

She reached up and put her hand on his lips. "That doesn't give us much time." She walked through the door and closed it behind her. Slowly, she stepped close to Tom and put her arms around him. "If you're gonna be gone for a long time, I want to make sure I give you a good reason to come home." She reached up and kissed him softly.

Tom swept her up and carried her to the bedroom. It was the quickest three days of Tom's life.

30 January 2003
Huntsville, Texas

TOM WENT UP TO HUNTSVILLE TO say goodbye, to make sure Cindy and the girls didn't go through the long, arduous wait at the airport and the stress of watching the unit get on the plane. Saying goodbye was always tough, but saying goodbye when you have to go to war is, by far, the toughest thing anyone with a family has to do. He promised the girls he'd be back. Sarah took it best, while Alicia, at three, was too young to understand. Jenny took it the hardest. She was just beginning to see her mom and dad get back together and now her father was leaving to go to some faraway land. Tom had to wipe tears away after he hugged her. She was crying harder than he had expected.

He rose quickly and grabbed Cindy, giving her a hug and a peck on the cheek. He took a moment to study her face, then turned away. He didn't want her to see his tears. How different this was from the first Gulf War. Just as he was beginning to get his family back together, he was off to war. As he drove away, he couldn't help but think how unfair war was, especially for the kids too young to understand.

Ten miles closer to Ft. Hood, he wasn't even sure if he understood. *Why would anyone in their right mind leave their family to go off and fight in a war?* He was smart enough to see the long-range implications of Saddam Hussein's rule. However, because "somebody had to do it" or "it's the right thing to do" just didn't hold water for him at that particular moment. The fact was, Tom Lawton was off to fight another war. All indications were that this one would keep him away from Cindy for a very long time. So the quicker the Cav got to Iraq and kicked Saddam Hussein's ass, the sooner Tom Lawton could get back to Texas.

31 January 2003
Gray Army Airfield
Ft. Hood, TX

MAJOR GENERAL WALKER, STANDING NEXT TO Lawton, had made it up to Ft. Hood to see his Texans off. The battalion was a little thin in some of the support areas, and they needed about three crews to get a full eighteen Apaches in the air. Tom Lawton was still proud of the fact that his squadron showed up en masse with 262 people and was as ready to fight as they could be.

Colonel Crane was already forward in a support role. Tom could picture Crane standing over some poor major in the 3rd ID Tactical Operations Center (TOC), trying to get him to spill the beans on how a different colonel was screwing up. One quick way to the top was to stab all the competition. Crane would lie in wait for just the right moment to drop a dime on another brigade commander so he could take his job.

Meanwhile, Tom watched as Colonel Ben Powell approached. Tom said under his breath, "Crap, sir! Here comes the fun sponge!" Walker covered his mouth to hide his snicker.

"Hello, General Walker." Powell turned to Tom and grunted, "Lawton."

Lawton dropped his salute and looked at Walker and smiled. "Nice day for a deployment, eh, sir?"

Powell, way too uptight for Tom, just nodded as if he had actually heard what Tom had said. "I see lots of long faces out there. Doesn't look to me like your guys are too excited about going over, Lieutenant Colonel Lawton."

Tom answered honestly. "Let's see here, sir. Most of my soldiers are leaving family behind, they're all leaving jobs behind. Most of those jobs pay the same or in some cases three times more money. They signed up to be in the Texas Guard and fight for the state, but they're fighting for the President. They've had half a dozen shots. They're headed off to war for an undetermined amount of time." He looked at Walker. "Can't understand why they're feeling down." Walker grunted and covered his smile again.

"I just hope they're ready to fight," said Powell with a frown.

"Sir, my guys understand one thing. Getting back home means going to Baghdad first. Just give 'em the word and we'll be there before the tanks!"

This time Powell grunted. "Pretty bold statement from a guy whose unit isn't even fully manned and barely got through the NTC! I hope they can do half of what you think they can, Lawton." He turned to Walker and saluted, "Thank you for coming to see us off, General!" Powell turned and stomped off.

Walker looked at Lawton. "I like you, Tom. I really do. You remind me of when I was young and stupid."

Tom took the general's quip in stride. "I really think we are better than Powell and Crane give us credit for."

"You're going to have plenty of opportunity to prove it, Tom." The general turned solemn. "Iraq was the cradle of civilization. Before it was hijacked by the scum that are ruining the planet, they believed in commerce and prosperity. They believed in the separation of religion and secular authority."

The general looked at Tom. "You just can't bring freedom and democracy to a country that has been decimated by a criminal for the past thirty years.

"You'll kick the shit outta the Republican Guard and you'll probably be in Baghdad quicker than you think. But you won't win the war until you can fly around the country without worrying about getting shot down by the locals. I wish you the best of luck in getting to that point." Instead of saluting, Walker stuck out his hand. "Don't do anything to make the locals hate you and you'll win."

Tom took the hand and said, "Thanks for the advice, sir. We'll be back as soon as we can. I'm thinking three months this time!"

Walker was not smiling. "Just do the job and bring them home, Tom. I'll see you when I see you."

Lawton wondered how soon that would be.

CHAPTER TEN

Got to get my armor on,
Stand up to the demons.
Got to get my armor on,
For the battle against the dark.

"Armor Jive"
-Dana D. Jacobson

8 February 2003
Camp Texas Kuwait

THE CAVALRY SQUADRON WAS SETTLING INTO a fairly good routine. After removing and painting over all the signs that said "Camp California", the unit was quick to focus on war preparations. The daily grind involved, mostly, keeping oneself occupied—eating, sleeping, training for chemical attacks, cleaning weapons, taking shelter when real sirens went off, cleaning around the area, and more chemical training. The unit was doing a good job of sticking together despite the fact there were no helicopters flying.

Tom's first serious issue within the unit was the question of arming the soldiers. The NCOs and the sergeant major had wanted to get live ammunition for the troopers. Tom resisted this request. He pointed out the camp was surrounded by towers with soldiers armed with .50 caliber machine guns and that the enemy was not knocking at the door. Tom remembered all too well what accidental discharges of weapons could do; more soldiers were likely to be injured here at Camp Texas than after they crossed into Iraq.

Just days later, a soldier from the 101st threw grenades into tents as the officers were sleeping and sprayed his camp with gunfire. Upon hearing this, the sergeant major just nodded at Tom.

The fact that the soldier who did the "fraggin" in the 101st was a Muslim quickly spread throughout Camp Texas. While all the soldiers were wary of the third-world nationals or darker-skinned foreigners that came anywhere close to the camp, Tom was pleased that none of his men gave any grief to the black soldiers in the unit. His troopers were smart enough to know the incident was an isolated event that would not be repeated in the Cav. You count on your buddy, regardless of race or religion, and Cavalry soldiers know they can trust each other.

The toughest thing to deal with while living in the tents was the shamals. These desert windstorms were a snapshot of hell for the troopers. Visibility dropped to zero, and eating, working, training, and even sleeping were impossible. All they could do was cover everything up, hunker down, and wait it out.

12 February 2003
Camp Texas Kuwait

THE EQUIPMENT FINALLY ARRIVED IN PORT. For the men of the 7/17th, having the aircraft was a breath of fresh air. The meals were starting to repeat themselves, so the news that the unit would be moving out to a "forward location" was received with open arms. What they didn't understand was that this meant leaving what little comfort Camp Texas afforded them to set up tents in the much less hospitable desert of western Kuwait.

Tom had one last meeting in a real building before leaving Camp Texas. Powell had called all his aviation commanders and senior NCOs together to give them a pep talk. It wasn't much of a speech.

"I know a lot of you men have never been in combat." Powell walked around the group of twenty men. He had a stern look on his face and was walking with his hands behind his back. Lawton noticed as he turned that the man had no patch on his right shoulder. Powell had never been in combat either. "It's going to be tough when we cross into Iraq. We don't know what to expect. Your men are going to ask a lot of tough questions. Don't let them see any fear." Tom sensed Powell was saying that as much for himself as he was for the assembled leadership. "We're all scared. But together, we'll get through this war!"

The crowd quickly dispersed after the talk. Tom heard one of his peers say, "Mark my words, that son of a bitch is gonna spend the entire war in the TOC!" Tom smiled and headed to join his men. He had a mental picture of Powell, hands behind him, stalking the Tactical Operations Center tent, screaming for information.

He knew the image was fictitious. Powell would be in a Blackhawk flying above the battle. If he was anything like Tom's first battalion commander, Barney Steele, he would be in an Apache shooting "Gomers" by the dozen. Then it dawned on him, Powell was not Barney Steele. Steele was a great leader. Powell was a pencil-pusher who would probably keep his ass safe, update the chain of command with his tactical prowess, and set the stage for his collar to wear stars. Part of getting his promotion plan was to make the AH-64 Delta-model Apache the premier fighting machine of Operation Iraqi Freedom. As an Alpha-model pilot, Lawton knew it would probably take a direct order from the division commander to get his unit into the war. If the fight were left up to Powell, Tom and the Warriors would be protecting the rear echelon with their pistols.

As Tom thought more about his boss, Colonel Ben Powell, rear-area support looked more and more like the safest place to keep his Texans alive. The thought set in as he whistled his way to his Humvee.

13 February 2003
AA Turban
Western Kuwait

TOM LAWTON WAS HAVING SERIOUS FLASHBACKS as he scanned the assembly area. AA Turban was nearly an exact replica of any of a half-dozen assembly areas he had lived in during the first Gulf War: flat, dry, dusty, dirty, and just plain nasty. If it weren't for the gentle depression of the Wadi two kilometers to their west, they might as well have already been in Iraq. The Wadi-al-Batan identified the border between Iraq and Kuwait. Fortunately, from two-hundred feet above ground level, pilots could see the definition of that little valley even with night-view systems. The Wadi was perhaps thirty feet deep at its lowest point and nearly three hundred yards across near AA Turban. It was a great limiting factor for any flights to the west. Everyone knew Indian country was across the Wadi.

The newer, younger pilots could hardly believe the unmistakable distinction between friendly and enemy territory. There was no enemy there. They could fly into Iraq without anyone even firing a shot. But Tom instructed all his senior pilots to never penetrate Iraqi airspace. They could get as close as they felt comfortable, but no one was to trigger any event that would draw Iraqi forces south toward their positions.

The unit became comfortable again as the flying took precedence over how shitty the living conditions were. Doing the job was always the best way to overcome any morale problems.

Even the MREs were satisfying. Tom finally tried one of the new "Meals, Ready to Eat." The sergeant major had described one as the "Four Fingers of Death," usually called beans and franks. By Tom's count, there were eight new meals that had not been available during his last trip to Kuwait. The only one he didn't care for was a kind of Chinese chicken dish—he tried to make sure he never got that package again. His driver, Specialist Tomkins from Helotes, Texas, was always willing to trade. To Lawton, any MRE (except the chicken) warmed up was edible, and Tomkins was always on hand to heat the food up in the Humvee. Not only was the kid a great driver, but he turned out to be a pretty damn good cook, too.

22 February 2003
AA Turban
Western Kuwait

DAILY THE ARMOR UNITS POURED INTO the area surrounding the aviation brigade. Tom and the Warriors actually started to feel comfortable with an entire three brigades of the finest Armor division in the world surrounding them. The 1st Brigade was in the north, the 2nd Brigade was to their west, and the 3rd brigade, mostly Bradley fighting vehicles, was in the south.

The armor tended to weather the shamals much better than the aircraft, but mother earth had a way of disrupting anything that seemed to go right for the division. If it wasn't sixty-mile- per-hour sandstorms, it was rain—every other day. As soon as they would dry out, it would rain again and the desert would turn back into one big mud pit. Any fighting holes the men had dug would be flooded. All the equipment took on the same reddish-brown hue of the Kuwaiti desert. As hard as the men tried, they could never keep all their clothing dry.

Tom took the squadron out for a late afternoon battle drill and flew over the division. Men, vehicles, and equipment carpeted the desert. An untrained eye would have difficulty telling one tank from another, or be able to figure out what unit was where, or which vehicles worked or didn't. He had not seen any persons of Middle-Eastern descent, or even any of the third-world nationals who had been picking up the trash since the unit left their hard-stand airfield three weeks prior. As long as the Russians weren't giving Saddam satellite imagery, and the French hadn't sold him any similar pictures, chances were good that the Iraqi Republican Guard divisions were still blind.

One other item significantly different for Tom from the first Gulf War was the availability of email. The men still loved to get to the phone tent, but every time they went, there would be a line. The TOC had two unclassified computers that allowed the troops to either surf the net or send emails using Hotmail accounts. It was a tremendous morale booster for anyone that had time to get online.

One email making it around camp was a particularly amusing account of accommodations for US Air Force personnel in Afghanistan. The individual sending the email was whining about having to share the shower and only having one every three days. He went on to complain that the workout tent wasn't big enough for all their equipment and the big-screen TV and speakers filled up one end of the morale and welfare tent. The Warriors did share a large TV in the chow tent, but they would have killed for a building for showering or anything that resembled a workout room.

26 February 2003
AA Eagle
Central Kuwait

TOM LAWTON WAS ORDERED TO REPORT to headquarters for a briefing on roles and missions. He had been eagerly awaiting this meeting because he wanted to know what Crane and Powell had in mind for the 7/17th.

The division G3 had set up a huge rock drill that walked through all the units down to squadron and battalion level. The colonel conducting the briefing was an Armor officer and he focused on armor brigades and the mech infantry units. Long on actions and timelines, he didn't want to hear any questions from the assembled commanders.

One curious armor lieutenant colonel asked what Lawton thought was a damn good question. "When can we expect the second stop for refuel and rearming?"

The colonel had already stated the first expected stopping point, but no one had brought up the follow-on FARP arrangements. The division's deputy G3 didn't seem too sure of the answer himself. "This is a movement that will depend on the activities of the enemy. We can only speculate on when and where the Day Two FARP will be. That will be disseminated in a follow-on FRAGO." Tom reassessed his initial thought. *This guy's clueless about the logistics support from Day Two on.*

The second thing about the plan that bugged Lawton was its failure to employ aviation assets in a continuous manner. They had planned on Deep Attack, but only as an on-call mission. That meant it would be at the discretion of the division commander and when he thought would be the best opportunity to exploit weakness in the Republican Guard.

The Deep Attack mission was the one mission the attack units did not enjoy. It required tremendously detailed planning, communications, and synchronization. It helped if the ground commander's scheme of maneuver was oriented on the mission, but Lawton looked at the G3's plan and thought it was way too aggressive on the ground. The aviation side preferred to have a well-defined, dug-in, positively-identified enemy. As fast as the division was planning on moving, the Deep Attack would probably be movement to contact operations against retreating Iraqis, followed by Army ground forces immediately occupying the ground the aircraft had just engaged. Plus there was no mention of Air Force assets. For years Lawton had been taught JAAT (Joint Air Attack Team) that involved Armor, Artillery, Army Aviation, and Air Force jets. A serious assumption was that all this firepower was synchronized. Assumptions in war have a way of getting people killed.

Colonel Crane called all his commanders together for a review of his unit's operations. He was direct in his guidance and obviously comfortable with the units he had trained and worked with. Colonel Powell, as the Aviation Brigade commander, watched from the background to pick up pointers on how he could best employ his helicopters to support Crane's task force. Lawton noticed Dick Crane was none too happy being a reserve force.

At least Crane's unit was identified and tasked with a mission. The Texas Guard Attack Helicopter Unit was not even mentioned in the operations. Lawton reviewed the written order and found the 7/17th was listed in the coordinating instructions as a support element to the rear-area commander. Not only was it a stupid role for an attack helicopter squadron, it was also an insult. Lawton was standing in line next to Colonel Powell when Crane finished.

"Colonel Crane, a moment of your time." Lawton stepped in front of his Brigade commander. "I didn't see a role for the 7/17th that," Tom tried to be tactful. "best utilizes my assets."

Crane knew exactly what Lawton meant. He smiled and nodded to Powell. "We discussed your assets, Lawton. We've got you right where you need to be for now." Powell nodded and gave Tom a condescending smile.

"All it says in the order is 'support element to the rear area commander.' I don't see that as much of a benefit to your Task Force."

"Well, do you want us to plop your Texans right up there on the first Cross-Flot, Lieutenant Colonel?"

Tom knew the mission as briefed was crap. Crane had Tom by the balls in front of Powell. Lawton wanted no part of it but knew the answer Crane wanted to hear. "If you need us to do that mission, we can do it, sir."

Powell spoke up as if he were making the decision for Crane. "We don't need you to join the active units for the Cross-Flot, Lawton. We think you can best help the Task Force by assisting Lieutenant Colonel Motley with the rear-area coverage. We'll be bypassing tons of enemy prisoners on the move to Baghdad. You can best assist him by being his quick-reaction force. You can do that mission just fine." He reached over and patted Tom's shoulder like he was a little kid.

Lawton fought every urge he had to scream, but the cards were on the table. And no lieutenant colonel in his right mind goes against two full birds. The bullets weren't flying yet, his men could handle the rear area support mission, and it was the safest place for them to be. As much as he wanted to prove himself and get his unit recognized, the sanity of playing it safe contributed to Lawton keeping his mouth shut. *Bring 'em all home* kept ringing in Tom's head. "All right, sir."

As he stepped backwards to leave, he said, "Sir, I just want to make sure you know I'm no Jeb Stuart." Jeb Stuart and his cavalry commander were nowhere to be seen when Lee attacked the Union forces near Gettysburg; many blamed Stuart for costing Lee not just the battle, but the war.

"If anyplace near Baghdad gets to be Gettysburg, we may need you, Lawton. But until we call, do your assigned job."

Tom said, "Yes, sir!" turned quickly, and headed for his Humvee.

Play it safe and bring 'em home. Tom smacked the hood of the Hummer. Logic told him to be happy. *Accept the mission and do the best you can. But we've come 18,000 miles to fight a war. The hell with playing it safe! We're good enough to be here and we're good enough to fight.*

5 March 2003
AA Turban
Western Kuwait

ONE OF THE BEST WAYS TO break the monotony of life in the desert was to go to the barbershop. It also gave Tom a venue for gauging his men's spirit and morale. On this particular day the barbershop was outside the B Troop Bandits' warrant officers' tent. Most of the Bandits were there and the word must have filtered to the commissioned officers.

The first topic of discussion was an article in "The Stars and Stripes," reporting the testing of a 21,000-pound bomb, the Massive Ordinance Aerial Bomb (MOAB). Soldiers quickly dubbed it "the Mother of All Bombs" to mock Hussein's calling the first Gulf War "The Mother of All Battles."

"I hear the Muslims ain't too keen on getting burned to death," claimed Chief Warrant Officer Two Jason Early. "Somethin' about fryin' keeps 'em from gettin' to heaven."

The S1, Lieutenant Terry Harper asked, "If that were true, how come so many of 'em blow themselves up?"

"They do that because they're offered 72 virgins and eternal life in paradise," Joe Petty replied. Petty, strumming on his guitar, had a nice spot in a lawn chair that had miraculously appeared.

"You can tell they ain't from Texas. I don't think there's 72 virgins left, 'cept maybe in Amarillo! And that's 'cause they run faster than their brothers!" Only Chief Warrant Officer Four Brian Trant could get away with that comment and still get a laugh. Most of the guys had sisters back in Texas but took the jab in stride.

Lawton faked a cough and shook his head. "Getting back to our enemies." The officers' chuckles died down. "I guess you could say that in just a few days, it may become our job to make sure those dudes get a chance at those virgins." Some guys laughed, but others understood the significance of killing an enemy.

"I'm not sure how many of you know, the Apache doesn't really have a stellar reputation." He looked around at the men. Some pulled their sunglasses down or looked over the top at their commander.

"I mentioned this before, but I need to reiterate this to you officers. Back in the first Gulf War, a pair of Apaches were flying cover for a

Blackhawk carrying medical personnel. Somewhere along the Euphrates River, the Blackhawk took massive ground fire from small arms. The aircraft crashed and rolled on its side. The Apaches, assuming no one survived the crash, bugged out."

Lieutenant Harper spoke up. "They didn't check the status of the crew?"

"Nope. They fired some rockets and the 30-mm gun, but that was it. The result was a captured pilot, crew chief, and female flight surgeon."

Captain Chase Freeman joined in. "They left a female to get captured?"

Tom jumped all over the comment. "It didn't matter that she was female! These are bad dudes we're up against." Tom looked around the room. "You can imagine what happened to her. Luckily, she was strong enough to survive the ordeal."

Tom let the comment sink in. "We will NOT leave anyone. If we have to send in a troop of Apaches and every one of us gets hammered, we're going after our people. Everyone understand that?" There were "HOAHs" all around.

Tom wasn't done. "The next thing that got Apaches a bad reputation was the deployment of Task Force Eagle for ALLIED FORCE." Trant nodded again. "When the Apaches were called on to take on Milosevic and the Serbs, they had problems.

"First of all, the unit was a task force, and they had to get a couple different units together to form the Task Force. Next, they took forever and a day to self-deploy around the Alps, through Italy, and across the Adriatic to Albania. When they finally arrived, the staging area was a muddy airfield that kept the unit focused on keeping clean versus being ready to attack the enemy.

"Then, when the training started, they crashed two Apaches. One might have been a wire strike, I don't remember offhand, but the other was due to a night-flying training error.

"We have a few more days of night flying and the boss is going to let us shoot a live-fire three days from now. We need to make sure all the weapons systems work and that we're ready to use them." The men all nodded. This was good information. It would be reiterated at the staff meeting later that evening.

"Now I have a question for you all," said Lawton. He looked around at the faces of the men getting haircuts and waiting in line. "Do you know what you're doing here?"

Captain "Bat" Talbot was first to respond. "It's to take down Saddam and his regime."

Next was Lieutenant Tony Harper. "We're here to find nuclear, chemical, and biological weapons that can be given to terrorists and used against the US or its allies." That got a lot of nods.

Petty stopped strumming his guitar and said, "We're here so other folks can drink Shiner Bock and bitch about the President." Petty's comment drew a laugh from most of the assembled crowd.

Tom nodded. "All very good reasons, and spot on. But Joe's reason is actually the most important one." Petty stood up and took a mock bow.

"We're here to bring freedom to a people who have never known freedom in their lives."

"You mean for Iraq, right?" asked Harper.

Tom Lawton shook his head. "No, I'm talking about the fight against all the people that want to take the United States down. I'm not just being paranoid here. Not only do our enemies want to see us taken down a peg, but some of our former friends and current friends would just as soon see us get hammered. They stand to benefit from there no longer being any superpower. Unfortunately, that is all shit that is out of our lane!

"At our level, we need to take care of each other, the unit, and even the kids on the ground. We can make a difference by understanding our role and being better at it than anyone else. We will get into the fight. Sometime, someway, we will be called on. Pass the word and be ready."

15 March 2003
AA Turban
Western Kuwait

TOM KNEW SOMETHING WAS UP WHEN Powell informed all the aviation units they could have a sports day. The Cav unit had an extremely successful gunnery. The aircraft had survived nearly intact, and now the maintenance workers could focus on getting them all fully mission capable (FMC).

Everyone in the unit felt better after they had a chance to unwind. It was a fun day as the troops participated in the many sporting events, going to the phones, or taking a quick trip to the PX.

Tom knew it meant something else. He had friends at Division Headquarters who kept Tom in the loop even when Powell and Crane didn't. The division was getting ready to fight. The general officers had told the Pentagon they were ready to go.

The final indicator came the next day. Five HEMMTs, huge tractor-trailer-like vehicles, showed up. One had MREs and water. The other four carried ammunition. The time had come for the 7/17th to go to war.

CHAPTER ELEVEN

I'm going to Galleywinter.
A place where all the cowboys ride,
A place where all the outlaws hide.
Away from the men who want to kill them for what they done.

"Galleywinter"
-Pat Green

19 March 2003
Border area between Iraq and Kuwait

IN SPITE OF WHAT HIS CHAIN of command thought, Tom Lawton did have a grasp of the bigger picture. He listened to the radio news and read "Stars and Stripes" every chance he could. He wasn't exactly sure why they were bumped up to Readiness Condition 2 (REDCON2). He'd been watching the entire diplomatic fiasco with the UN's and Turkey's assertion of democracy at a time so beneficial to Saddam. He couldn't help but think the Turks had sold out, believing they could keep the US not only from attacking Iraq from the north, but maybe even from attacking at all.

In Lawton's eyes, the Turks were one step above the French. In their attempts to maintain independence from the US and present the appearance of neutrality, both countries had sacrificed allied support from the US and had presented Saddam Hussein with a false sense of security. Hussein may even have been receiving information from some governments that gave him reason to believe he could remain in power.

Yet as much as the world situation seemed to be pushing the start of the war to later rather than sooner, Tom wondered, *Why the increased state of readiness?* The Aviation Brigade even had one unit of AH-64 Delta models at REDCON 1, and some scouts were flying the border.

Tom pulled his Humvee up beside his helicopter and stepped out to take in the night sky. *The desert at night is truly one of God's amazing works. I bet I could easily count a billion stars. The Arabian Desert in particular is especially breathtaking, there's so little man-made light to interfere.*

For an instant Tom was taken back to the first Gulf War.

He had gotten his ass chewed on a night like this for what his squadron commander had perceived to be Tom's failure to properly maintain the colonel's Apache. All the events on that fateful night had taken their toll on Captain Tom Lawton, so he had decided to take a little run across the desert with only the moon to guide him. The memory that he was buck-naked at the time brought a smile to his face.

He then remembered the first night they crossed into Iraq. They did not engage the Iraqis, but the squadron damn near killed two pilots when the weather had gone to hell. The beautiful night sky, so clear for a week, brought a tremendous rainstorm. When the unit returned from the mission, one Apache crashed. The pilots walked away, but the aircraft was a total loss. That was the night before the war officially started. Tom shuddered at the thought. Deep down he knew the 7/17th were trained well, but so was his Squadron back then. He decided to skip praying to the helicopter god and go straight to the Big Guy.

Tom walked away from his aircraft and sought the solace of the desert night. The night air was cool and it was perfectly quiet. He looked around and was surprised to see how brightly the stars lit the desert. *The squadron really is well trained—no lights from the tents, no music from radios, not even voices.*

Tom was at peace. Suddenly he dropped to one knee and put his helmet on the ground. As he looked up at the beautiful blackness and brilliant stars, he began to pray.

Long time, God. I'm sorry about that. I don't think I've prayed since Christmas. Been a little busy. That doesn't mean I've forgotten you. Tom inhaled the night air deeply and slowly let it out as he thought about what to say to his Savior.

I guess you know what we're gonna be up against here. I can't say I'm looking forward to it. I've got a lot of young guys here. Guys that don't want to be here. Hell, even some guys that shouldn't be here, but they are. They got jobs and kids and pregnant wives back home. But they left all that behind. To a man, they haven't bitched once about it. At least, not to me.

I'd ask that you take care of these folks, Lord. They're good people. They'd rather be back in Texas, doing the things that life is all about, but we're here, doing what our country has asked us to do. So if you can, please take care of them.

Tom stood up and put his helmet on. *And one other thing, if you can see to it. Please see that you get me back to Cindy and the girls. This may be a beautiful place you created here, but it ain't Texas. Amen.*

Tom turned and headed to where he thought he left his helicopter. From somewhere in the night he heard a noise. He couldn't make it out for certain. He quickly took off his helmet and looked to the sky. He had heard the noises before. He searched the night sky. He thought it might be jets. But as he listened, he looked to the north. In the night sky, he imagined he had seen something flying. *Cruise missiles?*

He remained still and soon heard the same sound. The missiles were miles away, but there was no doubt what it was. He put his Kevlar on and double-timed to his Humvee. *The war is starting.*

21 March 2003
25 miles south of Talil Airbase, Iraq

WHILE THE 3RD ID SET PRECEDENCE for speed of an armored force in the attack with their sprint across the southern desert of Iraq, the 7/17th was executing their assigned mission in an exemplary manner. Lawton directed Major Jon Wright to split the squadron into four teams of four aircraft each. That utilized sixteen of the Apache aircraft, leaving the only other operating aircraft for Lawton and Petty to fly. The eighteenth aircraft in the squadron was down hard for a transmission at Talil, so the troop maintenance officers cannibalized her for parts to make the rest of the squadron work. Aircraft 90-19478 would never fly out of Iraq; if she ever made it back to Texas, it would be on the back of a truck.

Tom had his original three Troops: Outlaws, Bandits, and Cowboys. Now he added the Desperados. The "D" team was a collection of leftover pilots, newbies, and outcasts, guys not in the unit long enough to have established a relationship. Out of qualified Apache pilots, Tom put Chief Warrant Officer Four Brian Trant in charge of the Desperados. As much as he could, Lawton kept Major Wright or himself in an overwatch position to provide command and control for Trant. He was more than capable of handling the job, but Lawton kept a special eye on the new team since they were a collection of vagabonds. He knew the captains would take great care of their own four birds and crews, but the Desperados needed a leader.

The four teams split into six-hour shifts to cover rear area operations, with the A Troop starting at midnight, the B at 0600, the C at noon, and the D at 1800. This had Trant and Petty flying at night. Other than Petty, Trant had the most experience with nighttime operations and was probably the best qualified to lead aircraft on the night missions.

The more the squadron flew, the better they got at communicating with each other. Each unit averaged at least four hours of flight time a day.

After the first week, Lawton had them stop recording ground time as flight time. Technically, if a helicopter's blades were turning after they had pulled pitch the first time, the pilots logged flight time. Tom did the numbers and realized the squadron would be pushing too many airframes forward into required maintenance if they counted their ground time. Yes, he was cheating time from the pilots, but he was easing the burden on his D Troop and Maintenance Chief Captain Darren Hodges.

The only other problem was getting into the fight. Supporting the rear area was important and they were doing good work, but it was getting old quick. Tom could tell when he talked to the pilots that they weren't happy flying rear area support, and he didn't blame them. He didn't much care for it either. It wasn't boring, but they were more a message than they were a deterrent. This was apparent when they made first contact.

Talbot's team was flying cover for a convoy. The team maintained communication with the convoy and flew in pairs. The red team flew on the western side of the convoy's route, the white team, the east.

The ambush wasn't well coordinated. It started with three of four men shooting AK-47s at the lead Humvee.

The convoy commander was on the radio to Talbot immediately, but he did his job and kept the convoy moving. Talbot's red team engaged the area where the attackers had initially fired from, using their 30-mm cannons. After two bursts from each Apache, the firing stopped.

On the eastern side of the road, the white team, led by Chief Warrant Officer Two Darren Bingam, engaged two Iraqi firing positions with 2.75-mm rockets. The engagement only lasted five minutes.

Talbot's team had successfully fired the first rounds for the 7/17th and had not taken any fire. He was cocky when he reported to Lawton how successful their first fight was. Lawton reminded them to fly over their target area and videotape the sites so the S2 could review the fight.

Videotaping engagements was a pet-peeve for Tom. He remembered how having video imagery in the last war had helped protect him from charges of fratricide. He made sure every crew turned in their videotapes to Lieutenant Tony Harper, so Harper could catalogue and record the target types and locations that the squadron engaged.

Harper had a sergeant who worked in a newsroom in Houston as a video technician and part-time cameraman. Sergeant Brett Johnson took the footage and started to produce a "greatest-hits" video that covered all the good attack shots the 7/17th had fired.

All the ground engagement footage by the Task Force was on a special tape. Lawton had not ordered this tape, but Johnson's talent couldn't be suppressed—the young man loved his job.

Crane viewed Sergeant Johnson's videotape of his tanks during a surprise visit. The colonel stayed around to watch the full twenty-two minutes of his men in combat. Johnson made a copy of the tape and gave it to the colonel when he left. It was the only time Lawton had ever seen Crane smile. Crane should have learned something that night, but later events demonstrated he didn't.

The 3rd Infantry Division and the 1st Marine Expeditionary Unit (MEU) set a historically torrid pace as they stormed across Iraq on the way to Baghdad. The embedded reporters provided instantaneous coverage of the actions and progress of US Forces.

Yet even with all the unprecedented coverage, stories were missed and actions of the troops, good or bad, would slip through unreported. As the battle lines became confusing, so did the conflict.

The tremendous momentum the coalition forces enjoyed in the first four days abruptly dissipated when the push to Baghdad slowed down to permit rearming, refueling, and rest. The incredible speed of the attack had put the forces just south of Baghdad, yet pressure against Saddam's Republican Guard remained necessary.

With the heavy ground units running low on supplies, Command finally decided to employ the attack helicopters in a Deep Attack mission against the dug-in Republican Guard. It may have been the only mission the Iraqi military could have defended against.

22 March 2003
Nasiriyah, Iraq

SOME OF TOM'S QUESTIONS FROM THE Division brief lingered. What was the ground element doing? Was the Air Force available? Could the artillery reach far enough to support the passage points? Lawton suspected that corners were being cut to maintain the momentum, keeping pressure on the Republican Guard with any means available. The ground guys were beginning to run into stiffer enemy resistance. Some convoys were getting attacked in the rear and it was time for a bold military action to regain the momentum lost during the rearm phase.

This attack had the potential to give the entire Iraqi army a knockout blow. The potential to create US aviation history was evident, and this was not lost on Colonel Ben Powell. If the mission succeeded, not only would the Apache shine as the premiere fighting machine of the war, but success would secure this colonel's star and keep the huge defense industry contracts for Army Aviation flowing. Powell could go on to lead Army Aviation for the next decade, if the mission was successful.

Lawton saw many problems with this particular Deep Attack mission, and he shook his head as he left the tent. Execution wasn't set the way Aviation was trained to be employed. The only good thing he saw was that there would be no friendlies in the target areas; every hot spot they picked up in their FLIR (Forward Looking Infra-Red) would be bad guys.

But the Air Force was not integrated into the plan, the routes selected took the Battalions too close to villages, it took too long for them to establish the battle positions, and they weren't coordinated with the ground forces. Plans for down pilot pickup were skimmed. Standard Operating Procedure (SOP) would be employed, they said. But there was nothing standard about flying 50 miles across enemy lines and engaging the enemy—especially an enemy that was ready.

The Brigade commander sent a warning to all the pilots that they must have eyes on the targets to engage, and their tapes would be reviewed. Lawton knew that this threat would make the unit hesitant to fire and made the rules of engagement (ROE) too restrictive. To top it off, due to delays in the FARP, the helicopters took two hours later than planned.

As for the 7/17th, they were relegated to their support mission. In a way, Tom was relieved. The Cross-Flot was dangerous and he admired the courage, dedication, and professionalism of each and every man that flew into the breach that night. Deep inside, a part of him wished he could've been with them. Even with his reservations, the potential the mission had to shorten the war was probably worth the risk. During the most daring attack in the history of helicopter aviation, Tom Lawton would be sitting on the hood of his Humvee.

25 March 2003
Talil Airbase, Iraq

THE RESULTS OF THE MISSION WERE mixed. The brigade-sized element of Apache helicopters had met the enemy, engaged, and destroyed numerous Iraqi Republican Guard tanks and vehicles. Pressure had been maintained against a dug-in enemy; however, estimates of just how many Republican Guard vehicles were destroyed was mixed. The command claimed the mission was a success in the next day's news conference, but in reality, the best news was that no one was killed.

The mission was a near disaster. The Command, in its haste to get in the fight, had taken short cuts. By not engaging aggressively with Artillery first and using Air Force support, the Apaches were left wide open to prepositioned air defense teams made up of every Iraqi man, woman, and child that could fire a weapon, from all locations, including schools. The Iraqis sent the Brigade home in tatters.

The lack of Air Force integration and minimal ground support contributed to the inability of the helicopters to accomplish a knockout blow. Consequently, the Deep Attack mission for Army Aviation would probably never be employed again.

The setback was no concern to the 7/17th. Tom Lawton made sure his men checked the guns whenever possible. As they flew south out of Talil, the aircraft used three vehicle hulks set up in the distance for target practice and to make sure their guns and rockets were okay. Hellfires were too expensive to test-fire. If the chain gun failed to fire or any weapon system malfunctioned, standard operating procedure prohibited the crew from continuing with their patrol.

The flying was generally fun, yet the mission was always dangerous. Convoys were coming more and more under fire as the enemy became emboldened. One convoy turned around and was subsequently attacked by Fedayeen or Saddam loyalists. The ambushed convoy had fought well but was overwhelmed. The media stories displaying pictures of the American prisoners of war quickly spread and were met with disgust and outrage. The dead appeared to have been killed at close range.

This news created a heightened sense of urgency to the mission and served to stiffen the resolve of the support units. Even they became aware they were in the fight, and it made them much more aggressive.

Crane's task force had been knee deep in fights with the Fedayeen and was getting trigger happy. The death of three soldiers, two in one particularly nasty ambush, had created a new atmosphere within the task force. Crane did not take the death of his men well. The task force had sworn a vow of revenge, and within days, the unit that had been the hunted became the hunter.

The Texas Guard squadron was doing its best to support the rear area. Lawton went to both Powell and Crane to offer assistance in the fight forward. The division was getting close to Baghdad and had only 50 percent of the attack helicopters back into the fight. For the second time, he was rebuffed. The first time was because the chain of command didn't have confidence in the unit. This time it was because the division did not want to risk the possibility of fratricide.

Just like the first Gulf War, this war had produced its own share of friendly fire deaths. Entire units had come under fire from sister units or other friendlies. It was a command decision that Apache aircraft were not allowed to mingle with the ground-combat units. Although fratricide was possible, Lawton disagreed with the decision.

The 7/17th was getting enough action for two units. They probably didn't need to get anywhere near heavy combat. The US forces owned the air, so there was virtually no chance any US forces would shoot at helicopters. However, at night, under night vision system conditions, it was possible to mistake a friendly Armor vehicle for a rogue Republican Guard tank. Plus, the ROE remained at visual identification of the target. The risk of shooting friendlies or Iraqi citizens was too high a risk, one Lawton did not want to take.

28 March 2003
Holding Area Quebec
Twenty-four miles southwest
of al Karjubal, Iraq

LAWTON AND PETTY WERE FLYING WITH the C Troop and had just finished in the FARP. They were sitting in the aircraft in a wide-open sandy area waiting for the other four aircraft to finish getting fuel. Up to that point, it seemed like just another day of keeping the convoys protected. It would end up like no other day they had ever witnessed.

Petty asked Tom, "Why are the Iraqis fighting so hard?"

Tom replied into the intercom, "What would we do if someone came into Texas and told us how to run our country? If it were us, we'd be killing a helluva a lot more of them than they are of us!"

That was when they heard the FM Command radio come to life about an ambush, and they could tell it was bad. Petty tried to say something but Tom raised his hand.

The radios screamed with confusion. "TANGO FOUR- SIX HAS THREE MEN DOWN! I SAY AGAIN, THREE MEN DOWN! WE NEED A MEDIVAC IN HERE IMMEDIATELY!"

The radio operator at Task Force 41 Tactical Operations Center acknowledged the call and asked for coordinates. T46 quickly yelled his location and reiterated he had casualties. The radio operator at the TOC verified the grid and urged T46 to "Hold on! Medivac is on the way!"

Tom was on his map in an instant and plotted the grid. They were only fourteen kilometers away. It was south of the town of al-Karjubal. Al-Karjubal was reportedly a Ba'athist stronghold where Saddam sympathizers took refuge.

Petty could see what Tom was doing. He quickly got on the VHF radio and told the Cowboys to hurry up in the FARP and get ready to head north. The other aircraft were not monitoring FM command while in the FARP. Within two minutes, Lawton had a flight of five and they were off. He notified the TOC of his relocation to support the MEDIVAC.

Within five minutes they were approaching the ambush site. Lawton had the flight pick up overwatch positions with two aircraft located one kilometer to the southwest, and the other two one kilometer to the southeast. He and Petty picked up a position directly between the two teams. He told them to turn on their video recorders and to watch for vehicles approaching or departing.

A minute later, they overflew the ambush site. It was one of the worst things they had ever seen. Three Humvees had been hit and two were burning. The MEDIVAC Blackhawk was on short final to a site just north of the ambush and ten soldiers were setting up a perimeter. The Blackhawk circled the area at just under one hundred feet and forty knots. When they circled to the south, Tom noticed the ten Abrams M1A2 tanks hauling up the road. Tom worked the Target Acquisition and Designation System (TADS) bucket and recorded everything he could.

When they circled back around to the north, Lawton used his TADS to search the buildings of the village a kilometer to the north. He saw the ditches on the sides of the highway and some vegetation that had provided cover for the ambushers. A river ran out of the village to the east and another road headed off paralleling the river in a south-easterly direction.

The river had trees and tall grass on both sides. He saw what appeared to be civilians fishing in the river.

Lawton followed the vegetation up to the village and noted the wall built over the ditch that surrounded the southeastern side of the village. The wall was about five-foot high and ran from the road east for about 800 meters before it ended. He didn't see any people whatsoever. Petty turned the aircraft turned back to the south and Lawton continued to record the activity at the ambush site.

Lawton watched the tanks stop and saw the tank commander jump off his tank and approach the MEDIVAC personnel working on the wounded. Two minutes later the tanks were rolling north into al-Karjubal. The seven remaining Humvees followed the tanks into the village.

Lawton turned his attention back to the ambush site. He felt sick to his stomach as he watched the Blackhawk depart. He turned up the FM Command frequency and listened to the situation report. Tango 46 indicated they had two men dead, one in critical condition, and four more wounded. Tango 46 also added, 'We had the Six element here and he has relocated into the objective to pursue the enemy.' Tango 46 did not mention the Cowboy element was also on site. They were too preoccupied with trying to save their buddies to notice the Apaches flying around.

Lawton and Petty stayed near the ambush site five more minutes and watched as another group of Humvees and a tow truck came up the road. There also appeared to be two Military Police Humvees in the convoy, likely there to map out the site of the ambush and control any crowd that might have assembled.

To the north, Humvees were coming out of al-Karjubal with Iraqi men walking in front with their hands held up in the air. Lawton was nodding when he said to Petty, "Looks like Crane already has his prisoners." Lawton moved his TADS over to the prisoners and increased his magnification. Petty maneuvered the Apache so they were only a kilometer away.

The prisoners were ordered across the ditch and were stood in a line against the wall. Tom started counting out of habit. He counted seventeen men, with more coming down the road. Tom zoomed in further on the prisoners. Some were old men and some were boys of only thirteen or fourteen. There was something ominous in the way they were being herded and lined up against the wall.

As Petty hovered the helicopter, he too could see. Petty's voice couldn't hide his nervousness. "You getting this on the tape, boss?"

Tom focused on the screen. "Uh-huh." He brought his magnification out and caught Crane jumping over the ditch. Tom could tell it was him because he was the only one with a 9-mm pistol—and he had it drawn.

Lawton made a call on VHF. "All Warrior elements, this is Six. Come to my location and pick up security." Then he said something that only Petty understood. "I want 32 and 34 to cover to the south and east. And I want 36 and 38 to cover me."

Captain Hector Sanchez answered the call, but he was confused. "Roger, Six. Understand, cover YOU?"

"Roger. From my present position, cover me."

Lawton had Petty move to within 800 meters of the prisoners against the wall. A tank came out of the village, came off the road, and through the ditch.

"Land, Joe! Land now!" Tom was almost yelling.

Petty lowered the collective. "Roger that!"

Lawton had his restraint harness off before the Apache hit the ground. He said into the microphone, "You cover me, Joe. You have the video, too. I hope nothing happens, but if it does—",he turned and looked at Petty,"—you shoot! Okay?"

Petty nodded.

Lawton unplugged his helmet and jumped from the aircraft. As he got closer, he could see Crane waiving his pistol in the face of a petrified Iraqi man. A boy ran up to Crane and was obviously begging for him to stop. Crane hit the boy in the head with his pistol. His men fired their M16s into the air to prevent the assembled crowd from charging. The tank turned to face the prisoners and took a position about one-hundred meters from the wall. Tom quickened his pace.

Crane pulled the man away from the wall and threw him down on the ground. The interpreter was yelling, Crane was yelling, and the Iraqi man was lying on the ground, begging for his life. Crane signaled for the tank to come closer as he pushed the interpreter away. He waved the pistol at the man's head and stepped back. The interpreter continued yelling.

Lawton was twenty feet away when he yelled, "COLONEL CRANE! WHAT ARE YOU DOING?"

Crane yelled back, "THIS IS NONE OF YOUR CONCERN, FLYBOY!"

Tom stepped closer. "If what's goin' on here is what I think, it is my concern."

"You don't understand! These bastards killed my men! You got that! They killed my men!" He was waving the pistol and walking in circles. "They're gonna pay Lawton, just like my men did!"

"You can't do this, sir." Tom stepped closer and put his hands up with his palms facing Crane. He was only ten feet away.

Crane erupted. He ran towards Tom and put the pistol right into his face. "I CAN DO ANY GODDAMN THING I WANT! YOU GOT ME, SHITHEAD?"

Crane was shaking as he moved closer to Tom, but he calmed slightly. "Some of these bastards killed my men! Some of them are gonna pay! Three of my men are dead, so I'm gonna make sure they lose thirty!"

Lawton didn't back down. "Prove it. Can you prove it, Colonel?"

Crane was silent. Tom shook his head. "When does it stop Colonel? Thirty here. Another three hundred in Baghdad! You don't have any proof that these poor bastards killed your men! Absolutely none! If you wipe out this entire village, you still may not get the guys that killed your troops." Tom lowered his voice. "But the word will spread that US troops massacred Iraqis, and we will never be able to walk around without having our back covered. You can kill me if you're pissed off. But if you kill anymore of these men"— Tom pointed at the civilians lined up by the wall— "they'll come back more determined to fight us every step of the way. We might never get outta Iraq if you do this!"

"I can do whatever I want to do!"

Tom spread his hands wide. His voice was calm. "Easy now, sir. You can't hurt these people."

The pistol got closer to Tom's face. "Why not, Lawton?
You gonna save 'em?"

"That's not why I'm here, sir."

Crane was confused. "Why are you here then, Flyboy?"

Tom turned his head slightly to look around the pistol. "I'm here to save you, sir. This situation is not out of control. You can walk away from this!" Tom dropped his ace. "I have control over the situation!"

Crane was still confused, but his anger diminished a little as he tried to comprehend what Lawton was saying.

"What do you mean?"

Tom still focused on Crane and looked him in the eye. He used his thumb to point over his shoulder. "Those aircraft behind me won't let you do what I think you want to do."

Crane looked past Tom, and Lawton could tell he saw the Warriors hovering behind him. "You gonna have them shoot me, Lawton?"

"Not if you get control of yourself, sir." Tom was trying his best to use military courtesy. He looked around and saw the situation was becoming clearer to Crane's men. Their guns were pointed toward the prisoners, but they weren't aiming them anymore. The Iraqi man continued to scream for his life, but the tank had stopped approaching.

Something in Crane's mind switched on and he started thinking again. He stepped back, but didn't lower the pistol. "You got those damn video cameras rollin', don't you, Flyboy?"

"Yes, sir," said Tom as flatly as he could muster.

Crane nodded. "All right, Flyboy." Crane put the pistol down. "You win this time. There will be other times when your ass won't be around. We'll take care of the Hadjis."

Tom wasn't sure if Crane meant the ones lined up against the wall or that he would kill other Hadjis later when Tom wasn't around. It didn't really matter. Crane was finally in control of himself. At least, partially in control of himself.

"Sir, I'm gonna go get back in my helicopter now." Lawton put his hands down and exhaled. He turned to see a Humvee sporting MP in large white letters pull up. He started to breathe a bit easier.

Crane stepped closer to Tom. "Don't suppose I can get that videotape you got there, eh?" asked Crane. His face was still red with anger.

Tom hesitated before answering. "I don't think so, sir." The MP's vehicle stopped and a large sergeant first class and three other men jumped out. "You can probably turn those prisoners over to the sergeant now, sir."

"These are the horrors of war, Lawton. Just like what happened to my men. And you're takin' their side."

"No! These are war crimes! And this is what we came here to stop. So just turn these poor bastards over to the MPs and take care of your wounded."

"Yeah. I'll do that, Lawton." He stepped even closer to Lawton and said in a whisper, "If I ever see or hear anything about that tape, you won't make it back to Texas."

"I'll make it back to Texas. But you pull anymore bullshit like this, and you'll make it to Leavenworth for a long tour." Tom didn't add "sir." He took a small step towards Crane and hissed, "And if you ever put a gun on me again, you better pull the trigger, 'cause next time, I'm not leaving!" He stepped backwards two steps, snapped to attention, and yelled, "By your leave, sir!" He didn't wait for a return salute.

Crane hollered out, "You watch your ass, Flyboy!"

Tom muttered under his breath, "I'll be watchin' your ass on a TV screen, shithead!"

Lawton returned to the 'copter, sat down in the cockpit, and motioned to bring the blades up to full speed. Petty looked at him in disbelief. "Damn, sir! I thought you were dead!"

Lawton leaned his head back against his seat and exhaled loudly. "Me too, Joe. Me too." He shook his head and continued to put his gloves on. "You got that little event on tape, right?" Petty smiled broadly and gave him a thumbs up. "Good! Let's go back to the Assembly Area. Maybe the sergeant major has dinner warmed up."

Petty shook his head. "Roger that, sir!"

Tom thought to himself, *Crane's comment about never getting back to Texas sure hit home. Getting home is the only thing that matters.*

Lawton reviewed the video during the flight back. Petty had captured most everything on tape. It would be obvious to any viewer that Crane had put his pistol in Tom's face and had been mistreating prisoners. The video could put Crane in Leavenworth for the rest of his life.

Immediately after the flight landed, Tom had all the pilots come to his bird for a debrief. They knew why they were there and not inside the shade of the TOC. Lawton moved quickly. He pulled the tape out of the recorder in the tailboom of the Apache. He tucked it into the bottom of his flight helmet bag.

Moments later, the final two crews arrived. He cleared his throat before he started. "I know you guys probably saw everything that went on back there, but I'm asking you to put it behind you and drive on."

Captain Sanchez was hot. "Putting that behind us is the wrong thing to do! Those bastards need to go to jail!"

Lawton bit his lip and shook his head. "Think about this, Hector." No one missed that Lawton hadn't called him Captain Sanchez. "If this incident gets reported, it goes to the press. There's embedded media in every ground unit out there."

"Except for Crane's Task Force!" Petty observed.

"That's because they aren't a front line Armor unit. Their mission is to clean up the trash in the rear with us, right?" explained Lawton. The men nodded, "If the word gets out on this, what happens? It gets out to the world and we either have to lie about it, or even worse, explain the truth. And I'm not sure I can explain the truth."

"The truth is, he was gonna kill that guy! Maybe all of them!" said Sanchez.

Tom shook his head. "We don't know that for a fact. We can't prove anything, so Crane can always refute it. He had over twenty men there and it would be their word versus ours. Just like you guys, they're gonna stand up for their boss if he needs it!"

"But you have the tape." Petty was trying to help. "You can show the tape."

"I reviewed the tape and some of it may be useful. But it probably could be torn apart by a lawyer defending a colonel in a wartime situation. So I don't know." Tom thought before he spoke again, sensing that Sanchez and Petty disagreed with his decision.

"The bottom line is, if word of this gets out, it becomes a public relations nightmare for all of us. It will become mis-information for the Arab press, and more soldiers will get killed by increased resistance." He saw they understood his logic. Sanchez was still shaking his head.

Lawton finished. "As far as Crane and me personally, I understand what he was doing. He won't do squat to me. He can't now." Tom tapped his flight bag. "No harm, no foul. Got it?" Tom got nods from everyone, even Sanchez.

"Let's go get some hot chow." The men slowly headed toward the tents.

Sanchez waited for the others to move out of earshot.

"I'm willing to keep this to myself, sir."

"I appreciate that, Hector."

"I know what I saw, and I know it ain't right. If you want me to keep quiet, I will." Tom nodded. "But if Crane so much as blinks at you wrong, sir, you let me know."

"He won't do shit, Hector. He was upset about his men."

"You'd be upset if any of us got killed, but you wouldn't do what he did!"

"You're pretty damn smart for a captain."

Sanchez nodded. "I got your six, sir."

"Thanks! Let's go eat." Tom smacked him on the back. Tom tried to put the day's events behind him. It was a long time before he fell asleep that night.

1 April 2003
Talil Airbase, Iraq

TOM SAT IN THE BACK OF the briefing room at ten after nine as all the lieutenant colonels waited for the O-6s to file in. The briefing was supposed to have started at 0900, but some kind of mission was being planned and half the division leadership was present.

The crowd was called to attention when the remainder of the leadership showed up. When Crane entered, he didn't even look at Lawton. Right behind him cruised Ben Powell. He did look at Tom, with a smile on his face. Suspecting that Crane had told Powell about the incident at Al-Karjubal, Tom felt his face flush as he took his seat.

The 3rd ID Deputy G3 presented the briefing. The Division was planning the final push to Baghdad and he explained the routes—aggressive with high expectations. The briefing took twenty minutes, and then the remaining crowd stepped to the back of the room for the tabletop rock drill.

Tom eyed Powell and Crane nervously. Neither man would look at him. It wasn't until the end of the rock drill that Task Force 41 and the Aviation Brigade, rather the remnants of the Aviation Brigade, were even mentioned. Their role in the Division's fight remained rear-area support. After the rock drill, the Brigades broke down into five groups at separate sand tables and war-gamed actions for the movement forward.

Because they didn't really have a mission during the Division's roll forward, Crane and Powell mingled with different units as they discussed operations. Tom headed to the snack area to get a Pepsi.

He heard a familiar voice behind him. "Lieutenant Colonel Lawton. A moment of your time, please?"

It was Powell. Before turning around, Lawton considered not acknowledging the colonel's voice. But Lawton knew he had no choice, so he turned slowly. "Oh, hello, sir. Buy you a soda?"

"No thanks, Tom." Lawton knew something was up. Powell never called anyone by their first name. "I'd like to talk to you about a little operation we're going to conduct."

Tom was hesitant. The "we're going to conduct" comment hung in the air like a noose. Again, he weighed the options and knew he had no choice. "All right, sir." "Come on over to table three when you get your drink." Powell slapped him on the back like he was an old friend. Something stunk and it was coming from table three.

After buying two Pepsis, Lawton finally headed over to the colonels' sand table. Powell smiled broadly and introduced him to the ten other subordinate commanders. Tom noticed Dick Crane was standing next to Powell, but he didn't share the same broad smile as the Aviation commander. Lawton knew most of the other men on sight—battalion commanders in Task Force 41 and the other two aviation battalions.

Powell started the meeting at the map with pointer in hand. He pointed to the routes the ground brigades would take as they moved on Baghdad, then to a line that separated the division sectors. "I want 3rd Attack to cover all operations in the western sector, and 1st Attack to take the eastern support. Jack, you need to make sure you tie into the Marines, here." He was looking at Lieutenant Colonel Jack Billingsly as he spoke. Billingsly commanded the 1st Battalion of the 3rd Attack Helicopter Brigade.

Powell continued. "Now everything from this point south," he pointed to the map again, "will be covered by the 7/17th." Tom looked at the area. It was huge—east to west fifty miles wide, north to south it stretched from 30 miles outside Baghdad all the way down to Talil Airbase. "You wanted in the fight, Lawton. Now, you're in it. It's a big mission, but I think it's one you can handle."

Lawton was pissed. It was a mission that 3rd and 1st Attack didn't have enough aircraft to handle together, much less the 7/17th by itself. He only had fifteen fully mission-capable aircraft. Tom could tell that he and the unit were being set up for failure. It took every ounce of his military discipline not to explode, but Powell could still sense Lawton's irritation.

Powell tried to calm Lawton down with a suggestion. "The area doesn't have to be covered twenty-four, seven. We need you to focus up in the north, particularly around these half-dozen villages or so."

Tom assessed the mission in light of this new guidance. The villages were fairly close together. If he didn't have to cover the area to the south, he could split the squadron in half and cover the northern area with six aircraft doing twelve-hour shifts. It was still weak. Tom frowned.

Then Powell added one more caveat. "You only need to cover it for three days and nights. By then, we're in Baghdad and reinforcements from Talil can cover the area." Powell looked over at Crane, who simply nodded. "We tried to tell the CG that we needed Delta-model Apaches to cover the entire rear area, but he wants to have those up north where the Division is sure to hit the remnants of the Republican Guard. There shouldn't be nearly as much action in the area you'll be covering. You guys can handle it, can't you, Lawton?"

Tom could tell they were tag-teaming the setup. He understood why Crane wanted him and the Cav to fail, and knew Crane had told Powell about the incident at al-Far- jubal. But he was on the spot in front of ten other officers. He didn't have a choice. "Yes, sir. When do we start?"

"Eighteen-hundred tonight," said Powell.

Tom nodded and saluted the colonel. As he headed out, he looked at his watch. It was 11:15. He needed to get back to the Assembly Area. He immediately called the sergeant major and told him to get all the Troop commanders and staff together. "Put the C and D element down for crew rest. We're flying tonight."

On the drive back to the Assembly Area, Tom kept going over the briefing in his mind. *Powell said he wants to use the Delta models. What a prick! If the newer Apaches don't get into the fight in Baghdad and perform better than they did during the Cross-Flot mission, Powell might not get his star. Anything Powell can do to prove the new-model Apaches' tactical prowess and their technological advances, he's going to do.*

Lawton's Alpha-model Apaches were still damn good. He was proud of the way they had held up to the elements. And he was proud of his unit, too. He thought they could handle the mission. It shouldn't be that hard, considering the enemy was getting routed. The Hadjis were on the run.

At that moment, Tom had forgotten his father's first rule of warfare: overconfidence kills a fool.

CHAPTER TWELVE

"Old Judge Jones"
-Les Dudek

2 April 2003
FARP TOPAZ
South of Najaf, Iraq

IT WAS A DARK OUT, 0115 in the morning of April 3rd, and Lawton and Petty were in the FARP getting more fuel. They hadn't talked for over ten minutes. Petty seemed tired and grumpy, and he had good reason to be so. He'd been on the controls flying 80 percent of the time at night using the PNVS and was getting worn out.

Lawton was thinking about how stupid he had been to have believed Powell's bullshit. It was their second straight night of flying the rear-area cover mission. Crane and Powell were taking turns trying to get the 7/17th to go into the villages and draw fire. Lawton resisted any order that sent the unit near towns. Only on special occasions, when there were known bad guys in town or friendly ground elements available to support the 7/17th, would Lawton approve entry into populated areas. When they did go in, they never stayed in town long. The Apaches didn't need to get anywhere near the villages to get shot at. The whole Task Force was getting shot at from everywhere.

The mission was turning into an aviation version of the repeated-day movie, *Groundhog Day*. Only it wasn't a comedy. It was becoming a recurring nightmare. The D team had been shot at all three nights since the mission started. The unit was down to six aircraft for their shift while the day team was down to five. To top it off, no one had gotten any real sleep in the last 96 hours.

Tom glanced at Petty in the mirror as the helicopter was being refueled. It looked like he was sleeping. *Let him sleep. None of us are getting what we need.*

Lawton looked at his map. He had marked it up with movements in almost every village where they had been taking fire, annotating the hot spots. He had so many marks on the map that he couldn't sort out which engagements had taken place when or where. If he didn't know any better, he would swear that Crane and Powell wanted him dead more than the Iraqis.

On one occasion, Crane directed the Apaches into the center of a town that Task Force 41 wouldn't enter even with armor. He told Tom that because there were no ground friendlies, he was clear to go weapons hot on anything in the town.

Lawton knew better. Up to that point, they had resisted as many calls as possible to get mired in urban warfare. The Cav knew the enemy was coming out at night to set up ambushes and put Improvised Explosive Devices (IEDs) on the roads, and they were having some success at catching the bastards in their tracks. The ground guys had engaged six different parties involved in mischievous activities at strange hours of the night, all of them out in the middle of nowhere. The night vision system of the Apache helicopter was state of the art, so the 7/17th would find them, radio the ground units, and then they would go after the bad guys. There really was no need for aircraft to go into any towns.

Tom laid his head back against the headrest. He swore he wouldn't close his eyes. He started to think about other things. Little things he missed, like laughing. And big things, like Cindy and the girls. He missed sleep, too. Maybe if he closed his eyes he could catch a quick couple of minutes. He popped one eye open and looked into the mirror again. Petty seemed to be awake. Lawton was positive he would handle any emergency that came up. It would have been easier to catch a few winks if the blades weren't so loud.

Someone was pushing his shoulder. The pushing wasn't so bad, but the yelling was what got his attention. His head snapped up as he shook himself awake. He looked to his right and saw a sergeant kneeling on the forward avionics bay holding his thumb up. He was yelling something. On the third yell, Lawton finally understood. The aircraft was rearmed. Tom gave him a thumbs up and shook his head once more to clear the remaining cobwebs.

At that moment, Lawton finally turned on his radio. They had turned them off while they were rearming. It was so much quieter without the constant chatter.

Tom spoke into the microphone. "Hey! Sunshine! You awake?"

Petty sat up in his seat like he had been awake. "UH! Um, yeah! Yeah, I'm awake! What's up?"

"Us, finally. How 'bout turning on your radios back there." Tom looked at his watch. *Crap. We've been off the net for over twenty minutes!*

They knew the second the FM Command radio came on, the shit had hit the fan somewhere. Tom told Petty to turn up the radio. One of the infantry companies was in a fight. From the sounds of it, it was a good one.

Suddenly, he heard his call sign on the UHF. It was Powell. He was yelling for "Warrior Six." Tom muttered "Shit." His boss had been looking for him while they were in the FARP with the radios off.

"Eagle Six, this is Warrior Six, over!"

"WHERE THE HELL ARE YOU?" screamed Powell.

"Just got done in the FARP."

"Are you up on FM Command?"

"Yeah, just now. Sounds like one helluva fight!"

"If you're in TOPAZ, you are only about a fifteen-minute flight away. I want you to move your element to the southwestern side of Najaf. We've got a company of infantry that is up to their asses in Fedayeen. They cornered them in a school on the southwestern side of the city. I need you to get in there and take 'em out!"

Tom wasn't thinking too clearly. *Get in "where" and take out "what"?* Before he could ask, Powell said, "There is a company of tanks from TF 41 headed there. They will be coming from the south, but it will take them over an hour to arrive. If you don't get there soon, those guys are going to lose the Fedayeen!"

Tom didn't understand the last statement either. *"Lose the Fedayeen?" Where? They were in the city; where else could they go?* He shook his head again. He needed to wake up.

Powell continued, "I'm counting on you to get in there and mix it up with those bastards! You need to keep the pressure on 'em until the tanks get there. Don't let 'em get away! You understand, Warrior Six?"

Lawton immediately answered, "Roger, sir! Keep the pressure on until the tanks get there!"

"Eagle Six, OUT!"

Tom shook his head. He had his mission. He wasn't sure exactly what it was, but he knew that he had to go to the sound of the guns. He'd wished he had recorded the order from Powell so he could replay it and verify exactly what he had just been told to do.

Fourteen minutes later, Lawton and Petty were leading a flight of six Apaches to a battle position on the southeastern side of Najaf. He had directed the flight to break up into three teams of two aircraft each. Lawton commanded the Red Team and would approach from the south. Sanchez and the White Team would come from the southeast, while Chief Warrant Officer Four Brian Trant and his two ships would approach from the west. There was a one-kilometer separation between each pair of aircraft.

Tom was listening to Delta 34 on the Command FM radio sending a spot report to Cougar Six. Delta 34 was the lieutenant in the town taking on the Fedayeen; Cougar Six was Dick Crane. Tom wondered what Crane was doing on the radio since he had been commanding the fight in the daytime; Powell usually commanded the night cycle. Powell was in a Blackhawk about twenty miles to the east overseeing operations in the Division's sector.

Lawton didn't have a clear picture about the chain of command for the fight, but he could tell two things. Delta 34 was getting his ass kicked, and Crane had been woken up.

Then he heard Crane report he was still thirty minutes out. The picture became clearer. Crane was in the company of tanks coming to relieve Delta 34. The next question was, where exactly was Delta 34?

Tom came up on the Command FM. "Cougar Six, this is Warrior Six. My element is in position southeast of Delta 34. I do NOT, I say again, I do NOT have visual contact with Delta 34."

"'Bout damn time, Warrior Six! Delta 34 is in the city. I repeat, in the city. You won't have contact with him unless you enter the town."

Delta 34 cut in. "Cougar Six, this is Delta 34! I need some help here now! They have large numbers of heavy caliber weapons and must be a hundred damn RPGs! We're getting our asses handed to us!"

"All right, Delta 34! All right, I understand!" Crane was quiet for a moment. Tom kept searching the outskirts of the city in hopes of seeing any sign of Delta 34. He looked out his window and saw the explosions inside the city. That would be where Delta 34 was.

Cougar Six came back on the radio. "Delta 34, you get out of there! You hear me? I want you to get out of there now!"

The radio was silent for about ten seconds. Crane said again, "Delta 34! Get out of there!"

Delta 34 finally came on the radio and yelled, "NEGATIVE, COUGAR SIX! Our route out is blocked by bad guys! We've got to stay here!" Lawton's first thought was *Shit.*

Delta 34 said, "I've got two Bradley's that are immobile and will set up a defensive perimeter with the other eight. The enemy is primarily firing from a large building about 150 meters to the north of my position. They are moving to encircle us to the west. How long before you get here, Six?"

"Still over thirty minutes out, Delta 34!"

Tom said to Petty, "You thinking what I'm thinking?"

"I think if we don't go help him out, there might not be anything to go help out in thirty minutes!"

"Roger that! You with me?" asked Tom.

"I ain't anywhere else, boss! I'll tell the other guys we're moving in and to not fire up any Bradleys!" Petty immediately tuned to their internal frequencies to notify the rest of the flight.

Tom interrupted Delta 34's request for Air Force support and said, "Cougar Six, this is Warrior Six, I'm moving my element in to support Delta 34!"

"NEGATIVE, WARRIOR SIX! NEGATIVE! You will not move in there! I don't want you firing up Delta 34!"

"Cougar Six, we will not fire at the Delta element! Break! Delta 34, this is Warrior Six. We are approaching your position from the southeast with six aircraft. Expect overflight in two minutes, over!" Tom tuned to UHF and told the other two teams to form on him, turn on their recorders, and go weapons free.

Petty was first to see the Fedayeen pickup trucks. They were coming straight at them. Lawton didn't say a word. He pulled the trigger on the 30-mm chain gun and promptly destroyed two pickup trucks.

The FM radio came to life. "Warrior Six, this is Delta 34! I see your fires. The destroyed vehicles were the ones trying to encircle our location. We are 500 meters to your east! There is a large building 300 meters north of our position that is full of bad guys. We could use more fire on that position!"

"On the way, three-four!" Tom switched to UHF and directed the teams to engage the building north of Delta 34 in pairs with running fire. "After engaging, break right and continue firing until the enemy ceases firing!" The crews roger'd the directions and set up for the attack, remembering that any aircraft hovering in an urban environment would be subjected to merciless ground fire. Movement was life.

Petty flew lead toward the red and orange tracers. Lawton fired just a little to the left of the building on the first run with cannon fire but nothing else. Lawton quickly relayed to the White and Blue Teams to go to his right and engage. Red Team (Lawton) couldn't break right anymore or they would have put themselves in the line of fire of the other two incoming teams. They switched to a left break after their engagement. That was the beginning of the confusion.

White and Blue Teams were on the money with rocket fire and 30-mm rounds on their engagements. Unfortunately, they both broke right as initially directed. Delta 34 radioed that the last four aircraft were right on the target. The enemy had not ceased firing and Delta 34 requested another attack.

Lawton agreed, so he and his Red Team came around for another strike. When they did, the team somehow got into the flight pattern behind the White Team. The Blue Team saw White turn to the north and picked up the Red Team turning at the same time, so Blue came to a hover.

Petty was smooth on the controls and radioed his wingman to follow. Petty gradually reduced his airspeed and the Red Team now followed the White Team into the attack route. White was on target with eight rockets and Lawton followed with three pairs of rockets and five 30-mm bursts. This time both pairs of aircraft broke right and came around to find the hovering pair of aircraft from the Blue Team.

Just as they started to get moving again, Chief Warrant Officer Four Brian Trant began hearing the small-arms fire hitting his helicopter. While he could barely hear the 'peck' of the AK-47 rounds, when the rocket propelled grenades (RPGs) hit, Trant knew immediately he was in trouble. The front and backseat warning panels lit up.

Tom heard Trant's wingman scream, 'YOU'RE ON FIRE, BRIAN! PUT HER DOWN! PUT HER DOWN NOW!'

Lawton and Petty rolled out as they were heading south away from the fight. Tom looked outside the cockpit in time to see Trant's aircraft skirting the rooftops with a streak of yellow shooting from his right engine.

Trant called a MAYDAY and rolled the helicopter onto a street that was only 100 meters from Delta 34. Tom tried to call Trant, but Trant was too busy flying his bird to answer. Next he called for Blue Chalk Two to pick up a defensive perimeter around Trant's bird and make sure they got out.

Delta 34 called Lawton on FM Command and said, "I've got the aircraft in sight and we are sending a Bradley to support his position! We are still receiving massive fire from the large building across the field from us. Re-engage as soon as possible!"

Tom said, "Screw this!" He switched to UHF. "Red and White Teams, this is Six. Set up for Hellfire engagement from Trant's position!"

The other three aircraft acknowledged. They came to where Trant's bird had landed. Lawton looked underneath his NVGs and saw that both pilots were out of the burning aircraft and heading toward the Bradley. The Bradley and Blue Two were firing suppressive fire to cover the pilots as they ran to cover. Tom's aircraft managed to keep the small arms shooters from engaging the other four aircraft as they set up for Hellfire engagements.

Lawton lined up the building where the flood of red, orange, and green tracers pierced the blackness. In seconds the aircraft were ready to fire. The direction was clear. "All aircraft, FIRE!"

It was the only time in the engagement that things seemed to go in slow motion. Lawton was focused on his missile and its impact point in the building. He selected a target, painted, assessed his distance, and got a solid box indicating he was ready. The missile quietly left the rail. Petty kept the aircraft steady as the 100-pound missile came off the wing. The smoke temporarily blocked Lawton's target, but the shot was true. He put it in a first-floor window.

For just a second, he thought he had missed or the missile had malfunctioned. Then there was a small explosion, followed by a much larger one. He looked up from his cockpit screen and saw four explosions in the building 1500 meters away. He made a call on the radio. "Re-engage!"

All four aircraft fired four more missiles into the building, destroying it and the two buildings that bordered it. Delta 34 made a radio call that indicated most of the firing had stopped, but there was still some coming from the northeastern portion of the area just engaged.

Lawton had the flight move forward slowly. They were now within 100 meters of Delta 34. The ground commander was now much more in control of the situation and provided direction to Tom as to where the enemy fire was coming from. The aircraft formed a perimeter over the Bradleys and with Delta 34's guidance, engaged any target stupid enough to fire.

After five minutes, Delta 34 sent three Bradleys north to engage the remaining targets. The tide had turned.

Delta 34 called Tom. "I've got some news for you, Warrior Six! Your boys are in with my 55 element and doing fine. A little shaken, but none the worse for the flight they had!"

"Thanks, 34!" He gave Petty a thumbs up. In the dimly lit front-seat mirror, Petty could barely make out Lawton's smile.

The FM Command radio came to life again. "Delta 34, this is Cougar Six. We are entering Najaf. What is your present position?"

Delta 34 answered Crane and Tom flew towards the commander. The Red Team found the M1 tanks and flew over them, bringing them into Delta 34's defensive position. Four tanks continued north to support the Bradleys' pursuit of the fleeing enemy. Tom called Crane and requested relief for his flight of five. They were nearly out of gas and four of them were low on bullets. It was the first time they had expended over 50 percent of their ammunition. Crane was brief with his response. "Roger, go home. Thanks."

Tom looked at Petty and said, "Did you hear that?" Smiling, Petty replied, "Yeah, but he's still a prick." Lawton, too, was smiling. "I'm guessing he wanted us to be dead. Let's get this thing full up again. I really am pretty tired."

Petty roger'd the guidance and called the flight. Two hours later, Tom collapsed on his cot. Even though they had lost an aircraft, the most important thing was that the crew was okay. The fact that they had kicked some bad guys' asses didn't hurt, either. For the first time in a long while, Tom was smiling as he went to sleep.

4 April 2003
AA Dallas
South Central, Iraq

THE BATTLE FOR BAGHDAD WAS OFFICIALLY under way. The 3rd Infantry Division entered Saddam International Airport leaving a path of destruction and death in their wake. The first thing the commander did was change the name of the airport to Baghdad International, as a psychological statement to the world and the Iraqi people that the liberation of Iraq was at hand.

Ninety-five miles southeast of Baghdad International Airport, Tom Lawton rolled over in his sleeping bag. It had been a long night and the sergeant major had let him sleep in. He looked at his watch. It certainly felt earlier than ten-thirty. He rolled out of the cot and rubbed his head. The hazy thought that the previous night's mission was a nightmare dispersed. The mission had been real. They had lost an aircraft.

Tom put the negative vibes away, grabbed his shaving kit, and headed outside to meet the day. The temperature was already a relatively crisp ninety-two degrees. The sergeant major met him at the wash point and handed him a Pepsi.

"Hey! It's cold!"

"Don't tell anybody, sir." The sergeant major was smiling. "We heard about last night's festivities. The whole squadron is psyched up. Captain Sanchez is over reviewing the tapes. We got crew chiefs, mechanics, even cooks popping into the S2's tent to watch the videos. You guys kicked some Iraqi hippy ass!"

Tom smiled as he shaved. "We did get some bad guys." But he also acknowledged the truth. "We lost an aircraft, too."

"OH, yeah! That reminds me! The pilots are back. They brought them in about 0700 this morning."

"Good deal!"

Suddenly they were interrupted by an out-of-breath specialist. "Sir, we have some visitors from Division inbound. They were asking to see you, sir. By name."

Tom wiped his face dry and looked at Martinez. "I don't like the sound of that."

"Sir, they should hit the TOC in about ten minutes!" The specialist raised his hand to salute and waited.

Tom turned, came to attention, and saluted back. "Thanks, Baker. I'm on my way." Tom turned to the sergeant major. "Takin' odds on whether this visit is congratulations for savin' those grunts' butts?"

Martinez shook his head. "Don't think I've ever heard of anyone from a ground division thanking any aviation guys. Too soon for that." Tom nodded in agreement. He had no clue what anyone from division would want this morning. His best guess was it had to do with the mission. His negative vibes returned.

"Sir, my name is Major Raymond Kline. I was sent here by Brigadier General Stoddard." Stoddard was the 3rd Infantry Division operations officer. "The General was debriefed this morning on the results of your engagement in Najaf last night. There are some questions that he feels only you can answer."

"Only I can answer?"

"Affirmative, sir. He told me to find Lieutenant Colonel Lawton and bring him to Headquarters. I'm supposed to get all your videotapes from last night's mission as well." Tom nodded towards the S2 to get the tapes. "Also, your unit is not to fly any missions until further notice."

Everyone in the tent became perfectly silent. "Bring me to Headquarters, eh?"

"Yes, sir!"

"Unit can't fly anymore, either?"

The major shrugged his shoulders. "That was the order, sir."

Tom stood up and grabbed his helmet. "It ain't good, is it, Major Kline?"

The major was hesitant, but Tom already knew his answer. "Um, no, sir. I don't believe it is."

Tom shook his head and yelled, "Major Suggs!" He looked at his executive officer, "You heard the man. No more mission flying. I still want you to fly maintenance missions, but I don't think they want us to shoot anybody." Tom shook his head. "You have the controls until I get back." Suggs nodded. "That may not be for quite some time, Bryan."

"Roger that, sir. We'll be here."

As Tom left the tent, he took a long look around the assembly area. After listening to Kline, he wasn't sure if he would see it again.

4 April 2003
Division Headquarters
Talil Airbase

TOM WAS ESCORTED TO A MEDIUM-SIZED conference room. No one told him anything. He was halfway through his bottle of Evian when three men entered the room. One was an infantry colonel named Adams, the second was a Judge Advocate General lieutenant colonel named Myatt, and the third was Dick Crane.

The three men joined Tom at the only table in the room. Adams went first. "Well, Lieutenant Colonel Lawton. We're glad you could join us on such short notice."

Tom fought the urge to be pissed off. From somewhere in his Texas heart, he managed a smile. "I didn't think I had a choice, sir."

Adams smiled back. He didn't want to prolong the meeting any longer than he had to. "You didn't." He got to the point. "We need to discuss the events from last night's mission. There is a certain amount of ambiguity in what was reported and what appears to have happened."

The word "ambiguity" hung in the air. Tom was straightforward. "Sir, we can take a look at those tapes, and with the audio, some interpretation, and maybe a diagram or two, we can sort it out."

Adams nodded and leaned back. "Yeah, we'll do that, too." He looked at the lawyer. "My friend here, Lieutenant Colonel Myatt, has been ordered to participate in our interview session."

Tom nodded at Myatt. "No problem, sir." Then a blinding flash hit him hard in his overly fatigued mind. He turned his attention back to Adams. "Why do I need a lawyer, sir?"

Adams answered, "We're not sure, Lawton. We need to listen to your view of what happened, compare it to what other people say happened"— he looked at Crane— "and figure out where the truth is."

It still didn't explain why Myatt was there. "And a lawyer is here to rule on who's telling the truth, sir?"

Adams sat up in the chair. "Myatt is here to determine if we need to conduct an Article 32 investigation."

Tom's heart sank. Myatt wasn't there to defend him. He was there to see if Tom needed to be put on trial.

"You know what an Article 32 is?"

Tom knew. "Yes, sir. To determine if there are grounds for a court-martial."

Adams looked down at the table. It was clear to Tom, that Adams didn't care for the mission he was given. "We hope it doesn't go that far. So if we could get down to it. We have a list of about twenty questions we'd like to go through with you."

Tom looked around and analyzed the situation. He was in deep shit and he knew it, but he smiled and said, "No sweat, sir."

Adams started the questioning. He wanted Tom's version of what happened from the time they left the FARP until they returned to base. To the best of his ability, Tom gave them his version of the mission, how it went down, why he did what he did, and what he saw less than twelve hours prior to the interview.

Ten minutes later, he was done and the questions came from Myatt. Tom could tell by the way he was asking the questions that Myatt was already predisposed. Someone, probably Crane, had told him a different version of the fight.

Crane had been quiet and solemn during the initial part of the interview. After Myatt started to question Lawton's version, Crane would occasionally throw in a few lines to "clarify" what he thought Tom said. Crane's additional comments were never really lies, but they were enough to make Myatt ask something else. After thirty minutes, Lawton was getting red in the face.

Adams was smart enough to pick up on Lawton's anger and interrupted Myatt's questioning. "That's enough for now, Bill. I think we have enough information. Let's give the colonel a break. I need to talk to you for a minute." The two men walked a short distance away.

Lawton finished his water. The interview had not gone well. Crane was obviously assisting Myatt in his questioning, and the questions were headed somewhere that Lawton couldn't quite figure out.

Dick Crane leaned over towards Lawton. He cleared his throat and said, "I, uh, I want to thank you for saving my guys last night."

Lawton was stunned. "Then why the hell aren't you turning this thing off? Everything I said, you amended or added to make my story look screwed up!"

"I was just adding clarity to the story, Lawton."

Tom shook his head, "No, sir! You were screwin' me. That lawyer listened to your version and not to a word I said."

"That's because you're tired, Lawton. I got my story to him early this morning when I was fresh from the fight. I'm trying to make sure the truth gets told."

Tom wondered how Crane could've been so fresh. He had put in nearly a twenty-four-hour day on the second of April. "I'd rather he got my truth, sir."

Crane sat back. "I'm gonna try and support you through this thing, *amigo*." Crane sounded much too white to be using *amigo*.

It just added to Tom's state of anger. He knew enough not to trust Crane. "I'll get through this without any help from you," he hesitated, "Sir."

Crane took the gloves off. "It doesn't look good for you, buddy. They're gonna try to hang you. You're gonna need me."

That was the moment of clarity Lawton needed. He instantly understood what Crane was doing. He wanted to make sure Tom didn't bring up the incident at al Karjubal, where Crane had nearly committed a war crime.

Lawton sat back and eyed the colonel curiously. Crane leaned forward and said softly, "I know what your unit did last night. And they did the right thing. You saved my guys and I owe you for that."

Tom could feel the setup. He leaned towards Crane and hissed, "I have no intention of bringing up anything else. So you don't owe me a damn thing!"

Crane turned red, stood up, and said, "That would be best for everyone concerned." He quickly turned and walked away. Tom leaned back in his chair. He was no longer in control of his fate. The video of Crane's behavior at Al-Karjubal stayed in Tom's mind. If things went badly, he decided right then that he would bring it to Myatt's attention.

Adams led Myatt back to the table. The decision was made. "Lieutenant Colonel Lawton, it is my duty to inform you that we have determined an Article 32 investigation is necessary. The first issue is: Did you disobey a direct order?" Lawton was nervous. "What order?"

"The order to not go into Najaf." Crane had answered. Lawton shook his head in dismay.

"Colonel Powell ordered my unit to go into Najaf when we were at the FARP." Tom squinted as he tried to remember exactly what Powell had said.

Adams continued, "The second part is to determine if you and your unit shot at and destroyed a mosque."

Tom shook his head. He couldn't believe it. "A mosque? That's what this is all about? A damn mosque?"

Myatt stepped in. "You're aware of General Order Number One, right, Lawton?"

Lawton knew the standing order. "Not to shoot anything that will piss the locals off! I'm well aware of General Order Number One!"

Adams smiled slightly at Lawton's off-the-cuff summary of the official order. Myatt was professional in his duties. "The order says we don't shoot civilians, hospitals, schools, or religious sites. Apparently, you violated that order."

Tom shook his head. "I was never told there was a mosque there. I was told it was a school or—" His mind was drifting back and forth to the mission. Then it hit him. "That shouldn't matter anyway! We were taking fire from those buildings!" He looked at Crane for help that never came. Lawton turned to Adams. "The enemy was in those buildings and we fired when we were fired upon!"

Adams summed it up. "The question comes down to who was in charge. Was it Colonel Powell telling you to go in? Or was it Colonel Crane, whose ground forces were in contact? We need to determine if you were aware of the no-fire area around the mosque in the village, or did you have the right to fire back? You understand why we need to do an Article 32?"

Tom shook his head, "Roger, sir." He understood he was in a world of shit.

7 April 2003
AA Dallas, Iraq

LAWTON WAS ALLOWED TO RETURN TO the unit, but they were still restricted to maintenance-only flights. Tom tried to convince Colonel Powell to let the unit do its mission, but he wouldn't listen. "We can't afford to have you or anyone in your unit make a mistake. The press is watching everything we do and word will get out before we can even get our story together. It's too risky."

Tom considered the irony of the comment. They were neck deep in a war, and fighting it was "too risky."

The 7/17th passed the time by working on their equipment and listening to the news. A nice rumor was floating around that Saddam and his two sons were killed by four 2,000-pound bombs dropped from a B1. They apparently had met at a restaurant in the upscale Monsul district at around three in the afternoon. For just a few hours, the camp was buzzing with the thought that Hussein and his two sons were dead. At least it boosted morale for a while.

The word had spread that the squadron commander was going to be on trial for murder, but Lawton quickly called a formation to dispel all rumors. He told them about the Article 32 investigation and what he was being charged with. He was grateful to know they all supported him. Some of the warrants were pissed off and wanted to go to the Headquarters and stand up for their boss. Tom told them how much he appreciated the sentiment but knew it wouldn't do any good. It was up to him to ride out the storm and get them back in the air as soon as possible.

The next day he was called back to Headquarters. The Article 32 hearing would start immediately—Headquarters wanted to have the matter solved at the earliest possible time, by either finding no mistakes were made, or the opposite. Either way, somebody would have to take the blame or the responsibility.

8 April 2003
Division Headquarters
Talil Airbase, Iraq

THE HEARING HAD ALL THE SAME players from the interview. One addition was a gruff older brigadier general named Carl Clay. He left no doubt who was in charge of the hearing. Clay called all parties involved around his table and gave the whole lot an ass-chewing before they even started. Colonel Adams, Colonel Ben Powell, Colonel Dick Crane, all were clear in understanding they were there to observe the proceedings and not interject. The bad vibe Lawton had been experiencing was still there, but he actually thought he had hope for a fair hearing. He should have known better.

Lieutenant Colonel Myatt had been assigned as the prosecutor. Tom's defender was a brand new major by the name of Darwin Hobby. The hearing started with the discussion of Lawton's orders. Lawton said he was clear in his recollection that Powell had ordered him to enter Najaf because Delta 34 was under attack.

Powell countered Tom's perspective by saying he wasn't really clear that Delta 34 was in Najaf. Tom shook his head in disgust. Powell had been receiving updates in the command aircraft all night. He knew exactly where Delta 34 was. Tom leaned over and mentioned to Hobby that if he was the commander on the battlefield that night, it was his responsibility to know where all units were, especially the friendlies. Hobby nodded and wrote notes on a pad. Tom looked at the major and waited for him to counter the testimony of Powell. But Hobby wasn't about to question a full-bird colonel. Tom sat back in his chair and shook his head. Any hope he had was quickly fading.

Then Myatt followed by asking Crane what his orders to Lawton were. Crane said he informed Lawton not to enter the city. Crane did not want to risk any potential fratricide.

Lawton couldn't argue with that. When asked why he went in, he told the truth. "I was in a position where I thought my unit could help. We were able to help the troops under fire, I knew Colonel Crane needed thirty minutes before he could enter the city, and I was positive I had heard Colonel Powell tell me to go in. I heard him say, Get in there and mix it up!"

Myatt countered. "Wasn't the ground commander in charge of Najaf? His call indicated he thought there was no need for aviation assets. Yet, you disobeyed a direct order?"

Lawton was pissed. Hobby went to grab his arm to calm him down. Tom shook him off, "Colonel Crane was not there! The situation required someone to assist Delta 34. The tanks were not available. We were! So we went in."

Brigadier General Clay turned to the row of colonels and asked, "Did you ever send the Apaches into villages or towns before?"

Powell and Crane squirmed and looked at each other. Powell spoke for them both. "In this urban environment, the helicopters weren't good. We learned that on the night of the 22nd, General. We didn't want to see anything like that happen with just a company-sized element."

Crane chipped in with, "And there was still the fratricide situation, General. We didn't need to have our aviation assets shooting at our tanks."

Lawton looked at Major Hobby, who said nothing. Lawton leaned back in his chair in disgust. Brigadier General Clay said, "All right, what else do we have?"

Myatt brought up General Order Number One. "Lieutenant Colonel Lawton, you are aware all Coalition forces are not allowed to engage the

Iraqi civilian population in accordance with the guidance provided by the commanding general, correct?"

Tom answered, "That's the gist of General Order Number One. No firing on civilian population, hospitals, religious, or historical sites."

Myatt turned to Clay. "As we will see in the video footage, Lieutenant Colonel Lawton and his men disregarded this order and attacked anything and everything in the city of Najaf."

Myatt pointed to a TV, VCR, and five videotapes. The lawyer took the first tape and put it in the VCR. The attorney fast-forwarded through most of the engagement to save time. Powell's orders were not on Tom's tape, but Crane was heard very clearly telling Tom not to enter the city. As the videos rolled, Tom watched the assembled crowd and could tell they were fascinated by the video footage. For a full two hours, the officers watched the value of 21st century technology. The tapes caught everything.

The video of the Apaches' attacks was fairly clear. It bothered Tom that the picture as seen on the television display was so much bigger than what he used in the aircraft. Even the Forward Looking Infrared (FLIR) images looked clear on the TV screen.

Unfortunately for Lawton, the video captured the unmistakable silhouette of a mosque just behind and to the right of the main building where the Apaches initially attacked.

After his crew was shot down, the audio revealed a definite change in Tom's tone. His verbal commands were stronger and more aggressive. The tape had captured his every word. He had not realized how much he had been cursing. The tone wasn't one of fear for himself; he was afraid for his men. His response was of anger. In fact, any observer could tell that losing the aircraft and perhaps a crew had made him totally pissed off. Lawton watched Clay and could read his body language; he understood what was happening. The colonels occasionally talked to each other, but never said anything loud enough for anyone else to hear.

During the second engagement, Lawton's video showed rockets going over the building in front where his crosshairs were oriented and heading toward the mosque in the background. Later videos would reveal two other aircraft had fired on the buildings with rockets. The videos showed at least ten rockets going over the front building and hitting the mosque. Without a clear picture of any impacts, all assumed the rockets were direct hits.

Tom could only shake his head. On the display in his cockpit, Tom had to admit he had never noticed the dome now clearly visible on the tape. He was never told there was a mosque in the engagement area, by Powell or Delta 34. He never saw the mosque while he was firing.

After all the video's were viewed, Lawton tried to explain the difference between the video image in the cockpit and what the board members were witnessing on the TV screen. He was met with cold grunts from Myatt and Clay. Lawton became animated and said, "When we're getting fired upon, General Order Number One is not applicable! Those sites were being used by combatants to shoot at and direct fire against us!"

Clay cut to the chase. "That's not how it's being viewed by the Arab population. The Arab media is all over this fight. They are portraying this whole incident as a massacre. You are being viewed as a murderer and killer of innocents. They are reporting up to 200 people killed. Mostly women and kids, Lieutenant Colonel Lawton."

Tom couldn't hold back. "General, if that was women and kids in those buildings, they were shooting at US soldiers. I don't think for a minute it was! But if it was, they damn well needed to get shot!"

Clay erupted. "Damn it, Lawton! You can't say that!"

Lawton wasn't done. "It needs to be said, General!" Clay sat back in his chair, still steaming. Tom continued, "The Fedayeen may have used some women and kids in those buildings. For all I know, the bastards probably brought a dozen or so non-combatants into the building the next morning and blew them away right before they brought in news cameras! I don't know! But the videos show them shooting at us, and we gave back the same as we took! So if you want to send me to Leavenworth for that—" Tom got quiet. He had tears in his eyes and he quickly wiped them away. He broke the silence in the room. "You do whatever it is you have to do, General. But I put the value of US lives at a higher degree than what those bastards in the media are reporting."

Clay was visibly pissed off. He stood up and glared at Lawton. "You don't hold the value of American lives any higher than anyone else in this room!" Lawton had crossed a line. "Whether or not you believe it, I'm on your side in this thing. That big mouth of yours is gonna get you to prison! If you just drank a small cup of 'shut the fuck up,' we might get you outta this without sending you to jail. But you have all the answers, don't you?"

He shook his head in disgust. "I need a break." The general turned and stomped out of the room. Apparently they were adjourning for the day.

Lawton saw the handwriting on the wall. He called to Petty to have his video of Crane's actions at Najaf brought to Myatt at Division Headquarters. After hearing their boss was losing, Sanchez and Petty got an email sent back to Texas. It was immediately forwarded to Major General Walker.

8 April 2003
Talil Airbase
Division Headquarters

REPORTS FROM ALL THE MAJOR NEWS networks focused on an incident in Baghdad where an al Jazeera reporter and his cameraman were fired upon while on the balcony of a hotel. They were reportedly killed by US Army tank fire. Tom sat in a chair in the chow hall watching the news, scratching his head. He couldn't see how a tank round could hit the fifteenth floor of the hotel and not completely blow the corner of the building away. He was inclined to think the reporters were killed by an Iraqi bomb or mortar round. But that's not what the press would report.

Lawton briefly appreciated that the world press possessed the attention span of a gnat. The reputed massacre in Najaf by an insane "Commander of Texans" that killed 300 women and children during prayers at a mosque had temporarily taken a back seat to the deaths of two Arab newsmen.

The Arab media was doing everything they could to slant the perception of the war towards the poor Iraqi people and all of Islam, while the US military was getting hammered by the world for liberating Iraq and supporting the Israelis against the Palestinians. Deep down, Lawton knew the war had jack shit to do with Israel. He was sick of hearing about WMD. Hussein and his sons needed to be dead. If the US and coalition could do that, the world would surely be a better place.

Since Clay needed to take a day off to mind his real job as the assistant division commander for logistics, the hearing was delayed. Tom had one bit of good news during the break. Word had come that Major General Walker was on his way to Iraq.

9 April 2003
Talil AirBase
Division Headquarters

THE WORLD WATCHED IN AWE AS a United States armored vehicle pulled down the statue of Saddam Hussein in the center of Baghdad. Crowds of Iraqi civilians showed up and joyously roamed the streets, aware that change had truly come to their country.

For Tom, the news that his mentor and leader was coming to Iraq was a small sign that things might be looking up. Major General Walker arrived late in the evening and quickly met with Lawton to gain his assessment of the situation. Lawton was quick to bring him up to date. He tried to explain both the situation in Iraq and his position in the hearing. He was honest when he told the general his personal situation was not good. Crane and Powell wanted his ass. Clay had been maintaining, at least on the surface, a show of impartiality, but Tom felt the cards were stacked against him. Hobby told the general he might not have options.

Walker told Tom to relax. He was there to help, not just Lawton, but "all his Texans." It seemed like a strange thing to say, but Lawton put the comment off as just the way his boss was. Tom tried to imply that it was not just the Arab press assisting in applying pressure. It seemed like some US press were out to see him hanged as well. No one from any press organization had ever received all the facts about what had happened.

It's easy for Walker to tell me to relax, Tom thought. *It isn't his ass on the line.*

They had to report to the hearing room at 0900 the next day. Walker was having breakfast with Clay and maybe even Major General Stoddard, the Division commanding general, in the morning.

As Tom watched the news of Baghdad falling, his mind switched from wanting to be there to share in that victory, to the fact that his career was probably over.

```
10 April 2003
Talil Airbase, Iraq
Division Headquarters
```

TOM LAWTON COULDN'T HELP BUT NOTICE the crowd in the hallway. This was the first time reporters had been present during the investigation. Tom could tell instantly which reporters were from the Arab press. Their faces were scowling grimaces unable to hide their hate. They had found out what had happened and now they had a face to go with the deed. A quick flash ran through Lawton's mind: *Did Crane let the media know what was happening?* He quickly dismissed the notion. *Crane has nothing to gain by having reporters ask about US actions in combat.*

As Lawton and Hobby pushed their way toward the conference room, an Arab reporter thrust his microphone into Lawton's face and, in broken English, asked him how it felt to murder women and children. Lawton stopped dead in his tracks. Hobby saw Tom's face flush red and quickly grabbed his arm to pull him down the hallway.

Lawton tried to turn, but Hobby yanked his arm and put his mouth close to his ear. "It won't do any good. Come on. You've got another fight that's more important."

The Military Police stepped in and kept the handful of reporters away from the doorway.

Crane was already in the conference room. He too was scowling. Colonel Powell sat in the front of the room. Tom saw the aviation commander was in a rather pleasant mood. "How'd you like all the new arrivals in the hallway, Lawton?" Tom put two and two together and realized Powell was the shithead that leaked the news of the investigation location.

Before Lawton could say anything, Clay, Walker, and to Tom's surprise, Major General Stoddard, entered the room. The players took their seats and Major General Stoddard called the hearing to order.

"I'm here today because we need to get this settled. We don't have time to be screwin' around anymore." There was noticeable silence as the general spoke. "Lieutenant Colonel Myatt, I've heard your side of the story," he nodded at the lawyer, "and I've heard the story from the colonel. What I need to hear is what the damn truth is. To be quite honest with you all, we are in deep shit because of Lieutenant Colonel Lawton's actions." Lawton noticed Powell suppress a smile as he looked at Crane. Crane remained stoic and expressionless as he surveyed the attendees.

"Lieutenant Colonel Lawton, I have some questions for you." The General had Lawton's undivided attention. "First and foremost, did you disobey the order not to enter Najaf?"

Lawton thought about his answer carefully. He was screwed any way he answered it. If he said yes, he was guilty of disobeying Crane's order and that was on the videotape. Even as justified as it was in his mind, in the eyes of military law, he had disobeyed a direct order. If he said no, he would be lying. He could try to explain to the general the same things he had said to Clay, but he knew that Stoddard had already heard everything. He went in to save American lives. That was worth any consequences. "Sir, I entered the city because it was necessary."

"That's not the question, Lawton. Did you disobey Colonel Crane's order?"

There was no sense to lying. "Yes, sir." There was some mumbling in the background.

"You felt justified in this action to save soldiers' lives, correct?"

"Yes, sir."

Stoddard nodded. "I understand you believe that Colonels Crane and Powell were out to get you. Would you mind telling me about that?"

Tom inhaled deeply. Stoddard knew way more than Tom expected. He looked over at Walker who was wearing a small smile. A light came on. *Walker talked to Stoddard! The commanding general knows everything from both sides. I've got an ally.* "General, I had a tape that caught Colonel Crane's actions upon entering the village of al-Karjubal, showing him in the process of performing criminal acts against Iraqi civilians." Lawton saw Crane shift nervously in his seat. Myatt looked down at his notes.

"Where is this tape now?"

"I gave it to Lieutenant Colonel Myatt for the investigation."

Stoddard looked at Myatt, who was quick to respond.

"Sir, the tape in question is not pertinent to the charges against Lieutenant Colonel Lawton. It has no bearing on whether Lieutenant Colonel Lawton disobeyed orders!"

Suddenly, Major General Walker stood up. "Sir, I think I can help you out here." The Texas adjutant general pulled up a flight bag and produced four videotapes. "It just so happens that the operations officer from

Lawton's unit has some videotapes from other Apache aircraft that were supporting operations in al-Karjubal." Myatt looked at Crane in disbelief. Powell looked at Crane and shrugged his shoulders. They obviously didn't have the lynching as together as they had thought.

Walker handed the tapes to General Clay. "Maybe if we review these, we can see if there really is a reason why Lawton feels these colonels want to see him, and maybe even the unit, out of the picture."

Clay stammered, "Um, yes, General. Maybe we should take a look at these."

Stoddard took control again, and looked at Tom. "Were you and your unit ordered into villages by Colonel Powell or Colonel Crane?"

"We had been ordered into different towns both nights prior to Najaf!"

Stoddard asked, "Why?"

For the first time, Lawton hesitated. He formed the words in his head before he said them. "I think the intent was for us to get engaged, sir."

"What does that mean, Lawton?"

Tom watched Crane squirm in his seat again. He swallowed and spit out what he was thinking. "I think the colonels wanted to see the unit do poorly." He hesitated but he couldn't stop himself. "Maybe even wanted to get me or my men killed."

Stoddard was instantly incensed. "What? Why? Do you know what the hell you're saying, Lawton?"

Lawton let go. "Sir, those tapes will reveal that my unit and I witnessed Colonel Crane threaten a civilian not only with a pistol, but with a tank."

Crane jumped out of his chair. "That's bullshit, sir. He's just saying anything to try and save his sorry ass, because he knows he's headed to Leavenworth!"

Stoddard waved the colonel back to his seat with one hand. "Can you prove this, Lawton? You can't just throw a serious accusation out there without offering some kind of proof."

Tom nodded. "Yes, sir, we have that. I believe the tapes General Walker has are tapes from my crews at al-Karjubal."

Stoddard shook his head. He gave the colonels a peculiar look. Lawton suspected the general had not expected bumps in the investigation.

Stoddard sat back in his chair. "We need to see those tapes. We are not going to hide any facts related to this hearing." He turned to Myatt and pointed. "I thought you had performed a preliminary investigation."

"Sir, we did. This is the first I have heard of these other tapes."

Myatt quickly added, "Sir, I'd just like to remind you that it is Lieutenant Colonel Lawton that is being investigated, not Colonel Crane."

Stoddard shook his head angrily. "I hear you, counselor. But we need to understand everything about the situation. That includes prior events and other circumstances."

Myatt nodded. Crane and Powell exchanged red-faced glances.

The general said, "Let's get on with this. Were you aware that you were given orders to fire upon a mosque?"

Without hesitation, Tom answered, "No, sir! I was told it was a school. That in itself is against General Order Number One, sir, and for that I am sorry. But the order, as I interpreted it as a commander in combat, is superseded to protect troops in contact with the enemy." He saw Stoddard nod. Tom took a calculated gamble. "Sir, at that time I believed it was a school, and there were enemy there shooting at our guys. Delta 34 said he was taking fire from there, General, so I ordered my men to fire."

Stoddard drummed his fingers on the table. "So would I." The general stood up. "We are in a tight spot here, gentlemen. I've got colonels that are giving me, let's call it, a skewed perspective of a fight that has extenuating circumstances." He walked around the room. "I've got a junior commander whose ass is in a sling for doing the right thing, and a media in a frenzy to see this thing as something that it isn't." He shook his head.

"I think I need to talk to Generals Clay and Walker alone. Gentlemen, if you would give us a few minutes." Stoddard returned to his chair next to Clay.

Walker stood up and walked over to Lawton. "Good thing I got here when I did."

"It ain't over yet, sir." Lawton was smiling when he spoke. "By the way, how did you get the tapes?"

"A Chief Warrant Officer Petty came by with Captain Sanchez and woke me up last night. To be honest with you, I haven't seen what's on the tapes, but it sure did get Crane spinning, didn't it?" Walker was smiling. "Let me see how this thing is headed, Tom. No promises, but I like your chances much better now."

"Thanks, sir! Thanks very much!"

Petty was outside in the hallway waiting when Lawton and his defense attorney came out. The hearing was taking a recess and the Warrant managed to join Tom and get the latest on how it was going. Petty's grin was ear to ear. "Thanks for getting those tapes to Walker," said Lawton with a huge smile.

"Nothing to it, sir! You'd have done the same thing for any of us, right?" It was the first time Petty had seen him smile in a week.

As they talked quietly outside the conference room, Lawton quizzed Hobby about the proceedings while the lawyer smoked a cigarette. Thirty feet down the hall, Colonel Ben Powell was talking to Crane. Crane's face was flush red and it was obvious that they were having a disagreement. They saw Crane point his finger in Powell's face and the armor colonel turned and headed toward the rest room. Powell exhaled and turned to face a group of reporters that had gathered.

The reporters shouted questions and Powell did his political best. One reporter asked how, with all the US technology, a unit of 'state-of-the-art' Apache aircraft could fire on a no-fire area?

Powell went to town, "The Apaches that were involved in the incident aren't 'state-of-the-art.' They are merely National Guard aircraft. They don't have the same equipment active duty aircraft have. If they had been active duty personnel in AH-64 Delta-model Apaches, this incident never would have happened."

Lawton scoffed at the notion. Crane never would have allowed the Delta-model Apaches to enter Najaf, either for fear of fratricide, or for fear they would get shot down. It had nothing to do with technology.

Powell continued, "My point is, the National Guard with their antiquated equipment, is not able to perform as well as a regular unit."

Lawton said, "You listening to this?" Hobby and Petty both nodded.

Powell excused himself from the reporters and headed down the hallway. He walked up to Lawton and said, "Would you care to hear a prediction, Lieutenant Colonel Lawton?"

"If it's yours, sir, not really." Major Hobby turned his head away and tried to act like he wasn't there.

Powell knew both the major and Petty were still listening intently. "I predict Lawton will be found not accountable for firing at the mosque."

Hobby turned and squinted. "Not accountable?"

Powell nodded. "Yes. Not accountable." Hobby looked at Lawton. Of course, being found not accountable is completely different from being found 'not guilty.'

"What's that supposed to mean?" Tom didn't bother to add the 'sir' to his question. Powell was being more condescending than usual.

"It means that this whole thing is nothing personal, Lawton. No commander deserves to get relieved for defending his men. You're getting a raw deal. Nobody knows if there were women and kids in there. That very well could have been Saddam Hussein's hideout you destroyed. But in the propaganda war, the Arab press will say it was a maternity ward you blew to hell. It doesn't matter to the press. I tried to explain to them that it was your equipment that was deficient. Not your ability as a commander."

"Thanks so much for your help, Colonel. But what you were trying to do was show that the Department of Defense needs AH-64 Delta helicopters. With any luck, your comments will reach some congressmen and they'll appropriate funds to buy more Apaches to create another Brigade and, just maybe, you'll get a star out of this war."

Hobby turned slightly, but didn't move away. The comment struck a nerve with Powell. He was no longer amused by the verbal jousting. He stepped aggressively towards Lawton and turned red in the face. Hobby quickly turned to get between the two men.

Powell hissed, "You're just a turd, Lawton! A pawn in a huge game that you know absolutely nothing about. The only good thing about you is you saved some American lives in that shithole town. A week from now, none of this will mean a thing. Nothing you've done will have mattered to anyone!"

Powell stepped backwards and recovered his composure. "Like I said, I don't think you'll be heading to Leavenworth. You should be looking at seven to ten years, but your guardian angel in there probably saved you from hard time."

"I didn't need him. Because if I go, I take you and Crane with me!"

Powell smirked. "It's true. You have created a little problem for Colonel Crane. But he's a good man. A warrior. He was doing what he thought would best help his men. Similar to what you did."

"That isn't anything like what I did and you know it!" Tom was turning red and it was his turn to step toward the colonel.

Hobby stepped between the two men again and put his hand on Lawton's chest. He looked into Lawton's eyes. "He wants you to take a swing." The lawyer shook his head, "You're better than him."

Powell continued. "Think about it, Lawton. His method was different. Yet he was doing what he needed to, to save his troop's lives. His method may not have been the most admirable way to do business, but it can be seen as justified by some people. We can't have our troops being picked off one by one. Crane was seeing to it that his men knew he would protect them!"

"By giving the entire civilian population of Iraq a reason to take shots at us? That's insane!"

"You want to know how I can tell he did the right thing? After that situation, we didn't receive any fire from anywhere in that city. He merely threatened to kill a few civilians. His method was effective, just like yours. But unlike yours, because you killed 'em all, Lawton. Whatever they were in that mosque— Fedayeen, Saddam loyalists, or women with babies—you killed 'em. So that little thing in al-Karjubal? That shit doesn't matter. What the press reports about you matters. That will have a significant impact on how we have to deal with the future of this war." Powell smirked, then added, "And the next."

Lawton stood back and shook his head. It made perfect sense. Nothing he said or did really mattered anymore. It was up to the generals, and he would be lucky if he didn't get court martialed. He answered with the only retort he could come up with. "Screw you, Powell. You two will have to answer for your bullshit! Maybe not today, but it'll come back to haunt you."

Just then, Brigadier General Clay popped out of the conference room and announced, "All involved parties, please come in."

CHAPTER THIRTEEN

I've got a half a mind to call her,
Half a mind to go.
Jump a big jet liner,
And wing it on my way back home.

"Texas on My Mind"
-Django Walker

STODDARD DIDN'T MINCE WORDS. "I'VE MADE my decision." He looked around the room. The silence was eerie. Lawton looked at Walker. He was not exactly happy, but he wasn't upset either. He caught Lawton's stare and remained expressionless.

"I don't want to give in to the media on this thing. They don't run my division. I do." He looked at Myatt and said, "We're not going to charge Lieutenant Colonel Lawton with anything. There will be no pursuit of any charges. His actions, in my mind, were justified. You write it up that way."

Stoddard turned to Lawton and said, "I guess you can say you're off the hook. I don't condone your actions. You disobeyed the direct orders of a senior officer. In any other situation, I'd have your ass!"

Lawton could tell he was going to be okay. He did a good job of keeping his smile suppressed. "Roger, sir." Stoddard looked over to Walker and said, "He's all yours, Jerry. If I never see him again, I would consider it a favor."

Walker nodded. He wasn't smiling when he said, "Thank you, General. Lieutenant Colonel Lawton, would you join me outside?"

Tom couldn't suppress his smile. "Yes, sir!"

Hobby stood up and stuck out his hand. "I guess I won't be seeing you, sir!"

Lawton shook his defender's hand. "Thanks, Major Hobby. I'd like to say it's been fun, but it hasn't. If you get up towards Baghdad, look me up!" Hobby nodded.

Out in the hallway, Major General Walker walked as far away from the reporters as he could. Tom followed obediently.

Walker was quiet, so Lawton started the conversation.

"I don't know how to thank you, sir."

"Thank me for what, Tom?" Walker was still expressionless. "Keeping you from going to Leavenworth? They didn't have any case against you."

Lawton was beaming, "That's right, sir. No case!"

Walker exhaled loudly. A pit formed in Tom's stomach. Something wasn't right. Walker turned and looked out a window at the Iraqi desert. "I cut a deal, Tom."

Tom was confused. "What do you mean, a deal, sir?"

"I told them I'd take care of you if they didn't pursue the court martial."

Lawton started to get angry. "You told them you'd take care of me? What does that mean?"

"We can't have a Texas National Guard commander get court-martialed, Tom. We just can't have that."

Lawton shook his head. "But, sir? You just said they didn't have a case?"

For the first time since Lawton had known him, Walker became angry. He wheeled and got close to Tom. "YOU DON'T GET IT, DO YOU?" Walker got control of himself. "You're missing the big picture, Tom! I thought you were smarter than that!"

Lawton was at a loss for words. "The big picture, sir? What the hell is that supposed to mean? Screw the big picture!" Lawton stepped back and eyed his boss and mentor. Then it all sank in. Walker really had cut a deal. "You sold out, didn't you?"

Walker didn't respond. "Would you listen to yourself? 'Screw the big picture!' You were on the brink of going to Leavenworth for a long time. You have some cock-and-bull story about what some O-6s are doing to screw your unit and get you killed. I've heard enough!"

"But it's TRUE!"

"ENOUGH, LAWTON!" He stepped closer and said in a lower voice. "Enough!"

Lawton was stunned silent. Walker continued. "Now listen to me. Here's reality. All you need to do is write an apology letter. We'll issue it through the public affairs guys."

Lawton could see what was happening. "An apology letter?"

"We need to apologize to the Iraqis for firing on the mosque." The General was already writing the letter in his mind. He started to walk in a circle as the apology came clear.

Lawton was shaking. Things were happening too fast. *My boss has cut a deal, now I have to write an apology letter? For doing the job I was sent to do?* Then the haze in his head cleared.

Lawton had to ask the question that was most important to him. He knew the answer before he asked it. "Do I get to keep my command?"

Walker didn't hesitate. "I'm afraid that's out of the question! It was part of the agreement that you could no longer command. I thought you understood that."

Lawton understood everything. "I see the big picture now, sir. By taking me out of command, they won't have me around to be a problem anymore. The Arab media gets what they want, and the Division gets what it wants."

"That's all they asked for."

There was still something missing. One piece of the agreement was not clear. "What did you get, sir?"

"I got to keep you out of Leavenworth."

"And?"

Walker knew better than to try and bullshit Lawton any longer. "I got to keep the name and the reputation of the Texas National Guard clean. The 7/17th stays in Iraq."

Tom shook his head. "Is this part of the big picture that I don't get?"

"You're damn right it is!" Walker regained his composure. "Yes! That is what it's about. If I can keep the reputation of the Guard as a good fighting force, with good leadership, we stay in the fight!"

"You mean you get funding," said Tom. He shook his head again.

"Yes, Tom. Funding. It means money for equipment and positions. If I can get jobs for Texans, if I can get something for the state and give something to the nation with a fighting force, this is what I'll do. I don't mind having the reputation that we have as Warriors— that we can fight. But we can't have a reputation that we don't fight fair. Now that may sound ugly to you, Lieutenant Colonel Lawton. But that's what my job is."

Tom shrugged. "Why'd you bring me into this?"

"I checked you out. I know about your record in the last War. You are a great combat leader. You fight. You are a 21st century warrior. And you win. That's what you do." The general paused and looked out the window. "Or should I say, did. You could have been a great asset, Tom."

"I'll never command again, will I?"

"Not in the deal, Tom." Walker exhaled audibly. "You have a choice. You can turn around right now and go back in that room and tell General Stoddard you want to take the court-martial. But I will tell you right here, right now. If you go to court martial, you will be found guilty. Not because you were wrong, but because you're testing the system. You're pushing something up a hill that doesn't have a top. This event needs to go away."

"Just like me, sir?"

Walker nodded. "Yes, Tom. Just like you."

Tom turned around and looked at the wall. He couldn't face Walker. He had respected General Walker completely. Deep down he understood the general's position. It all made sense. The whole "big picture." He was just a small piece of the big picture. And the whole thing was making that picture ugly.

It all seemed to make sense, in an ironic way. He was sent to fight a war, kill people, and when he fought it, he was on the verge of going to prison for doing what he was ordered to do. His men had done well. They were all alive and they would stay that way. It was over. It was time for him to accept it, and move on.

A question popped into his mind. "When do I get back to Texas, sir?"

Walker smiled. "We can get up to your unit, get your equipment, and be headed back to Austin within a week!"

Another question popped into his mind. "What about a change of command ceremony?"

Walker frowned. "Don't think that's in the cards either, Tom. Can't have it looking like you're getting rewarded for—"

Tom cut him off. "For killing the enemy?"

Walker was ready for the comment. "For killing women and children, Lieutenant Colonel." Walker had to make sure Lawton knew who was in charge.

"I don't want to leave my men to just anyone."

"They are not your men anymore," said the general flatly.

Game, set, and match. Tom really had no choice. The deal for the betterment of the big picture had been made.

Tom nodded. He exhaled heavily and the smile that had left his face a week ago was back. "You ever go tubing on the Guadalupe River, sir?"

Walker was confused. "No, Tom. Can't say that I have."

"It's probably the most relaxing thing a person can do." He drew in a deep breath. "I think that's the first thing I'm gonna do when I get back to Texas."

Walker smiled. "I'll go tell Stoddard." The general started up the hallway. "I know this isn't the way you wanted to go out. But it's better than what they had in mind for you!"

Tom Lawton could only nod. Deep down he knew what they had in mind for him was to be laying inside a burning cockpit. He and his men were too good at fighting to end up that way. He would no longer be an ugly part of the big picture. He had just learned the hardest lesson of war. The men that do the fighting are only a minor piece of that big picture.

12 April 03
Assembly Area Houston.
Central Iraq

TOM LAWTON DIDN'T HAVE MUCH TIME. He got in one last night's sleep, if you could call it that. He didn't really sleep much at all. He rose before six o'clock and finished putting his gear in his kit bag. He decided to only fill one. Leaving the other extra stuff for the rest of the guys seemed right. He didn't think he'd need a Kevlar while sitting on his couch watching the Astros kick the crap out of the Cardinals.

At 0615, Sergeant Major Martinez knocked on the imaginary tent door and came in. He had two cups of coffee. "I know you like Pepsi, but figured today you wouldn't mind too much. I put a bunch of cream and sugar in there."

Lawton nodded and smiled. "Thank you. I don't know what I'm gonna do without you taking care of me. You really helped keep me together, Sergeant Major. Not just here, but even before we got here, ya know?"

"Yeah, well, that's my job. I miss your sorry ass and you ain't even gone yet, sir!"

Lawton laughed and took a sip of the hot coffee. It may have been the desert outside the tent, but it was still chilly in the morning. "If I'd known coffee could be this good, I'd 'a' drunk more of it." Martinez smiled. Tom coughed a little to clear his throat.

"I want you to take care of these guys, okay?"

Martinez knew where Lawton was headed. "I think they'll be pretty good at taking care of themselves."

"One goal, right?"

"Bring 'em all home!"

Lawton nodded. "Bring 'em all home." His bags were packed. "If it wouldn't be too much to ask, could you give me a hand with that rucksack? I'll get the kit bag."

"Sir! Hold on," Martinez hollered. "You guys can come in now!

Into the tent came Hector Sanchez, Bat Talbot, Sam Gash, Brian Trant, and Joe Petty. Sanchez spoke first. "We thought we'd come by and see you off."

Talbot looked like a kid about to cry. "I don't know what to say, sir."

Lawton smiled broadly. "Good-bye is just fine, Bat."

The captain walked over and hugged his mentor. Lawton took a deep breath. "This isn't making it any easier, guys!" Lawton slowly pushed Talbot away and said, "You fly safe, all right?"

"No sweat, sir!" Talbot stepped back and let Sam Gash speak.

Lawton couldn't help but notice the captains bars. "DAMN, SON! Those railroad tracks look outstanding!"

Gash was flush red in the face. "I couldn't have gotten them without you, sir!"

Lawton shook his head and said, "I disagree, Sam! You are the best lieutenant I ever had. You take care of the next boss the way you did me, ya hear?" Gash nodded and stepped back.

Then it was Trant's turn to say good-bye. The senior warrant was fighting back tears. "You saved my life." He shook his head and added, "TWICE!" Tom fought back his own tears.

"Nothin' you wouldn't have done for me!"

Trant shook his head. "Above and beyond, sir." He pushed Lawton's extended hand away and gave his commander a hug. Unaccustomed to showing that much emotion, Trant quickly turned away and wiped his eyes.

It was finally Petty's turn to say good-bye. He seemed hesitant to approach him. "I can't believe this is happening."

Lawton was still managing a smile. "The biggest thing that has me pissed off is, I'll be eatin' ribs while you're over here gettin' your ass shot at."

Petty smiled back. "They can't shoot for shit and you know it." Lawton laughed out loud. It was more out of nervous tension than amusement. Lawton stepped forward and gave Petty a huge hug. It was the kind of hug you give someone when you know you're not going to see them for a long time. Maybe never.

Petty was covering his own tears when he choked out, "I wish you were stayin', boss!"

"Can't happen, Joe. Can't happen." Lawton smacked his back and inhaled loudly. "You keep 'em alive, Joe! I'll see you when you get home."

Lawton grabbed his bag. "Let's go, Sergeant Major. I can't handle much more of this!"

Martinez was at the tent door and said, "We just got one more good-bye, sir."

Martinez stepped outside and held the tent flap for the outgoing commander. "SQUADRON! ATTENTION!"

Lawton stepped through the tent. As he straightened, the entire 7th of the 17th Cavalry was standing before him at attention. Tom came to attention. Under his breath he said to Martinez, "Damn it, Sergeant Major!"

"They wanted to say, good-bye, sir. Don't deny them this."

Tom nodded. "All right, Sergeant Major." Lawton coughed loudly and yelled, "Squadron!"

The Troop leaders yelled, "Troop!"

"ATTENTION!"

They were already at the position of attention, but they stood straighter and held their heads higher.

Lawton yelled, "What are you doin'?"

"KICKIN' IRAQI HIPPY ASS, SIR!"

"Where you boys goin'?"

"ALL THE WAY TO BAGHDAD, SIR!"

"When you comin' home?" Lawton was starting to choke up.

"WHEN THE JOB IS DONE!"

Lawton fought off tears. "You sons of bitches better check your six! If the Fedayeen ain't on it, it'll be me with a boot up your ass!" Tom Lawton pulled up his hand for a final salute. "Keep your powder dry and I'll see you on the high ground, boys!"

Lawton choked out, "SERGEANT MAJOR! Take charge of the squadron!" He saluted Martinez, did an about face, and grabbed his bag. He quickly wiped his eyes dry and motioned for his vehicle.

Lawton quickly jumped in. Petty threw his bags in the back. "See ya, boss!"

Lawton stuck out his hand and fought back the tears. "Shoot straight, Joe, and kill as many of the bastards as you can!"

He quickly turned to the driver and commanded, "Let's go. I got a plane to catch."

The driver put it in gear and slowly drove by the formation. They were still holding the salute. He didn't look back. It hurt too much.

13 April 2003
Talil, Iraq

TOM LAWTON WAS SITTING IN THE terminal waiting to board the plane that would take him back to Texas. He took some time to walk over and talk with some of the wounded soldiers as they lay on their stretchers. They were all so young. He had to stop talking to them because it was making him angry. He began to have questions. *Was it worth it? Was what they were doing really worth the pain and suffering?*

He looked out the terminal window. The first thing he noticed was a new squadron of AH-64 Delta-model Apaches lining up for take off. Maybe Powell was getting the technologically advanced forces he thought he needed to keep some Iraqi mosque from being blown to hell.

At that moment, Tom Lawton didn't really care. He was convinced technology wouldn't win the war. Those new Apaches probably wouldn't make as much difference as a squad of infantry would be going into a village to build a school or guard a hospital—personal contact that would show the Iraqis how to take advantage of the opportunity they were being given.

The next thing Lawton noticed was an old Iraqi man and a boy walking by the terminal. The man said something to the boy as two American soldiers walked by. The boy drew up a smart salute as the soldiers passed. The two soldiers immediately drew up their arms and saluted the young Iraqi. The old man smiled and nodded.

Lawton smiled. He went to his rucksack and grabbed the small Texas flag he carried in the side pouch. He took it outside and gave it to the man. The man, in turn, handed it to the boy who promptly saluted. Lawton returned the salute and bowed to the older man. It may not happen in the old man's lifetime, but maybe by the time the boy was a man, Iraq would understand what Lawton knew. Every ounce of American blood being spilled in Iraq, including Texan blood, was an affirmation of America's commitment to liberty. And because of this, the children of Iraq might grow up knowing government by the people and, maybe some day, freedom.

EPILOGUE

I wanna go home with the Armadillos,
Good country music from Amarillo and Abilene,
The friendliest people
and the prettiest women you've ever seen!

"London Homesick Blues"
-Gary P. Nunn

31 August 2003
Stillhouse Hollow Lake
Harker Heights, Texas

TEXAS MONTHLY REPORTER ANNA MERCADO INTERVIEWED Lieutenant Colonel Tom Lawton within five months of his return from Iraq. Ms. Mercado was seeking more insight into the story Chief Warrant Officer Four Joe Petty had told.

The interview wasn't exactly what Ms. Mercado expected. The lieutenant colonel was thoughtful before he answered, rarely evasive, and for some unknown reason always maintained a smile. It was Sunday evening, and Tom Lawton was enjoying the lake view from the deck of the Lawton home. Cindy stayed in the house and did not take part in the interview. After the formal introductions, Lieutenant Colonel Lawton said, "I got a call from Joe Petty, so I know you already have the story you're looking for."

Anna Mercado sat back in her seat at the edge of the deck where she could observe Tom and still see the lake below. The lake was perfectly calm. The cedar that usually bothered the reporter was not nearly as active this night. "I guess I don't need my recorder then."

Tom Lawton sat down and popped the top on his Diet Dr. Pepper. "No problem, Ms. Mercado! I'll answer most of your questions."

She smiled. "Most?"

Tom slowly sipped his soda, then placed the can on the table. "You know what you're going to write. I can't change your mind. I don't even want to. Joe Petty told you the truth. I won't tell you anything different. You know about the investigation, and you know I didn't do anything wrong. So you don't really have a story."

Anna Mercado said, "I have a story, Colonel Lawton. The story of how a National Guard commander was targeted by active duty officers. And how his unit was picked as a scapegoat for war crimes just to push along advanced military technology procurement!"

Tom showed little emotion. The fact that his everpresent smile faded was indication enough he wasn't too excited about her story. "Can I call you Anna?"

She smiled and nodded. "Certainly!"

"Anna, I would love to support you and I appreciate your effort. But it isn't gonna change anything." Tom could tell she didn't want to hear that.

He leaned forward in his chair and continued. "The whole thing is part of a huge system, a system called the Department of Defense. An article like you intend to write, any article like that, won't touch that system." He could see she looked confused.

Tom tried a different approach. "Soldiers, sailors, airmen, and marines are just employees in the largest corporation on earth. They are hired to do a job. The job is expected to be the same for any reservist as it is for an active duty soldier. In my situation, I didn't do my job well enough for the system. It probably had nothing to do with my being in the Texas National Guard."

Anna Mercado was shaking her head. "No. You're not just a paragraph in a much larger tale, Colonel Lawton. You were the point of the spear where we are fighting against terrorism! You were directly responsible for saving dozens, maybe hundreds of lives in Iraq!"

Tom nodded but changed the subject. "Anna, did you try to interview Colonel Crane?"

The reporter pulled the pencil from her notepad. "He was not interested in helping me."

Lawton chuckled. "So he didn't tell you a thing?" She nodded. He shook his head, grabbed his soda, and took a big drink. He leaned back in his chair and looked out at the lake as the sun started to set. "I applaud your effort, but I think you're missing the target. The target should be the rest of the world. That's what you need to change, not the system."

Tom could tell she was still confused. He paused and looked directly at her. "I'll tell you what you need to print. There is a spirit in this country that no bastards can tear apart, a spirit made stronger the harder we are pushed. That's the positive side. Now for the bad news.

"There are three things you need to tell your readers. First, our country is at a critical point in history. It is coming down to an us-versus-them situation, and I don't mean just our nation. Us is all the peoples of democracy and freedom. And though the US is the primary target right now, the rest of the world needs to know they are targets, too. The enemy is Muslim fundamentalism and all fanatics who use religion to corrupt the minds of poor, uneducated people who have no options."

Tom stood up and looked across the lake. "The enemy certainly isn't George Bush. It's not Alec Baldwin, or Eminem, or the Dixie Chicks. The enemy is the sons of bitches livin' under rocks or in caves that want to take away our freedom. Freedom that allows Rush Limbaugh and Al Franken to make money taking verbal pot-shots at each other while 50 percent of America scratches their head, not knowing who's telling the truth. They, the enemies of America, are using our own laws against us. They are targeting Jews and Christians because we have allowed ourselves to be easy targets. We are so comfortable with our lives that we have forgotten how to fight for what's right!"

Tom changed the subject. He noticed his face had become red. "It was right to shoot the mosque! The bad guys were exploiting it, thinking we wouldn't fire at it. It is right to shoot any bastard that picks up a gun in Iraq and shoots at us. It's right to shoot them before they make an improvised explosive device. It's right to go against all the shitheads that support them financially, with safe havens, or transportation, or use a camera to tell lies. I believe in preemption. Until America understands this fight is a war, and begins to treat it like a war, we will continue to go through the bullshit the networks put out on TV." He sat back down in his chair and exhaled loudly. After a moment his smile returned.

"That's the big picture as I see it, Anna. You want a story? You explain that to the world. Hell, a bunch of folks in Washington don't even want to hear we're at war! Nobody wants to hear it." His gaze returned to the lake.

"I'm going to tell the world, Mr. Lawton. I understand what needs to be told."

"Here's the second piece of information for you. Army aviation must change. The enemy is better equipped than we give them credit. They know our tactics, and we're way too decent to destroy all the palm groves to weed out the scum that want us dead. The free world and the liberal media would never tolerate us doing what needs to be done."

"You just did what needed to be done, right?"

Lawton nodded. "Yeah. Otherwise, we wouldn't be talking together right now."

"The third thing that must be known is that our reserve system must grow. Not just by a million people. We need to have a reserve force of five million folks ready to defend this nation." He saw Anna's jaw drop. "Yeah, five million might be enough. The draft should be mandatory, and 30 percent of Americans should be required to train to fight for America.

"The training should be on how to fight, use computers, speak multiple languages, be healthy, mentally and physically, understand global economics, and be socially and environmentally savvy. Right now, the greatest country in the world could do this. We have the money. What we don't have is the understanding of the need for change."

"I don't know if people will agree with your views."

"Just tell the truth, Ms. Mercado. Let America digest it. Sooner or later, the light will come on. I just hope you're more persuasive than I am." He smiled broadly.

Anna Mercado said, "I will let them know, Mr. Lawton." She closed her notepad and stood up. Her story was complete. "For what it's worth, I think what you did was necessary. I'm sorry for the way you were treated, and I will continue to get the story out. The story will be about you, about the war, and what's going on in the world."

Tom Lawton nodded. "I'll be here, Ms. Mercado. I'm still in the Guard. I'm still serving my country, and if she calls for me, I'll fight for her. I still have another fight left in me. Next time, we're gonna need to take the gloves off."

Tom smiled again. "Right now, there's over a hundred thousand great young Americans that need our support. There's gotta be a few more stories for you there."

Anna Mercado stood and Tom walked with her to the door. "Thank you for your time, Mr. Lawton."

Tom exhaled loudly. "They're coming for us, Ms. Mercado. That's the truth that you need to print."

She nodded and walked into the warm Texas night. Tom Lawton went back inside and turned on Fox News. Maybe they would show some Apaches flying over Baghdad. God, he wished he was there.

U. S. Army Aviation is currently being reevaluated in all phases of operations. New tactics, techniques, and procedures are being developed to maintain the role of aviation on the battlefield.

Major General Jerrold Walker was retired in a very lavish ceremony on the steps of the capitol building in Austin. He currently lives in Bandera, Texas and runs a bed and breakfast.

Chief Warrant Officer Four Joe Petty and his band the Ramrods are currently touring Louisiana. Their management company in Kerrville, Texas is getting funds together for their first video "Dangerman."

Colonel Richard Crane was removed from command soon after Lieutenant Colonel Lawton's departure. He currently fields questions as the public affairs officer in Fort Richardson, Alaska. His retirement paperwork has been approved.

Colonel Ben Powell left Iraq in May and is currently assigned to the Training and Doctrine Command. His primary task is to rewrite Army Aviation training and tactics for the Aviation Force XXI. He is expected to be on the next brigadier general list.

Tom Lawton is currently coaching women's basketball at Temple High School. Once a month, he commutes to Austin where he performs his Guard duties as the recruiting officer for the Texas National Guard. He no longer flies the AH-64 Apache.

ENDNOTES

i Copyright 2001 by Curb Congregation Songs (SESAC), Mike Curb Music (BMI)/songs of Moraine Music (ADM. By Mike Curb Music)(BMI). Available on the CD Three Days by Pat Green.

ii Copyright 1977 by Sony Music Entertainment, Inc. Available on the CD Say No More by Les Dudek. www.lesdudek.com

iii FMC means fully mission capable. This is a status given to an aircraft that is capable of flying day, night, and with fully operational night vision systems and fully functional weapons systems.

iv MOS—Military Occupational Specialty is the code applied to a specific job or duty. Such duties include helicopter mechanic, cook, military policeman, etc.

v Copyright 2003 by Greenhorse/EMI Blackwood Music (BMI), Cooke's Trust (LTD)(SESAC). Available on the CD Wave on Wave.

vi CG in this case is the Commanding General of the First Cavalry Division.

vii Round out units are reserve units expected to augment active duty units in the event of war.

viii Gunnery Table are scores assigned for aircrews based on weapons proficiency. Scores are assessed as an individual, crew, and team for both day and night. Without successful accomplishment of basic gunnery tasks, an individual or crew cannot progress to more accelerated/aggressive tables (scores) or multi-ship operations.

ix "Who's To Say," written by Pat Green, Walt Wilkins, and Mark Winston Kirk. Copyright 2001 Greenhorse Music (BMI), Curb Congregation Songs (SESAC), Mark Winston Kirk (ASCAP). Available on the Three Days CD by Pat Green.

x Copyright 2002 by Walt Wilkins (Curb Congregation Songs (SESAC). Available on the CD Poetry.

xi Copyright 1998 by Dana D. Jacobson (ASCAP)/Joseph & His Brothers Music. The CD Cover Me, Lord is available at Joseph and His Brothers Music, 13014 North Run, San Antonio, TX 78249.

xii Copyright 2001 by Greenhorse Music (BMI), and Curb Congregation Songs (SESAC). Available on the CD Three Days by Pat Green.

xiii Lyrics are a variation of "All Right Guy" by Todd Snider. The song is on the CD, Songs from the Daily Planet.

xiv "London Homesick Blues/Home With The Armadillo," by Gary P. Nunn. Copyright 1997 by Campfire Records, Bulverde, TX. Available on the CD What I Like About Texas by Gary P. Nunn. www.hepcat.com/campfire/gpnunn

xv "Poetry," by Walt Wilkins. Copyright 2001 by Western Beat Records (SESAC). Available on the CD Rivertown. Pat Green's version is also available on the Pat Green CD, Wave on Wave.

xvi Copyright 2001 Greenhorse Music (BMI). Available on the CD Three Days.

xvii Copyright 2001 Greenhorse Music (BMI), and Spunker Songs/Universal-Polygram International Publishing Inc. Available on the CD Three Days by Pat Green. Website: www.patgreen.com

xviii Copyright 1997 by Joseph and His Brothers Music. Available on the CD Cover Me, Lord by Dana Jacobson is available at: Joseph and His Brothers Music, 13014 North Run, San Antonio, TX 78249

xix A training technique involving a picture, sculpted sand table, or graphics for rehearsing battles.

xx Copyright 2001by Greenhorse Music (BMI). Available on the CD Three Days by Pat Green. www.patgreen.com

xxi Copyright 1977 by Sony Music Entertainment, Inc. Available on the CD Say No More by Les Dudek. www.lesdudek.com

xxii Copyright 2001 Djangold Music (BMI). All rights reserved. Used by permission. Available on the Django Walker's debut CD, Down the Road. Also available on the CD, Three Days by Pat Green.

xxiii Copyright 1997 by Campfire Records, Bulverde, TX. Available on the CD What I Like About Texas by Gary P. Nunn. Used by permission. www.hepcat.com/campfire/gp- nunn.

AUTHOR'S BIO

MICHAEL T. GREGORY GRADUATED FROM THE New York State University College at Cortland in 1980. He had considered becoming a coach or teacher, but a good Oneonta Army recruiter (and the opportunity to fly helicopters) convinced him to join the Army.

For over two decades, he served his country in numerous capacities. His duty stations included Germany, Saudi Arabia, Iraq, and Kuwait, as well as stateside assignments in Rucker, Hood, Knox, and Kelly AFB, including a six month stint as a company commander in the Persian Gulf War, where he led 36 men and oversaw several night-attack missions. A firm believer in the spirit of the Cavalry, Mike Gregory's love of military history ensured the Troopers he served with had his unequivocal loyalty, honesty, and trust. He finished his military career as an Information Operations analyst working global activities.

Mike is now a retired US Army officer with two novels under his belt. His first book, Desert Skies (1999), is a historical fiction of company command in the first Gulf War. "It's loosely based on what I went through." He hopes the book will function as an educational tool, helping "people understand a little bit more than what they got from CNN."

His second book, Hoopman (2003), is a fictitious account of an older military retiree, Chuck 'Hoopman' Hayes, who gets a chance to play college basketball. It doesn't take Hoopman long to figure out his team is hiding a dark secret. But Chuck Hayes has the courage to take on the criminals that threaten his teammates and his dreams, even if it costs him his life.

Originally from upstate New York, Mike is one of the many that has 'seen the light'; he, his wife, and three daughters call Boerne, Texas home. He spends most of his off time traveling around Texas, giving book signings, or working on his jump shot.

Other Books
by
Michael T. Gregory
Fiction
Desert Skies:
A Story of "Champions" in the Gulf War
The Legend of Hoopman
All of Michael T. Gregory's books are available from
1st World Library (www.1stworldlibrary.com)

www.ingramcontent.com/pod-product-compliance
Lightning Source LLC
Chambersburg PA
CBHW031014190726
48286CB00003BA/839